DRIVEN TO DISTRACTION

GAMBLE RACING
BOOK 1

RENÉE DAHLIA

Driven To Distraction

Copyright © 2022 by Renée Dahlia

All rights reserved.

Cover art © 2022 Justin Lanjil https://wickedlittletongue.art/

DRIVEN TO DISTRACTION
RENÉE DAHLIA

A race to the finish line, and a family secret ...

Car racing driver Ondrej D'Grieg has one goal in life. Be a champion. To achieve that he needs to focus. That's why Ondrej has no time for his father's insistence on him being involved with some old family drama about a missing rare car. He can ignore the mystery, if only Hudson, the historian investigating it, wasn't so distracting.

Hudson Lockley has a research job to do, and falling for the son of his employer is a no-no. But only one thing is more fascinating than this puzzle; Mr D'Grieg's famous racing car driver son, Ondrej.

When their interest turns to kisses, then more, the race to figure out this attraction between them starts. But a small mistake could cause a crash that breaks both their hearts.

ABOUT THE AUTHOR

An avid reader, Renée Dahlia writes contemporary and historical queer romance. Renée is a bisexual cis woman who is fascinated by people and loves to explore human relationships, with a side of humour, through her writing. Renée has a degree in physics and mathematics, using this to write data-based magazine articles for the horse racing industry. Her love of horses often shines through in her fiction, and she loves a good intrigue and to escape the real world in the pages of a book. When she isn't reading or writing, Renée spends her time with her four children, usually watching them play cricket.

FOREWORD

Welcome to DRIVEN TO DISTRACTION, the first book in the Gamble Racing series.

If you love gay sports romance with a coming out theme, workplace tension, rich/poor, and a little mystery thrown in, Driven to Distraction is the book for you. This series contains a few mystery plots that continue between each book; however, I have tried to make each book a stand-alone read.

Please note this book contains forced outing (off page).

This book is written in Australian English and some spelling and phrases may be unfamiliar to American readers.

If you are keen to keep up to date on new releases and, more importantly, sales, I recommend you sign up to my newsletter at reneedahlia.com or follow me on social media.

I hope you enjoy reading this book!

Renée

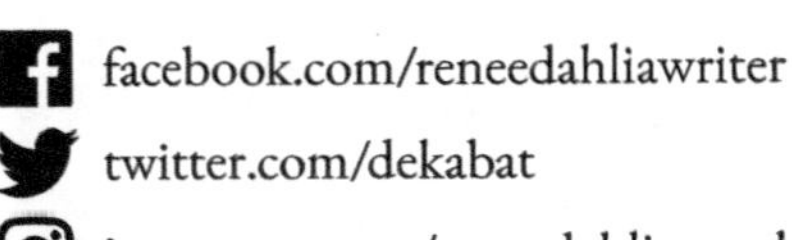

facebook.com/reneedahliawriter

twitter.com/dekabat

instagram.com/reneedahlia_author

bookbub.com/authors/renee-dahlia

patreon.com/reneedahlia

CHAPTER 1
AUSTRALIA

Ondrej had become accustomed to the gut-wrenching pain of being alone while surrounded by people. He braced himself for more of the same as his throat thickened. Heat haze rose from the asphalt, created by the Australian summer sun, and he zipped down the front of his racing suit as he walked into the pit garage after parking his car by the weighbridge. Today should have marked the beginning of his rise back to stardom ... except he'd just finished eighth in the Australian Grand Prix.

"Ondrej. Awesome drive." One of the mechanics called out and Ondrej fist pumped him as he walked past. After consistently finishing at the tail of the field for a whole season, he ought to share the jubilation on the faces of everyone in the Gamble Racing Team. He didn't. He expected to win. Two years ago—a lifetime in S1—he'd been a key member of a winning team, but so much had changed since then. Ondrej went through the motions in the garage easily, outwardly smiling, and blank on the

1

inside. Gamble Racing was one of the smaller teams in Series One with around six hundred employees. Less than a quarter of them were here in Australia, supporting him—the number one driver—and his rookie team-mate, Paulo Sanchez. Ondrej shook hands with each of the mechanics, thanking them for their hard work, and listened to them all gush over the way he'd driven today. Eighth wasn't worth this amount of praise. They should wait until he'd fought his way back to a podium finish.

"Great drive, Ondrej." His race engineer, Jaxxon, slapped him on the shoulder and pulled him in for a masculine sporty hug. It was almost worse to have someone touch him like this; with such familiarity and joy. "I told you the crash in quali wouldn't matter."

"It matters." Ondrej pulled away from Jaxxon. "I might have done better than P8 without it, and the mechanics wouldn't have spent all night fixing my car." Australia—the first race of a new season—should be all about hope and new beginnings.

"Most passes by any driver today, Ondrej. Own that. Next race, use it." Jaxxon wasn't just stroking his ego. He knew his stuff. But no one here understood the longing that came with wanting to be himself and being utterly unable to. Ondrej was gay. A simple fact that stole his goals. He would never be world champion in this mid-field team. No other team wanted a gay driver. If he thought about the unfairness of his situation, his chest compressed as if he'd been winded in a heavy crash. So he didn't think about it. He painted on his arrogant sneer and gave everyone the ego they expected from an S1 driver.

"I was third fastest in Q1. I shouldn't have needed to

pass seven people to get a good result." He'd crashed at the end of the first qualification drive—clipping the apex curb in turn one and spinning out—meaning he didn't drive in Q2, so he'd started fifteenth on the grid for today's race. Bloody twitchy new car.

"Bloody drivers and their impossible egos. Getting points in a mid-field car should be good enough." The team owner and boss, Socrates, stuck out his hand and Ondrej shook it automatically.

"Is mid-field good enough for you?" Ondrej was too good to follow other cars around the track. Two years ago, he'd finished third on the championship table, in a team that won the constructor's title. Before he'd been unceremoniously sacked for being gay.

"Today it is. You've just scored Gamble Racing's first points in four years." A world champion driver in the late eighties, Socrates had a typical S1 pathway as a wealthy white Brit. He stood out as different to all the other, mostly white straight European drivers in S1 history as the only openly gay man in S1. There were rumours about others, like retired driver and media personality Freddy Hipton-stall, but never out. Even Socrates hadn't come out until long after he retired from driving, when it didn't matter anymore. When Ondrej's old team had dumped him, Socrates had stepped in and offered him a seat in the worst team on the grid. If Socrates knew the reason why Ondrej had been tossed away like garbage, he'd never mentioned it. Being gay wasn't something people openly acknowledged in S1.

"History is irrelevant in S1." Jaxxon was one of the few people Ondrej took advice from. He was a brilliant strategist, and he knew how to fight for what he wanted. Jaxxon was a Black man who'd grown up in one of the poorest suburbs in Liverpool and he had ambitions. Jaxxon wouldn't be content until he was Team Principal. Having a race engineer who matched Ondrej's desire to be the best was the only good thing about ending up in this team. "The only thing that matters is how to take today's success and improve on it."

"Eighth today, podium in two weeks at Bahrain." Ondrej made it sound like he believed it.

"This year's car is very fast." It was hard not to sneer at Socrates who'd finally sacked his old Lead Engineer Reginald Whitehall after years of terrible performance, and replaced him with a young gun, Victor Tsui, who'd completely redesigned the car for this season.

"Yes." Ondrej didn't want to get into this argument now. Victor's car had a lot of potential. Once they got the balance sorted, it would be quick *and* drivable. Right now, he needed some space to clear his head. Socrates was right. After last season's awful results, Ondrej should be thrilled with this year's car. He plastered on a smile and continued his way through the team before heading to his trailer.

"Brilliant drive." Papa looked up from his laptop as Ondrej stepped inside. "This year's car is so fast. Are you pleased?"

"I should be." Ondrej could always be honest with his father and agent. It'd always just been the two of them with no secrets. Ondrej trusted Papa with his career and his life.

"You should be, and I can see that you aren't. You are worth more than this."

"Thanks, Papa." He collapsed into a chair, staring blankly at the wall ahead.

"Yes. I've noticed that you've been very hard on yourself since..."

"Since I was sacked for 'inappropriate behaviour with a staff member'?" Ondrej had hooked up with one of the mechanics in his old team, Alex, a couple of times, and his old boss had caught them kissing in a storage cupboard. It had been a fucking bad choice—definitely ill-thought-out on his part—to tempt fate at work. Gamble had offered him a seat, and he'd been desperate enough to accept. The worst team on the grid was better than not driving at all. Now ... after a year of following all the other cars around the track, he wasn't so certain he'd made the right choice.

"Yes. You are an adult ... and I think we mopped up that mess quite well."

"You don't judge me for that?" Ondrej cursed the question. For over a year, he'd skirted around this subject with Papa.

"I think that if he'd been a woman, no one would've cared. The standard placed on you is unfair. No one should blame a driver for needing to let off steam. S1 is a high-pressure environment. You need some ... ahh, release. Your mother always needed that."

Ondrej cleared his throat. He knew his parents must have had sex at some point—his existence was evidence of that—but he really didn't want to think about it. "Papa."

"She did." Papa's gaze glazed over, like it always did when he reminisced about Ma.

"How is the Bugatti project going?" Ondrej had to change the subject, even to one that he found irritating.

The weird heat along the back of his neck must be the reason that Papa never wanted to talk about what happened with Alex either. This was the problem in working so close with family; some things were awkward to talk about when considered with a father/son dynamic, not an agent/driver one.

"The last historian was very disappointing, as you know." For years, Papa had been searching for the missing Bugatti. He was obsessed with it. Ondrej sighed. When he was a kid, the idea that his great-grandfather had been gifted a rare car was thrilling. Now he was a disillusioned twenty-eight-year-old, he knew the car would never be found, but he tried to indulge Papa, because as far as hobbies went it was fairly harmless.

"Find another." Ondrej would have to meet them and ensure they weren't going to get Papa's hopes up too much. Just like driving Victor's car, it was a balancing act between letting Papa have hope and not destroying his dreams.

"I did." Papa's eyes lit up. "And better still, he works for a company who has a queer friendly website."

Ondrej leaned forward. "You found a gay historian?" Ondrej imagined some pompous old balding man in a dapper pin stripe suit with a purple silk handkerchief in the jacket pocket. Each of the twelve historians who had tried—and failed—to find the rare car had been retired.

"If I find you've match-made me with some dull bookish old man..." He grinned as Papa's eyes widened. "I'm kidding."

"I would never. Love is too distracting from your job. We've already seen what happens when—" Papa didn't need to finish that sentence to reinforce that Ondrej couldn't be gay at work. Not if he wanted to be in a team capable of winning races. No one ever told the straight drivers they couldn't think about sex when they weren't in their race car.

Two days later, Ondrej parked his Maserati outside his childhood home and once again stared at the perplexing text from Papa.

Papa: I've taken a leaf from Socrates' book with this new historian.

Ondrej assumed this referred to Socrates being gay and the new historian also likely being gay. He walked inside, holding his breath, ready to cringe at Papa trying too hard. All his breath whistled out in a rush. Seated at the dining table was a stunningly handsome white man, who was probably the same age as himself. Papa's eyes gleamed with his usual excitement; that this time, this historian would finally be the one to do the impossible and find the fucking car. Logically, it'd probably been melted down during WWII and made into machine guns. Logic didn't seem to matter to Papa when it came to this topic.

Ondrej stared at the man, unable to speak. He was nothing like Ondrej had imagined. The man's vibrant red hair was swept back off his face in a fashionable cut, and he wore wire rim glasses balanced on a straight nose. The gentle patient expression on his face made him look incredibly kissable, and when combined with the blue sweater that clung to his broad shoulders, Ondrej struggled not to stare hungrily at him. It'd been months since Ondrej had fucked someone. Hell.

"Ah, Ondrej. I'm so glad you are here. Please meet Mr Lockley, he's just arrived from England to solve our little mystery."

"Hello. Pleased to meet you." Ondrej didn't offer his hand for the historian to shake because his words were a lie. He wasn't pleased. He was confused as fuck. Papa had said he wasn't match making, that love was distracting. Ondrej wasn't looking for love, but he definitely could spend more time with someone so smoking hot. After a couple of short breaths, he couldn't find it in himself to be annoyed at Papa's choice. Confused, yes? Irritated, fuck no. More like intrigued.

"Let me read you this letter and you'll see what I mean." Papa turned back to Mr Lockley, who nodded his agreement. Ondrej had read this letter often enough that he could probably recite it. The thin yellowing paper had a crest printed at the top, and the writing was that old fashioned scrawling script with a few ink blotches at random.

February 12, 1940

My dearest friend,

I do hope this letter reaches you under these most difficult of conditions. We have now been in England for the past few months, safely ensconced at the estate of the wonderful Lord Benburgh, who you may recall raced against us both in the Le Mans of '37. He kindly offered us safe passage when this infernal war broke out, and we leaped at the chance. I am writing because I have one regret and I was hoping you might assist me.

If you recall that race in '37, our mutual friend Robert Benoist gave me La Voiture Noire, a Bugatti

Atlantis (chassis number 57453), as a prize when I won. We had a good couple of years, enjoying driving the somewhat experimentally designed car around France. What a car! So elegant in design, with an engine that purred. Unfortunately when we had to rush over here, we were forced to leave her behind. I rang Robert before we left, and he promised to try and collect La Voiture Noire from our old place of residence. I won't include the address here, but you visited there on several occasions. The house with the stone front wall, and the rather impressive elm tree in the front yard. Robert mentioned he would try to store La Voiture Noire back at the Bugatti factory. I haven't heard from him since, so I'm not sure if this was achieved. Given the increasing problems, I was rather hoping I could ask a favour of you. Would you mind checking our garage for La Voiture Noire, and if she's not there, checking the factory? If you find her, I have included the spare key. I hope that you would relocate La Voiture Noire to a safe location, and in return for such a difficult mission, she is yours to keep. She was a gift to me, and I gift her to you, because such an incredible machine surely deserves to be kept safe from those who dare invade our beloved France; the location of many of my race victories and a place dear to my heart.

Yours always,

William Grover-Williams.

"Papa, you know that letter only means the car existed until the war started." Ondrej used to dream about this car and the letter, hoping that it had been saved. There were only three Bugatti Atlantis cars still in existence—only four were ever made—and the sleek long design was still one of the most beautiful vehicles ever designed.

"Ondrej, you know that isn't true. We have a letter from my grandfather's sister that says they were planning to leave France and drive the car to a safe location."

"That doesn't mean they drove the Bugatti, or that it arrived anywhere safe." He flicked a glance at Mr Lockley who kept his gaze firmly on the old papers spread all over the table.

"I believe it does." Papa's smug expression tipped him over the edge. He didn't want to know what the fuck game Papa was playing at by introducing him to a handsome man. He breathed in slowly. Papa might not realise what he'd just done; it wasn't like they talked about Ondrej's preferences. If this was anyone else in S1, Ondrej would've assumed he was being manipulated. He really didn't need more doubt. Doubt was the enemy to victory.

Ondrej rubbed his eyes. "Good luck, Mr Lockley, and Papa, I sincerely hope you find the answer you want." He marched out of the room and slid back into his Maserati for the two-hour drive along the coast to his apartment in Monaco. In ten days, he needed to be in Bahrain. He had ten days to find his old certainty. Victor had designed a fast car. He had no excuses except those in his own head.

CHAPTER 2

BAHRAIN

Having a client with decent money was a rarity, so when Mr D'Grieg paid for a flight to Bahrain to watch his, quite frankly, rude son race, Hudson said yes. As far as he could tell, they would never find the car, but his sister and business partner, Mackenzie, said he should try his best. If they got a few perks along the way, that would be good too.

Mr D'Grieg had given him the swipe key for a hotel room and told him to meet him there for a late afternoon meeting, and now he stood outside. It would be easy to think that his client had more money than sense, but Hudson didn't want to underestimate him either. One way he coped with his childhood was to find the good in people. The chances of being misled or ill-treated by someone, or even becoming the victim of fraud, were low, and he'd rather trust someone's goodwill than to miss an opportunity because of a natural tendency to dismiss it. He swiped the card and pushed the door open.

"Oh." Hudson gulped and nearly stumbled on the edge

of the rug. A spectacular man stood on the other side of the room, wearing only a towel slung low around his hips. Damp short brunette hair curled at the top of his surprisingly solid neck. On his left shoulder blade was a tattoo; a car with angel wings and the number 36 printed on the driver's door. Three championship cups sat on the bonnet of the car. Lean muscles stretched across his shoulder blades, a hint of rib, and a narrow, tapered waist all drew Hudson's eye. The man slowly turned, giving Hudson a delightful display of athletic beauty. His shoulder muscles adjoined lean biceps and perfectly sculptured pecs. He lifted his gaze to discover that Ondrej D'Grieg—his client's son—was the owner of this distracting physique.

"I'm sorry. Should I go?" He should. He was most definitely interrupting something.

"No. Did Papa invite you?"

"Yes." Hudson refused to be intimidated by the intense glare on Ondrej's face. Holy mother of goodness. Those eyes. A blue so deep they were almost black, and the stern intense expression threatened—welcomed—Hudson in a virulently sexy way. If this man commanded him, Hudson would follow him anywhere.

"He's wasting your time."

"Isn't that his right?" Hudson had met Ondrej only once, ten days ago in the briefest of meetings. Ondrej had refused to shake his hand, said something rude, then disappeared. Hudson had been so focused on Mr D'Grieg's puzzle that he hadn't registered how smoking hot Ondrej was. It wasn't until the meeting ended and Hudson was back at his hotel that he discovered the truth.

It was only natural to look Ondrej up on the internet

because he was a researcher and he needed to know who his clients were. Mostly he'd spent his research time staring at photos of Ondrej and his eyes—eyes that were a lot more intense and dramatic in real life—and his research had stalled, distracted by images. It wasn't all just eye candy; Hudson did have the basic facts sorted. The family had oil money, from a Norwegian branch of the family according to some website, and Ondrej had been a teen driving star in France. From winning a European karting championship at aged sixteen, he'd driven in the lower levels of formula racing until he signed with a major S1 team at age twenty. Now twenty-eight—three years younger than Hudson—he was a global star, or something like that, with a net worth that was unfathomable to Hudson. Hudson understood racing and the way people strived for victory as part of the general psychology of human aspiration because he'd been fostered with the Trews, racehorse trainers in Newmarket, for a few years, but the world of car racing was new to him.

Ondrej tilted his head slightly, then straightened again. "Come here."

Heat flushed across Hudson's skin at the command. Holy fuck, what he wouldn't give to have this man's hands on him. His knees buckled a fraction, instinctually wanting to kneel before him. With every step closer, Hudson's breath quickened. *Settle the fuck down, Hudson, as if someone in such a masculine job would be gay.*

"Tell me about yourself."

"About me or my business with your father?"

"Start there."

"Five years ago, my sister Mackenzie and I started Ancestor Investigations. We specialise in putting together family trees and stories. She runs the business side of it, and I do the historical research." As far as jobs went for someone with his qualifications, it gave him a lot more freedom than working for an institutional museum or in academia.

"Okay, Mr Lockley. What are your qualifications?"

"Please call me Hudson. I have a master's degree in history." He had a feeling Ondrej wouldn't give a damn about what he'd specialised in—lavender marriages in the Victorian era—so he simply stuck out his hand instead and Ondrej shook it once. It took all his concentration not to shake out his hand afterwards to get rid of the electric tingles left by Ondrej's touch. He kept his gaze low, not wanting to show his reaction to Ondrej, but that meant he ended up staring at the bottom of Ondrej's towel and his bare legs. This rampant chemistry would likely confuse anyone straight and Hudson didn't need the reminder that his reaction didn't fit here.

"So, Hudson, you take your fancy education, and you entice families into thinking they are related to royalty, or that you can find priceless artifacts, and they pay you to fly around the world?"

Hudson blinked at the accusation. How cynical of Ondrej. He slowly raised his gaze to meet Ondrej's hard stare. "I wish. No, mostly, I hunt through public records, like births, deaths, and marriages to put together an accurate family tree. I try to find mentions of people in newspapers and create a narrative for the family." Mackenzie took his research and packaged it into a booklet. People adored their books, and they often ordered extra copies for all their family members. He loved that aspect of his job; creating family connections for people, telling the stories that were often ignored or untold by the history books. Every tiny detail about ordinary lives brought him joy.

"This job is a great opportunity for you."

"Honestly, yes. Most of our clients can't afford to fly me to Bahrain, or anywhere, for a meeting. This is highly unusual for me." In the month since he'd signed Mr D'Grieg as a client, he'd been to Mr D'Grieg's home in France, and now Bahrain. Ondrej stepped closer and Hudson was surprised to discover that Ondrej was shorter than his own six feet. Not by much—only an inch—but his presence in the room had been so big, he'd assumed Ondrej was taller than him. Ondrej stood so close that Hudson could feel his breath on his face.

"Let me make this clear to you. One." Ondrej held up his hands and tapped one long finger with another. "Papa is obsessed with this car. Two. The hunt for it is pointless. Three. I will not have him hurt by some prick who gets Papa's hopes up." A shadow passed quickly over Ondrej's face, fast enough for Hudson to dismiss it as his imagination. Hudson's face burned with heat at the proximity of Ondrej's naked chest, not to mention his passion for his father's wellbeing. There was something so elementally attractive—sexy—about a man who cared deeply for his family.

"Promise me you'll let him down gently."

"Understood." Hudson could barely talk under this onslaught of hot-headed commanding male before him. If he moved an inch, they'd be kissing. Focusing on the words Ondrej was saying was difficult. He really wanted was this man to kiss him. If he was a betting man, he'd go all in on this man being arrogantly outstanding in bed.

"Promise."

"I promise." Hudson's voice cracked a little.

"What do you promise?"

Fuck, he wasn't a child; as evidenced by the very adult sensations taking over his body. "I won't get your father's hopes up and I will let him down gently when I can't find the car."

"Good. And lastly. I will not have our family plastered all over your business as advertising. You will not use my name on any communications." Ondrej turned on his heels and went back to staring out the window. The last comment hadn't been necessary. Ancestor Investigations had signed a confidentiality contract with Mr D'Grieg that had included a clause that they couldn't mention this investigation or any family member of Mr D'Grieg in their marketing or social media. When Hudson had signed, he hadn't known who Ondrej was, and now Mr D'Grieg's insistence at complete confidentiality made sense. They obviously protected each other. Hudson closed his eyes until the yearning went away.

When his heart stopped pounding, Hudson checked his watch. Mr D'Grieg should be here soon. Hudson glanced around the room—looking everywhere except Ondrej's naked torso—then placed his briefcase on the coffee table. This hotel room was more of a suite than a simple room and came complete with a proper lounge area and coffee table. The luxury was far beyond his usual standard of living, and he tried not to be too awkward in the space as he prepared for Mr D'Grieg to arrive. Since receiving this commission, he'd reviewed all the documents owned by Mr D'Grieg, including all the reports from the various other historians who'd tried to find the car. It put Ondrej's concerns in context, given how many times Mr D'Grieg had gone through this process. Hudson backed himself to find the little details that other people overlooked and maybe this case wasn't completely hopeless. He might not find the car, but he could contribute something new to the research.

The door opened. "Ondrej, get dressed. Have you offered our guest some coffee?"

"Papa. I'm not putting on a goddamned tux until I have to. And no, he is not our guest." Did Ondrej plan to stand around in a towel for an unknown amount of time? And why was he going to wear a tux? What did that have to do with motor racing? He'd learned a lot in the last two weeks about the Le Mans races pre-WWII and William Grover-Williams, but even he could guess that life as a modern-day race car driver was probably very different to a bunch of aristocrats playing with emerging technology.

"Mr Lockley. Please excuse my son. He gets very... focused on a race weekend."

"I hope you don't mind me asking, but why the tuxedo?" Hudson kept his voice low, unwilling to let Ondrej know his ignorance.

"There is a sponsors dinner and press conference tonight, then tomorrow there will be two practice sessions."

Hudson glanced over at Ondrej, who gave no indication he'd heard their conversation. "It's nice that you can support him like this."

"I am his agent. Besides, family should support each

other, don't you think?" Mr D'Grieg was quickly becoming one of Hudson's favourite clients.

"Yes. Thank you for inviting me this weekend. I've never been an event like this before."

"We have a couple of hours to go over your research before tonight's dinner. I trust that you'll be able to entertain yourself tonight. Tomorrow you will join me in the guest's section above the pitlane."

"Thank you." Hudson found Mr D'Grieg's generosity a little overwhelming, so he opened his briefcase and pulled out the glossy report Mackenzie had created from his research. "Shall we get started?"

Mr D'Grieg glanced sideways as Ondrej collapsed elegantly into a chair beside his father. The resemblance between the two was strong, although the older D'Grieg had much paler blue eyes and a softer expression.

"What are you waiting for?" Ondrej asked, after less than half a minute's silence.

Hudson swallowed back a retort and simply handed Mr D'Grieg the report. "This report is a compilation of all the research done to date. You won't find anything new in there—"

"Well, that was a waste of time."

Hudson raised his eyebrows at the sharp retort. "Not at all. It would be waste if I ignored all the research done to date by others and spent months redoing it. By putting together this document, it collates all the work you've already had done and identifies any potential gaps in research. Those gaps will give me clues as to where to continue on with the work. Let's not reinvent the whole wheel here."

"That makes a lot of sense." Mr D'Grieg smiled and even Ondrej's face relaxed a little. Was that a tiny movement at the corner of his lips? Almost the beginnings of a smile?

"This report begins with the letter, and then I've created a timeline of all the research done to date and over-laid it against a basic WWII timeline. If you open up the report to the third page, you'll be able to follow the timeline along." Hudson was quite proud of the way they'd presented this information. It took a bunch of disparate pieces of research and put them into a logical timeline. "As you can see it begins with when Grover-Williams left his home in France. Each date on the timeline has a summary comment and a page number. If you flick to that page in this report, you'll find all the details around that research. For example, here in 1943, the factory was bombed." One of the previous historians had obviously specialised in WWII because he'd included a lot of unnecessary detail about the war and not very much about the missing car. Hudson had kept it all for this report, although some of it didn't appear to relate to the problem at all.

"Does this help at all?"

"Yes. Applying a logical timeline to a puzzle helps figure out potential lines of enquiry."

"For example?" For someone who apparently thought this search was pointless, Ondrej was oddly curious.

"One previous historian included a lot of information about German army supply lines. I hunted through every-thing he'd done on the assumption that he'd found discov-ered that perhaps the car had been repatriated to Germany using their supply line trains."

"Unlikely."

Hudson shrugged one shoulder. "This puzzle is all about the unlikely options, and honestly, it's not even that unlikely. During WWII, the Nazis stole an incredible volume of art, historical artifacts, jewellery, collectable items, basically anything that might be of value that was easy to transport. Their supply line trains were renowned for transporting supplies to their armies and stolen goods back to Germany. There's actually a high chance they stole the Bugatti from the factory in France and transported it to Germany."

"Did you find any evidence?" Mr D'Grieg was a little breathless.

"Not yet. It doesn't mean that didn't happen, it's just that the historian who researched that option couldn't find any evidence. And that's what I'd expect too. Thieves tend not to record what they were doing." Hudson shrugged.

"That's logical," Mr D'Grieg said.

"Most of the stolen art from WWII has only been recovered when descendants of those who took it tried to sell it; and many of the original owners have been left with nothing but a protest, especially if they can't provide provenance for the object."

"Provenance?"

"Proof of ownership. You are lucky because you have a letter from a known owner gifting the car to your family member. Not everyone in a war situation was so fortunate. Either the ownership records were destroyed, or they simply didn't exist in the first place. Do you keep a complete list of everything you own and update regularly?"

"No. But I have photos."

"Photography during WWII was still an expensive

hobby." Hudson didn't particularly want to get into this argument; if they were paying attention they'd understand that photography wasn't accessible to most people in that era. "If we could continue, please go to page thirty-seven in my report. I've listed the potential gaps here. I've already visited the former Grover-Williams property in France. The house remains, although the original land has been sold off and in-filled with other housing. Behind the house, in the backyard is a small hill." Hudson wanted to do more research around this house and the odd way the subdivision had been created, because that hill was out of context to the rest of the landscape. He didn't understand why the developer hadn't just bulldozed it, but why spend money bulldozing a hill when it could be easily be left in the backyard? "I've noted a few research questions around that house. As you can see in my notes, the garage that originally housed the car in 1937 has since been demolished for the subdivision."

"I have no interest in the garage, only the car." Mr D'Grieg's voice showed the same irritation as his son relied on.

"I imagine that you will be familiar with all the information in this report. I've merely presented it in a new fashion, and aside from my visit to the Grover-Williams property in France, there is nothing in here that will surprise you. This is only my first report, and as I said at the beginning of this meeting, it is a compilation document that brings together all the information you have already sourced."

"What happens next?" Mr D'Grieg asked.

"Next I follow the leads I've noted in the final pages of

the report and when I'm done, we can meet with an update." Hudson glanced at Ondrej. "Honestly, you don't need to fly me anywhere. I can post you the report and we can talk on the phone."

"I like our meetings. I propose we meet again at Baku at the end of the month." Mr D'Grieg ignored his proposal not to meet in person. He'd have to look up where and what Baku was; a place, presumably.

"Make it after the race." Ondrej said.

Mr D'Grieg obviously knew what Ondrej meant as he nodded. "Good plan. Let's meet on the Monday after the race. Thank you, Hudson. I'll have my PA email you with tickets. Please enjoy your evening, and I'll see you tomorrow for FP1."

"Okay." Hudson assumed that comment ended the meeting, so he packed up his briefcase and stood. "Thank you." He needed to research what FP1 meant and where in the world was Baku. He ought to be focusing on the Bugatti mystery, because if they were meeting at the end of the month, he had only four weeks to find new information to present to his clients. It shouldn't take long to figure out the basics of what Mr Grieg and Ondrej were talking about and then he could focus on his actual job. Although Ondrej was one hell of a distraction. All that intense tightly held control in one gorgeous package. Shit; the last thing Hudson needed to imagine now was Ondrej's package.

Mr D'Grieg stood and shook his hand. "I look forward to reading your report in detail."

Ondrej also stood and held out his hand for Hudson. He took in a short breath to settle his heart rate, then shook Ondrej's hand. Once again, the same jolt of energy raced up his arm and this time, he braved holding Ondrej's gaze to see if he noticed. Ondrej's eyes widened a fraction. Hudson couldn't breathe. He was in so much trouble.

"I'll see you tomorrow as agreed." He bolted out of the room before he did something ridiculous like kiss his client's son in front of his client.

CHAPTER 3

"**B**rilliant drive, Ondrej." Socrates, Gamble's team owner, gushed through the phone. "I was spitting mad after Shanghai."

"Paulo is a rookie." Ondrej had been fucking furious in the seconds after his team-mate had crashed into him, just after leaving the pit lane on lap thirty-two. It'd fucked up his race, and he'd finished at the tail of the field. After yesterday's result, it mattered less, and Ondrej was more able to recognise that rookie drivers fucked up sometimes. Paulo would learn.

"All up it was a shit outcome for the team, no points for the weekend and Paulo's car needed a rebuild." They'd already discussed this at the team meeting after Shanghai, it really didn't need to be rehashed.

"He drove well yesterday." Maybe Paulo had learned his lesson, especially since he came off second best in the incident at Shanghai, spinning out into a wall. Ondrej was nearly at the top of the stone spiral staircase that led to the room at the top of the castle here in Baku. It wasn't its official name, just what the drivers called it. The castle section of the track.

"Great drive by both of you, mate. We are starting to look like a proper mid-field team again. Our sponsors are thrilled."

"Good news."

"Just keep it up, stay focused like yesterday. I'll see you in Spain in a week." Socrates hung up before Ondrej could remind him that he had simulator time booked for two days time, so he'd likely see him then. Having a retired driver as team boss was usually great because he understood the routine during the season on an intimate level. Now the race in Baku was over, he had eight days before he needed to be in Spain for pre-race preparations, and the team's Head Engineer Victor had some additional testing he wanted done in that time.

"Stay focused." Ondrej whispered to himself as he stopped at the top of the stairs. On the other side of that door was Hudson, and Ondrej had spent too many hours in the two weeks since Bahrain thinking about Hudson. At work, he always found it easy to switch into driver mode. Like all the other drivers, he put his life on the line every time he drove an S1 car, and he knew how to clear his mind for the concentration required. The red-headed historian only infiltrated his thoughts during down times, like when he was while travelling between race venues.

Ondrej pushed open the creaky old wooden door and stepped into the room at the top of the castle. He hadn't been up here since his rookie season when his old team's boss had told him to get a different view of the castle section.

"Hi."

"Hello. Can you believe how incredible this place is! Built in 1136." Hudson rested his hand reverently against the ancient stone wall and closed his eyes. His red hair had grown a little longer since he'd last seen him and it flopped over his forehead. Ondrej wanted to brush it back. Fuck. The last thing he should be thinking about was this. He couldn't fuck up his career again; last time he'd kissed a man near a racetrack—Alex—it had gone terribly wrong. In hindsight, he'd let his cock make the decision. Never a great idea. Having the team boss walk in on them kissing in a storage cupboard had resulted in them both getting the sack. Intolerant fuckwit.

"It can't be that special. They let us race right next to it." Relying on sarcasm usually helped his control.

Hudson's eyes flew open, flashing behind his glasses. "I was stunned to see that. And only a small sheet of what? Plastic? Covering the wall to stop you destroying it."

"Hitting that wall would destroy the car before it would destroy a fortress wall." Ondrej shrugged. Turns eight to twelve at Baku was a technical part of the track and unforgiving if a driver made a fractional error. Those sections were his favourite to drive because the precision required at speed was the thing that made him one of the best twenty drivers in the world.

"How can you be so flippant about that?"

"About?"

Hudson dragged his hand through his hair and Ondrej's fingers tingled. Damn it. He couldn't thread his fingers through Hudson's vibrant red hair. Not now.

"About crashing, I suppose, and also … this is a historic monument. It's literally a UNESCO world heritage site."

"We can coexist."

Hudson's nostrils flared. "Part of me wants to scream at the idea that you get so close to the walls with your destruction machines, and part of me agrees. History isn't static and it should coexist with modern life."

"Such a dilemma for you." Ondrej adored the open expressiveness on Hudson's face. He obviously cared deeply for his argument as patches of colour broke out on his cheeks, making his freckles look darker. He wanted to kiss each one. Fucking hell. During the racing year, it was difficult to get laid. The schedule was intense, he had almost no time alone, and there were too many eyes on him all the time. In the off-season, it was easier to travel under a pseudonym and laugh it off when people 'recognised' him. He was well skilled at telling people that they weren't the first person who thought he looked like that S1 driver.

"I'm just not sure that coexisting equates to crashing heavy vehicles into historic buildings."

"You do realise that the track is a public road so people who aren't good drivers manage to drive past this fortress every other day of the year. It's still here after—" Ondrej paused, not knowing how old the Baku fortress was.

"A thousand years."

"Yeah. I don't see the difference in risk." A slow bad driver was at higher risk of hitting the wall as a skilled fast driver. Hudson ran his hand through his hair again and Ondrej sucked in his breath. He really needed to stop doing that if he didn't want to be shoved up against his fucking precious thousand-year-old stones and kissed thoroughly.

"I don't understand you."

"Understand this." Ondrej lived for taking risks; carefully managed risks that allowed him to drive the world's fastest cars. With a quick glance over his shoulder to check they were alone, he strode over to Hudson and pushed him back against the wall. Before Hudson had a chance to react, Ondrej kissed him. The shock on Hudson's face quickly changed, and Ondrej fucking loved that millisecond when Hudson chose to respond positively. The switch was perfect. Hudson kissed him back. Fuck yes. He'd read all those little glances from Hudson correctly. Ondrej pinned him against the wall, one hand on the cool stones, the other wrapped around his neck, and when Hudson shifted to push his thigh between Ondrej's legs and rubbed his hard cock against Ondrej, he got the same thrill as when he hit the accelerator on the starting grid ... but with much less control. His heart pounded loudly as their tongues tussled together. Hudson tasted like mint and sex and Ondrej wanted to drag him back to his hotel room. Screw who might see them. He leaped backwards. What the fuck was he doing? The last time he'd kissed someone at work, he'd ended up thrown away like garbage. He couldn't do this again. Hudson stood there panting, his chest rising and falling quickly, matching Ondrej's own frantic rhythm.

"Shit. Papa will update me on your meeting." Ondrej bolted away from Hudson before he kissed him again. He ran down the spiral stone staircase as fast as he could. What the fuck had he been thinking? His bloody cock was going to get him in trouble. Again.

"Ondrej." Someone spoke his name and it pierced the fog in his head.

"Alex?" Ondrej came to a screaming halt; if he'd been in his car, it would've been a huge lockup with smoking tyres. "What are you doing here?"

"Working."

"But..." Didn't Alex get sacked too?

"I found another job with a different team." He pointed to his cap, one of the other mid-field teams. "Same as you, really. Gamble Racing are going well this season."

"Yeah. I can't really talk about it."

"I'm not expecting you to give me insider information, Ondrej. Just because we ... well, I'm just glad it worked out well for you."

Ondrej gulped. He stuck out his hand for Alex to shake. "And for you too." He started to walk again, but Alex cleared his throat.

"Hey, I'm really glad I bumped into you here. I just wanted you to know that I've met someone." Alex gave him a strange look.

"Congratulations." Ondrej didn't really understand why Alex thought he might care. They'd hooked up a couple of times ages ago; it'd hardly constituted a relationship.

"Cool."

Ondrej finally got over the shock of seeing Alex so soon after running from Hudson and empathy filled his chest, slowing his heartbeat. Alex had a new job in S1 and a partner. "Is your new team okay to work for?"

Alex seemed to know what Ondrej was asking. "I was up front in my interview with them, and you know what the team boss said?"

"What?"

"We have over six hundred men working in our team. Using statistical probability, at least fourteen of them are gay."

"And that was it?" Ondrej was stunned. Obviously Gamble Racing would be okay with him being gay; if he ever admitted it. Socrates, the team owner, was openly married to his long-term partner Mike. As a contract-less driver, he'd been actively pursued by Gamble, meaning he hadn't needed to convince them to take him. Papa dealt with all the contractual side of things, so he could focus on racing. For Alex—who didn't have the same draw power— to be so bold was impressive.

"Yep. Direct quote. Pretty cool, huh."

"And?" Ondrej waited for the inevitable.

Alex shrugged. "Then we just did the interview and I got the job."

Ondrej's whole world seemed off-centre. "That's surprisingly open of them." It was different for Alex though; he wasn't a brand. As a mechanic, Alex was just a cog in the machine that was S1. An important cog, sure, but there was no one writing press releases about Alex every day during the season. No media following him around, wanting to know about his private life, making guesses at his relationship status every time he sat next to a beautiful woman at a sponsor's dinner. He was amazed that after eight years of writing the same nonsense gossip articles they weren't tired of it.

"I did get told that they frowned on office relationships because they wanted everyone's focus to be on the job and with the team working and traveling so much together, they would prefer to avoid that potential source of tension."

Alex confirmed Ondrej's experience in S1. It was okay to be gay, just not at work where it would affect the team. Perhaps it wasn't so different for them both.

"I'm glad you found another job. It'd be a huge loss to S1 if you hadn't. Good luck in Spain." Ondrej relied on years of media training to spit out some kind of vague answer, before he brushed past Alex and continued his way down the stairs. He needed to get far away from Hudson, and from Alex, from all temptations—old and new—and do as his boss said. Stay focused. Papa could have his meeting with Hudson and Ondrej would read the report some other time. It wasn't ideal because Papa's enthusiasm about the missing car would go wild without Ondrej keeping it tampered. He was used to being the rear wing for the project. In his car, it provided downforce and made the car easier to control. Not this time. He couldn't let himself be in the same room as Hudson, not now that he knew what his mouth tasted like, what the hard length of his cock felt like when pressed against him. The warmth of the skin on the back of his neck and the soft tendrils of his hair on the back of Ondrej's hand. Most of all, the moment when Hudson had softened between Ondrej's body and the stone wall would haunt Ondrej. It felt like Hudson would willingly give Ondrej everything, and it was far too fucking tempting. For his own good, he needed to stay far away, and that meant trusting the Hudson wouldn't take advantage of Papa. Fuck. None of this was ideal.

CHAPTER 4

SPAIN

"How's Spain?" Mackenzie's sing song voice came through Hudson's ear bud clearly.

"It's beautiful. Barcelona is incredible. How is this my life?" Hudson leaned against a stone wall outside the front of the stunning hotel that Mr D'Grieg had booked for him. The warm summer sun shone off the glassy water of the marina, and elegant people stepped off giant expensive yachts to promenade along the footpath. He had spent all morning exploring the city and should really go to his room for a quick shower before his meeting with Mr D'Grieg but being outside in this lovely weather held much more appeal.

Mackenzie laughed. "Next time, I want the eccentric rich client who flies me all around the world."

"Deal."

"What?"

"The next one is yours." The fancy lifestyle his client kept adorning him made him rather uncomfortable. He had smaller goals, smaller ambitions, and those were only two reasons among many for why he really didn't belong with these people.

"Good. I like that you assume there will be a next one. Now just remember who is keeping this business going while you are swanning about among ancient buildings." Her teasing tone made him grin, despite the little reminder that he tended towards anxiety and negative thinking. She was the only person in his life who was allowed to remind him to reframe negative thoughts into positive ones because she faced the same battle to look forward and find joy.

"Always." Hudson was always amazed how Mackenzie took his dull lists of information and created glossy reports for their clients. In the last two weeks, he'd ended up down a whole bunch of dead ends. It'd been frustrating and his report was flimsy.

"Now, seriously, how are you? When is your meeting?"

Hudson relaxed. "I'm fine. The meeting is in a couple of hours."

"And? What is that I hear in your tone?" Bloody older sisters who know everything.

He sighed. "I'm worried that I have hardly anything to tell them. Like my report in Baku was mostly crap— just more confirmation of other people's work—and it's only been two weeks since then. I have nothing to show them. I don't deserve all this fancy stuff they are giving me." He'd spent far too much time thinking about Ondrej's mouth and the way his body felt pressed against his. And now his lack of productivity would be found wanting.

"Stop that." Mackenzie pulled out her Mum voice. The one she used when he'd been a bratty teenager and she'd been his guardian, and the one she used on Henry and Harriet, her three-year-old twins.

"What?" Even though he knew what she meant. *Stop putting himself down. Stop saying he didn't deserve attention. Stop worrying that if he wasn't good enough, they'd end up being moved again.* They'd both been in and out of foster care—sometimes together, sometimes apart—and as soon as Mackenzie had turned eighteen, she'd applied for guardianship of him. He'd been fifteen and as he'd gotten older, it continually amazed him how much determined confidence Mackenzie had. She refused to let anything keep her down.

"You are worth this. We are worth a client like this. If anyone can find that car, it's you."

"It's probably scrap metal."

"So what! I don't care if you never find the car, but I do care about one thing, Hudson. You. And you will enjoy this."

"Okay."

"I mean it." Her determination made him want to believe her. She hadn't come out of foster care completely unscathed, but her husband, Brian Le, had encouraged her to go to therapy which had helped turn many of the wounds into healed scars. Still there, but no longer bleeding. Hudson had tried a few times but had never found a therapist he connected with. It was probably his fault. He didn't really like talking about himself.

"I believe you. I'll take some photos of the flower festival for you."

"Whatever. All I want is to see you enjoy yourself. Stop hiding in books." Mackenzie loved to tease him about his reading habit. She knew it was his way of controlling the world around him, a way to escape the reality of all the changes that came with being a foster kid.

"I'll have you know that my love of history and books is the basis of our whole business." He grinned, imagining her rolling her eyes. It felt good to tease her. Nicer than worrying constantly about how he wasn't going to measure up to Mr D'Grieg's expectations; or worse, to Ondrej's expectation that he'd 'let Papa down gently'. His breath was unsteady.

"Shit. Harriet. Harriet. Stop that. Damn it. I have to go. Harriet is trying to feed Henry dirt from the pot plant."

"Bye." Hudson hung up and leaned back against the stone wall overlooking the marina. He'd forgotten to tell Mackenzie about the Torre Agbar, a phallic looking building that locals apparently nicknamed the suppository, according to the tourist brochure he'd grabbed from the concierge this morning. Mackenzie loved that kind of whacky modern architecture. For him, something built in 2005 had zero appeal. It was too new. Old things appealed because they were solid, unchanging through the mists of time. Mackenzie's joking voice rang in his head; 'no prizes for guessing why!'

He'd spent the morning exploring the Gothic Quarter, and he had plans to check out the Gaudi architecture tomorrow during practice. Now that he'd kissed Ondrej, he wasn't sure his nerves could cope with watching him dice with death. Watching him at previous races had been exhilarating—the skill required to guide an S1 car at such incredible speeds around those tracks blew his mind. He closed his eyes and smiled with the warmth of the sun on his face.

He couldn't stay out here forever; the curse of red hair meant his skin burned easily.

But oh God, that kiss. It'd been glorious. Over and over, he'd relived that moment when Ondrej had pushed him up against the Baku Fortress Wall and kissed him thoroughly.

"Hello." Speak of the devil! Only one person had that voice and Hudson immediately opened his eyes and stood up taller. Ondrej walked towards him, dragging a small suitcase.

"Hey." What the hell was he doing? This was the biggest opportunity for their business, and he was risking ruining it by kissing the son of their client.

"When did you arrive?"

"Last night."

Ondrej raised one eyebrow. His stunning eyes were hidden behind sunglasses and Hudson was glad for the reprieve from his intense critical stare.

"I know. Mr D'Grieg is too generous." They were due to meet tonight before dinner, and Hudson had expected to head home again afterwards, but Mr D'Grieg had included the whole weekend, and a room in an incredible hotel near the marina. During the racing, he planned to sit on his balcony and get some research done so he had something concrete to talk to Mr D'Grieg about.

"You'd better be worth it."

"I am." Hudson breathed in. Had Ondrej seriously just hinted... No. Had he just instinctively answered with such confidence? "I meant the history stuff. I am good at that."

"Papa wouldn't hire someone who he didn't have faith in."

"Okay? I'm..." Hudson clenched his jaw. He didn't

need to demonstrate his uncertainty to his client's son. "I'm…"

"You're what?" Ondrej waited for a moment, but Hudson couldn't form words.

"Nothing. I mean, I'm not nothing. It's nothing for you to worry about."

"Come." Ondrej walked into the hotel with the doorman welcoming him by name. He dumped his suitcase and walked over to the front desk. They handed him an envelope and welcomed him in such an efficient manner that Hudson barely had time to blink. Before he knew it, Ondrej had stepped into the lift. He waited with his hand resting against the door until Hudson caught up. As soon as he stepped inside, Ondrej swiped the hotel card and the lift rushed upwards.

"Um, what just happened?"

"What do you mean?"

"When I got here, it took ages to talk to the front desk and get my room sorted. You just walk in here and they hand it over?"

"Perks of the job. I've stayed here every year for eight years. The team makes the booking and I turn up." Ondrej didn't sound thrilled by it.

"Is it hard to be recognised all the time?" Like, being able to walk into a hotel and not wait to be served sounded great, but it couldn't all be perks? Could it?

Ondrej barely moved. "Is it hard to be named after a car?"

"What?" Hudson blinked. "Did you just say I was named after a car?" He had no memory of his birth parents, which was probably a good thing according to his care records.

"Haven't you watched that kid's movie? One of the cars is named after a 1950s NASCAR winner; the Hudson Hornet. The lower chassis allowed better handling and drivability." For the first time today, Ondrej's voice lifted from flat and exhausted into something resembling passion.

"I was a teenager when that movie released. Why are you watching kid's movies?"

"I fly a lot."

"What?" Hudson had never flown as much as these last few months since taking on this job.

Ondrej bent his head, so he stared at Hudson over the top of his sunglasses. "Lots of flight time means lots of movies watched."

"Right, of course. It's not something I've done much of."

"Flying?"

"Yeah. We didn't really travel when I was a kid." Unless moving between foster homes and changing schools counted. "When I went to France to meet Mr D'Grieg, it was my first time on a plane."

"Ever?"

"Yes."

"You hadn't left England before that?"

Hudson grinned. "It is possible to take the train to Europe."

Ondrej nodded once, and the slight encouragement was enough to make Hudson want to babble at him happily.

"I'm basically a history geek. Whenever I had enough money saved up, I'd head to a new city. New museums, new knowledge. I love it all." When he'd been thirteen, he'd gone on the train with Rose of Gardenia to Chantilly, and it had opened a whole new world for him. The racetrack was stunning with the historic Chateau as a backdrop. He might have spent the whole time looking after the horse, but he knew he had to come back and explore one day. Rosie had run fourth in a group race and been sold to Japan where she'd become a broodmare. She'd be in her twenties now, old for a horse.

"Racing from one place to another like the Hudson you are named after."

"Sure. Something like that." Hudson didn't know how to answer that. He really didn't want to discuss his childhood, and luckily he was saved from the awkward moment by the lift doors opening. Ondrej stepped out. The doors started to slide shut again and Hudson took a half step forward then stopped. Ondrej waved his hand between the doors and they opened again.

"Come."

Hudson followed, because what else was he going to do? Disobey the son of his best client. Yeah, sure. It had absolutely nothing at all to do with the fact that Ondrej's command lit up his skin and made him want to obey. They walked down the hallway until Ondrej stopped and swiped his card to open a door. As he followed Ondrej into his hotel room, he scoffed under his breath. So much for keeping a distance between Ondrej and himself. Mackenzie's words bounced around his head. When she said "Enjoy yourself. Stop hiding in books", she probably didn't mean get on his knees and suck Ondrej's cock. Surely his face was bright red because it felt fucking hot.

Ondrej stood in the middle of the hotel room with the sun streaming through the window behind him, casting his face into shadow. The curled ends of his messy brown hair glowed in the light.

"Kiss me."

Hudson blinked. "Excuse me?" After Ondrej had bolted after their kiss in Baku and then had no contact with him, Hudson had assumed they just weren't going to mention it again.

"You liked it last time." Arrogance painted Ondrej's tone. It was true. Hudson had liked Ondrej's kiss. A lot.

"You can't just expect me to obey you. Come. Kiss me." Hudson mimicked Ondrej, because as much as he loved being told what to do, he wasn't a push over either.

Ondrej shrugged. "Your loss." He tossed his sunglasses onto a chair and the blaze in his eyes made a mockery of his dismissal.

"Yours too."

Time stretched as they stood staring at each other. It took all of Hudson's strength not to buckle, and he wasn't even sure why he was fighting this so hard.

"Why were you smiling?"

"When?" Hudson touched his mouth. He hadn't been smiling, had he?

"Outside, when I arrived. You were smiling."

Hudson grinned. Did he dare tell the whole truth? That he'd been dreaming of sucking Ondrej's cock? No, he couldn't say that.

"Yes, smiling just like that. Why?"

Hudson had a choice; he could mention he'd been talking to his sister and completely kill the mood. Or he could be brave and give Ondrej what he wanted. His heart skipped a beat. Did he really want to be another notch on an S1 driver's bedpost? Surely a man like this, who had fame and fortune, could have anyone in his bed. While he was cogitating, Ondrej walked towards him. He reached up and brushed his thumb across Hudson's lower lip.

"This smile is very kissable."

Hudson breathed in shakily. "Then kiss..." *me.* He didn't have time to finish the sentence before Ondrej pushed him up against the hotel wall with a soft thud. Ondrej's mouth covered his, and the soft pressure stripped away all of Hudson's earlier concerns. It didn't matter if he was one of many in Ondrej's life of fame and plenty. All that mattered was Ondrej's kiss, and his hard fit body pressed hard against him. It was a sensation overload and exactly what Hudson wanted and couldn't ask for. He stroked his hands up Ondrej's sides, then spread them over his shoulder blades. Ondrej kissed him lazily, as if he had all the time in the world. Hudson opened his mouth and let Ondrej savour him. For someone whose life revolved around speed, this kiss was slow and luxurious. Different to the urgent kiss at Baku. He adored both versions; Ondrej in a rush and this one; Ondrej taking his time. Hudson pushed his leg between Ondrej's thighs and hinted that he should move them across the room to the bed. Ondrej didn't move, just deepened the kiss with extravagant strokes along Hudson's tongue. It was decadent, a reflection on the life Ondrej led, and one that Hudson had no experience of.

"Stop." Being pushed against the wall the way he was, he had to slide his head sideways to end the kiss.

"Why?"

"I can't do this." He couldn't enter something so potentially uneven.

Ondrej rolled his eyes. "Technically, neither should I."

"What?" Hudson's brain switched direction so abruptly, he wondered if he had a concussion. It was one thing for him to doubt this; quite another for Ondrej—who acted like he knew what he wanted—to agree with him. This was a bad idea. He stood there, still pressed between the wall and Ondrej, trying to pull enough breath from his aching lungs to be able to speak.

"I know why I shouldn't do this, but why can't you?" Ondrej raised one eyebrow and Hudson scrambled to catch up. He placed both his hands on Ondrej's chest with some difficulty given their proximity. It was a mistake; he'd planned to shove Ondrej away and now with all the lean muscle under his hands, he wanted to lean into it instead.

"Why can't you?" Ondrej asked again.

"Um, I—" *Come on, brain.* He squeezed his eyes shut to try and remember why, but all that happened was his other senses came to life. Ondrej's heady scent wrapped around him, a masculine overload.

"Why shouldn't you?" Eventually, Hudson deflected the question back.

Ondrej stepped away, leaving Hudson's hands hanging awkwardly in the air. "Seriously? Do you even have to ask that?" Ondrej waved his arms around the room and Hudson quietly dropped his to his side. Hudson remembered why he couldn't do this.

"I'm—" Ondrej paused.

"Rich, famous, and way out of my league?" Hudson stated the bleeding obvious.

Ondrej shook his head. "I'm gay."

"And?" Kissing him had already told Hudson that Ondrej was either gay or bisexual.

Ondrej paced back and forth in this massive hotel room. "Sponsors, team bosses, fans... They don't like it."

Suddenly all of Hudson's concerns seemed minor. It wasn't that Hudson wasn't in the same class as Ondrej—although that hadn't changed—but that Ondrej's entire job required him to be closeted.

"I thought sports was more inclusive now?"

Ondrej sat on the bed and Hudson had the urge to comfort him. No, they didn't have that relationship yet. Yet? Maybe never.

"S1 is a very... masculine sport. They've been grappling with racial inclusion for a while now—"

"Surely that's important?"

"Absolutely it is. I didn't suggest it wasn't." Ondrej scratched his forehead. "Being gay is complicated in this sport. The race organisers have an LGBT inclusion policy; it's just that most of the fans would prefer that I wasn't."

Hudson's heart broke a little bit. "You just pretend you aren't?"

"For a long time, that was easy to do..." Ondrej didn't finish the sentence. He just stared out the window at nothing.

"Until it wasn't." Hudson guessed.

"Yeah. That's why I want this, and I can't." Ondrej's tone offered no option but to agree, while Hudson's brain bounced with delight at the notion that Ondrej wanted him. Ondrej jumped to his feet, once more stunning Hudson with his athletic ease. Before taking on this project, he'd assumed that drivers would be good at sitting, that it was all vision and reflex, but Ondrej was pure athlete. Lean, fast, strong, and at ease with his body.

"Aren't we a pair? I shouldn't do this because you are the son of my client. It has the potential to screw up the business I run with my sister, and I shouldn't be putting that at risk for anything." Not even for the hottest kiss he'd had in his life. He wasn't going to discuss how wrong it felt to kiss someone who could have anyone, and how hard it was to not feel diminished by their financial differences. All his life he'd been placed last in anyone's priorities except for his sister Mackenzie. She gave him enough love to allow him to know his own worth, even as the world continued to remind him of his place. Ondrej inadvertently gave him the same self-worth; that Ondrej could pick anyone in the world and he picked Hudson. It was heady.

"Why are you here? If you shouldn't do this, simply respond with no when I ask."

Hudson pushed himself off the wall, shaking his head. "No. You can't put this all on me. How dare you? You asked first."

Ondrej's eyes flashed, and Hudson tried not to melt.

"Because I'm a fool." Ondrej's voice cracked, and he went back to staring out the window. "Because your smile makes me want to break all my promises to myself." His whisper was so low, Hudson wasn't quite sure he'd heard correctly. His knees actually melted. Oh fuck. He went to swallow, and his dry throat hurt.

"My smile?"

"You should go now." Ondrej waved vaguely in his direction, not giving any reaction to Hudson's question, or any indication that he'd floored Hudson with his... admission?

"I need to get ready for tomorrow's practice session without distraction." Ondrej was distracted by Hudson? His heart soared—again—for a second before the weight of knowledge crashed around him. But what could he say? Please drive safely. It was on the tip of his tongue; he better not bloody crash before Hudson had a chance to explore this... whatever this was between them. A couple of smoking hot kisses didn't give him the right, and besides, this was Ondrej's job. Hudson had his own job to do too.

"Okay." He turned to leave. A strong hand landed on his shoulder. Ondrej spun him around and pinned him with that intense gaze of his.

"You won't tell anyone?"

"No. I promise."

"Good." Little pinpricks of colour appeared on Ondrej's cheeks. "When are you meeting Papa?" The change in subject, while Ondrej still had his hand on Hudson's shoulder, was rapid. Hudson wasn't accustomed to feeling left behind like this, and he wasn't sure he liked it. He'd always prided himself on being street smart and book smart. Naivety had no place in a foster kid's life. Ondrej had a way of jerking between subjects that left him unsettled. He was being ridiculous. It wasn't the topics that had him unsettled; simply this incredible man who admitted to wanting him. He wanted to believe he was worthy of being wanted by someone as amazing as Ondrej; wanted it with every fibre in his body.

He swallowed. "He hasn't given me a formal meeting time yet. He told me to watch practice with him tomorrow and we'd discuss my progress during the day." Hudson was looking forward it. Hopefully Mr D'Grieg's questions and a whole day of being quizzed on his reports would help him figure out the next piece in the puzzle. He wasn't ready to admit that he'd only found dead ends so far, even though that was the truth.

"Remember what I said."

"Yes. I promise to let him down gently." Hudson held a couple of promises in his hands now. What a responsibility.

Ondrej nodded slowly, then a slow grin broke across his face. "Besides, it gives you an excuse for when you find nothing." The cheek of it.

Hudson squared his shoulders. "I won't need that." If he couldn't find the missing Bugatti, no one would. Being good at historical fact finding was the one thing he was supremely confident in.

"Twelve other historians have failed to find the car."

Hudson laughed. "I'll be lucky number thirteen." Mackenzie was going to love knowing they were the thirteenth to try and solve this puzzle. "I don't believe in luck. Only hard work."

"Then we have that in common." Ondrej's gaze flicked up and down Hudson's body, leaving a trail of heat. Damn him.

"Is that what you do when you aren't racing? Practice." Hudson cringed at the obviousness of his question. Of course, Ondrej would practice, spending hours driving the car to get better at it. It was his job to be fast and precise, that didn't come without a lot of training. And look at him; he obviously spent a lot of time in the gym.

"No. We only drive the car on race weekends. That's why they have the practice sessions."

Hold on, what? Hudson stared at him. "Are you telling me that before you drive insanely fast around a track next to other fast cars that you only get three hours of practice?" He'd researched this; FP1 meant free practice one and there were three one-hour sessions on a race weekend leading into the qualifying session where drivers aimed to have the fastest lap to get the best race starting position.

"Yes."

"But that doesn't seem like nearly enough."

"It's the same for everyone."

"So? And you just accept that?"

Ondrej shrugged one shoulder. "We can train in other ways without being in the car itself. I do hours on the simulator, but it's the rules. Every team is only allowed to drive the actual race car on the actual racing surface during the free practise sessions."

"And that's safe?"

"It's not about safety. It's about fairness."

Hudson wanted to kiss him or hold him tight; just in case he didn't get the chance to do it after tomorrow's practice session. Having been to a few race weekends now, he knew he wouldn't see Ondrej between now and Sunday night after the race. He disappeared into his work zone, and Hudson was okay with that because the risks he took required that level of intense focus.

"If I don't see you around, good luck." Hudson hoped it wasn't unlucky to wish Ondrej a safe race. Wasn't that theatre who had superstitions about that? Did car racing have the same thing? Ernie had once shaved all the tail hair off one of his horses because the filly had been given too much weight for a race, and "if it was good enough for Tesio, it's good enough for me."

Hudson bolted out of the room before he stayed and asked far too many questions. As he paced down the hallway to take the lift down to his own room, he realised that one or the other always left the discussion speedily without resolving anything at all. Did Ondrej really want him? Him? Ondrej could have any queer man in Europe. Why him? And why now? Hudson recognised the beginning of an overthinking spiral and walked faster, as if he could outpace his own thoughts.

CHAPTER 5

MONACO

"Try not to look so bored." Jean-Pierre, his former team-mate and reigning World Champion, thumped him on the shoulder. Ondrej had escaped tonight's dinner with Monaco's royal family to stand alone on a balcony overlooking the marina. It wasn't boredom so much as loneliness. Papa had gone home, Hudson was wherever he lived, and Socrates and most of the team had travelled back to England after the race in Spain. His car needed a rebuild over the next ten days, thanks to a crash and DNF in Spain, before Monaco's race and the mechanics would be working frantically back at the workshop in England to fix it. It was only early in the season, and he'd already crashed too much. This damn car was so hard to drive. The complaint would go unnoticed because the car was fast. He would just have to learn to manage it.

Meanwhile, he was in Monaco having dinner with sponsors and royalty and other important people. It would be great if he had someone beside him. Someone to go home with, instead of his very nice, very empty apartment here. It was far too easy to imagine Hudson, in all his red-haired bespeckled glory with his sexy as fuck British accent. A couple of kisses and Ondrej had lost his mind a little.

Ondrej grinned. "JP, how are you?" The press had always made a big deal of them being rivals in a strong team, but the truth was that Ondrej liked and respected Jean-Pierre. He was a fair competitor, a brilliant driver, and a genuinely nice guy in a sport that loved tactical politics.

"I'm good. Going great this season." JP was top of the points table, so he was somewhat understating his success. He'd won the last two seasons and was on target to win again, even at this early stage in the season.

"Congratulations. You've been driving well and the car looks fast."

"Yours too. What a shame you got hit out in Spain last weekend."

Ondrej shrugged. "Just a racing incident." He was still a bit sore a few days after being shunted off the track during a re-start. Not finishing the race meant no points for the weekend and that annoyed him more than anything else. His car was fast enough to get points every weekend and he didn't think that was too much to expect from himself or the car.

"Hey, about what happened?" JP glanced around him, but they were alone on the hotel balcony.

"Yeah?" Ondrej stared out into the night sky, not acknowledging that he knew JP wasn't talking about his result in Spain anymore. The lights at the marina glowed against the flat sea, and the city looked amazing with the mountains shrouded in dark night shadows.

"It was shit, yeah. You didn't deserve to get discarded like that, just because you are..."

Ondrej breathed in slowly as JP spoke about how Ondrej had been sacked from their team. "Gay."

"Yeah. I just wanted to let you know I didn't agree with the decision."

"It's fine, JP." Ondrej knew JP couldn't have stood up for him without also losing his seat, and with his first championship on the line, JP's hands were effectively tied. "Thanks. I know you couldn't have done anything, so don't sweat it."

"I was about to win the championship."

"Hey, relax. I would've done the same if things were reversed. Winning means more than anything. I don't hold it against you. You worked hard for that championship." Ondrej would win his own championship one day, following in his mother's footsteps. Her dream was his dream.

"And you worked bloody hard too. We wouldn't have won the constructors title without you, and you pushed me hard in every race. What they did to you wasn't cool."

Ondrej shrugged, not wanting to show the mixed emotions swirling in his belly. "Sometimes life is unfair."

"You can't tell anyone this, but I had a secret meeting with Socrates the day after you got dumped." JP shuffled nervously.

"Excuse me?" Ondrej wasn't sure he'd heard that right. Had his former team-mate met with his new team's boss? Ondrej's whole perspective on the shitty situation spun, like a roulette wheel that had come loose and was about to fly across the casino.

"Um, well, it was super shit what they did, and the timing fucking sucked because all the contracts were already signed for the next season. I couldn't do anything to help you with our team, but I figured I could at least try with another one. And Socrates, you know, he's gay too, so I thought he might understand even if he couldn't help."

"Thank you." Ondrej's voice cracked. Without JP, he wouldn't have had a seat for last season, and perhaps this season too. JP had basically saved his entire career and taken a huge personal risk to do it. Gamble had already signed two drivers for last season, and they'd ended up moving Lucien Grenville to their Series E team so they could have Ondrej. Ondrej had literally taken Lucien Grenville's S1 seat from under him, which most of the press had construed as a dog act. He would've agreed with them except he'd just had the same thing done to him by his old team. In this world, with its intense rivalry, there would always be someone who lost out. It'd been him and then it wasn't him.

"You are too good a driver to miss out on a seat. What they did to you wasn't right."

Ondrej blinked hard to hold back the heat behind his eyes. "I owe you, JP."

"No, you don't. I wish I could've done more, but you know—"

"I understand. This game, it's cut-throat, and you didn't have to help me."

JP pushed him on the shoulder. "Yeah, I did. Without you pushing me to be better, I'd still be a lazy mid-field driver."

"Hey, mid-field drivers aren't lazy." Ondrej laughed.

"Yeah, some of you just have shit cars." JP grinned too. The lights from the marina shone on his dark blond hair. He wasn't conventionally handsome, but like all the drivers, his eyes glowed with intensity.

"Not this season."

"No. I don't suppose you'd return the favour and tell me about the new engine mods that everyone is gossiping about."

Ondrej winked. "No. Socrates and Victor would have my head on the block if I mentioned anything about that."

"There is something?"

"There's always something. Come on, let's get back inside before people notice us out here."

"Yeah, Sofia will be wondering where I am." JP's wife was a fashion model, and the pair of them adored each other. He missed their easy friendship.

"How is she?"

"Really good. So... you and Alex, is that a thing?"

Ondrej shook his head. "No."

"You need someone to care for you, man. A partner to share the load with. You should meet my brother, he's gay."

"JP..." Suddenly, JP's help made a lot of sense and Ondrej relaxed properly for the first time tonight.

"Not like that. He's happily married to his husband, but I'm sure he's got hot friends."

"JP!" Ondrej threw his head back and laughed. "I don't need you to match-make me. I'm fine."

"Then there is someone? I guess it's awkward, right, because you can't really be public about it. Not after all that fucking mess."

Ondrej nodded. All of that was true.

"Come over for dinner tomorrow. Bring him." JP patted him on the back again, then walked off, leaving Ondrej alone on the balcony to process everything JP had just spilled. Ever since he'd been dumped as JP's teammate, he hadn't spent any time with JP. JP was right. It was awkward and he hadn't wanted to try and keep his friendship with JP in case he aligned with his toxic boss. It'd all been devastating enough without having it confirmed that he'd lost a mate too. To know that JP had gone to Socrates and helped Ondrej get a seat blew his mind. JP had risked a lot to help him—risked his first championship and his contract with his team—to go behind his shitty boss's back to help Ondrej.

Drivers might be the face of S1, the ones risking their lives to provide fans with sport and entertainment, but the real money was in the constructor's championship. And to many of the teams, drivers were disposable. Discarded when they didn't do as they were told. The least Ondrej could do to return the incredible favour JP had given him was to turn up for dinner at JP and Sofia's penthouse apartment tomorrow. With Hudson? Fuck, that was so tempting. Could he take that risk?

Tonight's conversation had informed him that JP wouldn't judge him, that he was a much-needed friend on the grid, and what was the risk anyway? Well, that much was obvious. Someone in Monaco might see Ondrej and Hudson together and realise that they were more than friends. The media focus in Monaco for this race was always more intense than any other race. The fans were closer to the action here—closer to the drivers—thanks to the way the street circuit threaded through the city. He could barely move this week in Monaco without someone asking for an autograph or making up some story about him. He blew out a long slow breath.

One thing he'd learned early in his S1 career was to ignore what the press said about him. In S1, everyone else assumed they knew more about him than he did; who he was, what motivated him, what he was best at, and most frequently they talked about what he couldn't do, wouldn't achieve, and most of all, they speculated on where he would finish in any race. And that was without looking at the fan memes. If the fans found out he was gay, the commentary would escalate beyond the rampant nonsense people said now about him. He probably should go to JP's place alone tomorrow.

———

Temptation—Hudson in a dark blue suit—stood beside him in the elevator on the way up to JP's apartment. Ondrej wished he had no regrets about flying Hudson to Monaco for dinner tonight. He'd smuggled him out of his apartment and into a cab without touching him, and now Ondrej's skin prickled in a combination of anticipation and stress.

"I can't believe I was hunched over my computer in my room this morning, and now I'm in bloody Monaco about to have dinner with a champion." Hudson muttered to himself, apparently amazed at this circumstance.

"You didn't have to say yes."

Hudson scoffed. "Um, would you say no to this? This is

probably going to be my only chance to experience this. Would you give up a once in a lifetime experience?"

"Are you so mercenary?" Ondrej was glad for any excuse to keep Hudson at a distance.

Hudson threw his head back and laughed. "No. Fuck. No. Why invite me here if you believe so little of me?"

"JP told me to bring someone. I assumed you were available." Ondrej skirted around the truth. He wanted more kisses—and more—with Hudson and he was happy to use JP's dinner as a reason to get him here in Monaco. So much for distance. He really was kidding himself. For that first stunning moment when Hudson had been seated at Papa's dining table, Ondrej had wanted Hudson, and all his good sense about staying focused on work fled whenever Hudson softened against him. Every time he obeyed one of Ondrej's commands, Hudson wormed himself into Ondrej's life. He was temptation personified because he gave Ondrej the impression that he could have everything he'd ever wanted ... if he was just brave enough to ask. If he was bold enough to face the distraction the press would create if he was publicly out. He had imagined it a few times lately. He'd talk to Alicia Blasi first; of all the journalists, she was always kind to him because she had been a rally driver like Ma. She'd make it bearable. It didn't matter; he couldn't risk his career like that.

"I could've been busy."

"Doing?"

"Don't be rude. I was busy doing the job your father is paying me to do."

"And?"

"I brought my laptop with me, worked on the way here and I'll work on the way home again."

"Relax. I'm not here to police how much work you do. Honestly, it's all a waste of time anyway."

Hudson frowned. "You don't think the car can be found?"

"Twelve of the best historians that money can buy couldn't find it. The odds aren't good. And you've been working on it for three months and found nothing."

Hudson's cheeks went pink. "There are still a few questions that need answering. I might not find the car, but I will discover what happened to it and give Mr D'Grieg some closure. I promised."

The fucking earnest way Hudson said that made dragging him here completely worthwhile. Ondrej wanted to shove him against the wall of the elevator and kiss him thoroughly. Unfortunately the lift doors opened and it was time to introduce Hudson to JP as his boyfriend.

"By the way, JP thinks you are my boyfriend." Ondrej didn't wait for Hudson's response. He just knocked on JP's door. Hudson leaned closer, his mouth grazing Ondrej's ear.

"I like the sound of that. Do you agree with him?"

Ondrej swallowed. Whenever Hudson stepped out of his shell and did something like that, it set Ondrej's skin alight with need. Luckily—or unluckily—he was saved from answering when JP opened the door.

"Welcome, welcome, come in." JP waved his hands and they followed him inside. Ondrej walked quickly and turned so he could watch Hudson's face as he took in the stunning view over Monte Carlo. His eyes widened behind his glasses, and he walked slowly towards the open glass doors leading to the balcony.

"How are you, Ondrej?" Sofia pulled him into a hug and kissed both his cheeks. "It's been so long since you were here with us."

"Yes, too long. I wasn't sure—"

Sofia glanced at JP. "That's his fault. I told him to tell you before now, but no, he was focused on winning—"

"As he should be."

"Yes, and he didn't want you to feel obliged to him. I said, that's silly JP, Ondrej is your friend. He will appreciate knowing that you are on his side. I can't believe what they did to you. It's so unfair."

"Thank you, Sofia. I'm sorry I didn't reach out to you both." He'd been so sure that their silence meant they'd agreed with their team boss, and he'd struggled with the whole ugly incident alone.

"And who is this lovely man you have brought with you?"

"Hudson."

Hudson spun around, blinking rapidly. "Forgive my manners. The view is spectacular."

Sofia smiled. "Welcome to our home."

"This is Hudson Lockley. Hudson, please meet Jean-Pierre Lavigne and his beautiful wife Sofia." Ondrej found his manners and watched as JP shook Hudson's hand and Sofia kissed both his cheeks, the same friendly way she'd done to him.

"Call me JP. Any friend of Ondrej's is a friend of mine."

"Thank you."

Ondrej slung his arm around Hudson's waist. "And try not to look too overwhelmed."

Hudson cleared his throat. "Before you ask, yes, my name is like the car."

"Ondrej does love a good car." JP smirked and Ondrej wanted to smack him on the shoulder. Fuck he missed their friendship.

"Would you like some wine?" Sofia opened a bottle of Chianti and started to pour it into four glasses. Ondrej nodded. He had a limit of one glass per night between races, and none on the two days leading into a race weekend. Obviously, he didn't drink during race weekends. He needed to have every fibre in his body fit and precisely tuned to focus on driving successfully, and he'd never do anything to negatively impact on his reflexes.

"Yes please." Hudson leaned a little against Ondrej, just like a boyfriend might, and Ondrej liked it far too much. So far tonight—and yes, they'd only just arrived—he had a taste of what his life could be like if he was allowed to be himself openly. JP probably didn't know what a gift he'd just given him. Fuck, he couldn't get all emotional now. He took the glass from Sofia with a nod of thanks and sipped slowly, savouring the way the tannins danced on his tongue.

"Come and sit on the balcony. I'll bring out the entrée soon. Our chef has made socca topped with truffle oil, and then a light bouillabaisse for the mains, and I thought we'd skip the dessert and simply have a cheese course." Sofia led the way with JP trailing behind her. The champion driver reached out and touched her hair as they walked, his fingers twisting around her long black curly hair as if he needed to be connected to her. Sofia had grown up in Milan with an

Italian father and a Ghanese mother, giving her incredibly striking looks that she used to advantage in her modelling career. Like Ondrej, JP was a white Frenchman. They'd driven together as kids, all through the ranks, and had gone to the same specialist high school; friends first, then teammates. When Ondrej had been sanctimoniously discarded, he'd lost his friendship with JP too, and that hurt almost as much. JP might be a world champion race car driver, but in looks, he was nothing special. Shorter than Ondrej and slim, his most obvious feature was his huge nose. He left his hair unkempt with straggly dark blonde stubble to match as if he was too important for slick grooming. Ondrej's stomach pulled oddly. He wanted what JP had for himself; someone who would risk everything for him and who needed to be with him, the same way JP and Sofia had each other. He sat down, placed his wine on the table, and casually leaned back so no one would guess the churn inside him.

"They have a chef?" Hudson whispered in his ear. "Do you?"

Ondrej smiled. "No. I'm sure they only use a chef's service when they have guests."

"Right, because that makes total sense." Hudson moved away from Ondrej—leaving behind an emptiness—and sat stiffly in his chair.

"I love this week," JP said.

"Do you? I find the pomp and ceremony of Monaco to be distracting."

JP waved his hand. "Sure, that part is a problem. No, I love this. Summer evenings on this balcony with my Sofia, with the whole world being busy down there, and us just being together."

"You are so sappy." Sofia giggled with a little blush across her cheeks. She jumped up. "I'll just grab the socca."

"I hope you don't have any allergies," JP asked Hudson who still looked a little unbalanced.

"Um, no, but am I allowed to ask what socca is?"

Ondrej smiled. "It's a famous street food here in Monaco. Kind of like French crepes but savoury."

"And made from besan flour, not wheat flour." JP said.

"That doesn't make it much clearer." Hudson made a little self-depreciating gesture. It amused Ondrej how well he managed to confidently fit into any space even when it was obvious that he was out of his depth. He had a way of observing people and finding a way to listen to them that allowed him to belong easily.

"Besan flour is chickpea flour. It has a nuttier taste than wheat flour."

"I look forward to trying this famous street food." Hudson stood up and walked towards Sofia who was carrying a large platter. They had a quick conversation and Hudson disappeared into the kitchen.

"He's a little overwhelmed by us?" JP asked.

Ondrej tried not to balk at the question, even though he'd whispered the same thing to Hudson earlier. The problem was he didn't know enough about Hudson to answer it adequately. "What makes you say that?"

"Nothing. I remember the first time I was invited into Louis Kingston's house; like here I was, a rookie meeting a multiple world champion. It was a lot."

Ondrej relaxed. "Nah, Hudson isn't much of an S1 fan. I doubt he cares about your championship status."

"Is that the attraction?"

Ondrej shrugged one shoulder. "Sure. I mean, it's nice to spend time without someone who sees me for me, you know."

JP nodded solemnly. "Oh yeah, that makes total sense."

"What makes sense?" Sofia placed the platter in the middle of the table, and Hudson followed with a pile of plates and cutlery. He set them around the table with a practiced hand. "I hope you aren't talking about work. Tonight is a car free night. No shop talk."

"Ah, but darling, the politics are so fascinating."

"I get it and I know you haven't been able to chat to Ondrej for ages, but no. Not tonight. We have a guest."

"I don't mind," Hudson said.

"It's probably for the best. JP will ask me a million questions about Victor's designs that I can't answer, and the rest will just be JP having a whinge that I won't answer him." Ondrej winked at his friend who guffawed back at him, shaking his head.

"Fuck, I've missed you."

Ondrej felt exactly the same way. "How's the new teammate?" JP's new teammate, Grigor Anthony, was exactly who Ondrej had expected to be picked for that team. Competitive, crafty, and generally a bigoted prick.

"Hey, no S1 talk. Tell me Hudson, how did you meet Ondrej? It can't have been during the season?" Sofia changed the subject and Ondrej held his breath to see what Hudson would say.

"His father has employed me to help him with some

family history research." Hudson's careful response warmed Ondrej's chest, but his political phrasing didn't help as JP laughed.

"Fuck me, is he still trying to find the Bugatti? I mean, it's tempting as fuck, right. Imagine driving it. A car like that is sex on wheels."

"Yes. I don't want to talk about it."

JP raised his wine glass. "Then we won't. Have something to eat, and Hudson, please tell me your first impression of Ondrej?"

Ondrej glared at his friend's teasing tone and was rewarded with another smirk.

"He was rude, dismissive, and refused to shake my hand."

JP bellowed with laughter and Sofia was struggling to hold back a giggle as Ondrej wanted to squirm under the table. He glanced quickly at Hudson who was grinning at him. The tease in his expression instantly turned sent a flush of lust down his spine. He breathed in slowly and hoped no one noticed the way his heart thudded in his chest.

"Of course, the second time we met, he..." Hudson flushed and Ondrej had to think about what had happened. Oh, it was at Bahrain and he'd just showered after arriving from the airport. "He, um..." It was gratifying to know his naked form had a memorable effect on Hudson; well, they'd almost kissed that day, so it shouldn't be a surprise that the chemistry he'd felt hadn't been one way.

"—he wasn't any less rude, but one thing gave me hope. He made me promise to be gentle with his father when I couldn't find the Bugatti, and that simple care for a family member was—" Hudson swallowed. Holy shit. Ondrej wanted to pull Hudson into a hug and just hold him tight. JP and Sofia were staring at Hudson with their mouths gaping slightly.

"Anyway, I probably shouldn't admit this, but caring for family is kind of a thing for me."

"You have a great family?" Sofia asked.

Hudson shook his head. "No. I only have my sister. Um —" Hudson sighed.

"It's okay. You don't have to talk about it if you don't want." Ondrej had no clue about Hudson's family. He desperately wanted to know, but now didn't seem like the right time. Hudson didn't seem to think so either, as he reached forward and used the cutlery to take a couple of socca from the platter. He placed them carefully on his plate, and Ondrej wished he had some handy topic to talk about. Everyone copied Hudson and ate quietly.

Eventually Hudson swallowed his mouthful and lifted his head. "Delicious. Thank you. So, um, I'm a foster kid." Hudson stared down at his plate again, and kept his gaze low as he spoke rapidly, almost like he was reciting a data table from an engineering output. "My sister and I were placed into care when she was five and I was two. I have no memory of my biological parents, except what I've read in my case notes. I was in sixteen different homes until I was fifteen and my sister adopted me." Oh, that explained how Hudson could fit into any space easily. He'd had a lot of practice at it.

"I'm so sorry." Sofia spoke first. "That sounds really rough."

"Anyway—" Hudson drew the word out and it was

obvious he didn't want to talk about it anymore. "I really admire people who demonstrate care for their family members. For obvious reasons."

Ondrej reached under the table and rested his hand on Hudson's thigh. "Whether you find the Bugatti or not, I'm glad Papa employed you to find it."

"Oh, so sweet."

"Shut up JP. As if you aren't the sappiest asshole around Sofia." Ondrej blurted and they all laughed.

"True, true. I don't know why she puts up with me." JP leaned over and kissed Sofia on the cheek and Ondrej wanted to do the same to Hudson.

CHAPTER 6

udson couldn't believe he'd mentioned that he was a shitty foster kid with no money and in such company. He also couldn't believe the way they just rolled with it. He'd expected them to sneer, just like the wealthy elite who owned the horses his best foster parents Ernie and Doreen had trained. For the rest of the evening he kept waiting for Ondrej's friends to judge him and nothing came. The food had been incredible; the fish stew was the best he'd ever tasted, and the wine was obviously expensive. He'd drunk too much—Sofia kept refilling his glass whenever it emptied—and now he leaned against Ondrej in the back seat of a taxi on the way back to his apartment.

"I like your friends." Oh, fuck, he was pretty drunk; on that edge beyond happy control and heading towards sloppy. It was a good thing they'd left now before he'd had one glass too many.

"So do I."

Hudson wanted to blurt out that he liked Ondrej too.

His tongue curled around the words and he managed to hold them back. Now Ondrej knew about his past, about how poor and pathetically nobody he was, he'd just be the gold digger Ondrej had accused him of.

"Come on, let's get you in bed."

Hudson woke with a start. Had he fallen asleep on Ondrej's shoulder during the ride back to his place? Oh no. He stumbled out of the taxi and let Ondrej led him through some glass doors and into an elevator. Soon enough he found himself steered into a bedroom, and he flopped on the bed. Ondrej tugged at his clothes and Hudson tried to help.

"Just stop."

Hudson froze, then Ondrej finished undressing him and tucked him into bed. As he drifted off into a happily drunken sleep, he could've sworn he felt Ondrej's lips on his forehead, and his whisper, "If you weren't so drunk…"

Bright fuzzy light made his eyeballs hurt and Hudson flung his arm out towards his bedside table to grab his glasses. When his arm discovered only air, he ended up flailing about trying to orient himself.

"Settle down, you'll hurt yourself."

"Ondrej?"

"Good morning." Oh shit. Last night came flooding back and Hudson wanted to hide under the covers.

"Would you like your glasses?"

"Yes please." Could this get any more embarrassing? "Um, did I…" Hudson wasn't even sure what he was asking? All he could remember was the whisper of Ondrej's lips against his cheek. Did they have sex and he didn't remember? Because that would be both ridiculously pathetic and a real shame. He wanted to be wide awake and alert when that happened.

"Did you drink too much of Sofia's wine, say cute things, fall asleep in the taxi, then collapse in bed? Yes."

Hudson breathed out. "Okay." None of that sounded like he'd embarrassed himself too much. Or maybe he had; what 'cute things' had he said?

"Here you go." Ondrej handed him his glasses, and once he had them on, Hudson blinked up at Ondrej who stood there holding a glass of water. "Drink this. Here is some paracetamol."

"I'm not that hungover. I just forgot where I was for a moment." Hudson didn't expect Ondrej to believe the nonsense that fell out of his face. He certainly didn't.

"Okay. Shower is that way. I can order up some breakfast. Any preference?"

"Whatever you want is fine."

Ondrej disappeared and Hudson wanted to bury himself in the pillows—the incredibly soft plush pillows on this luxurious bed. This whole room was like an expensive hotel; from the giant bed and the gentle painting on the wall of a landscape and the soft curtains that billowed slightly in the breeze. He shouldn't waste time lying in bed. Since living with the Trews for three years, he'd formed the habit of getting up early to muck out boxes and help get the strings of horses ready for riders, and the early rising habit had stuck. Mackenzie always found it hilarious that he bounced out of bed early in the morning, especially when she'd first adopted him and he'd been a teenager. The Trews were by far his best foster family, and the only ones he kept in contact with. Before them, the longest he'd stayed with one family was fourteen months and the shortest was eight days. Life was temporary. He should get up and going so he could enjoy every moment here in Monaco while it lasted.

After he'd showered, Hudson felt a lot better, and slightly smug about it too. He hadn't been that drunk after all, just sleepy and giggly. It ought to bother him more that Ondrej—uptight, intense Ondrej—had seen that side of him, and yet he was comfortable with it, especially as he was certain he remembered Ondrej's soft whisper before he'd fallen asleep last night. He dressed and walked out of the bedroom into a stunning lounge room. Okay, he'd see it last night when he'd arrived from the airport, but Ondrej had hustled him to get ready and he hadn't seen more than glimpses.

"Wow. That's incredible." The apartment had a balcony and huge glass windows that overlooked the bay and the casino which sat on a rocky outcrop jutting out over the sea.

"Yeah, I like it. Most of the S1 drivers have a place in Monaco."

"I can see why. The outlook is spectacular."

"It's practical to have a base that is central to the majority of the races, and of course, it's a tax haven." Naturally, wealthy people would think of factors like that.

"Also the view." Hudson couldn't stop staring at it. A buzz sounded.

"That'll be breakfast." Ondrej disappeared from his peripheral view for a few minutes. Hudson didn't mind the wait; he had the view to stare at.

"I got a traditional English breakfast for you. Soak up some of last night's indulgence." Ondrej placed paper bags on a little table on the balcony, and Hudson followed. The summer Mediterranean breeze was warm on his skin. Ondrej fussed about unpacking the food and plating up for him.

"Coffee?"

"Of course." Hudson tried to drag his gaze away from the view. Gosh no wonder they call it Cote d'Azure, the blue of the sky and sea was breathtaking, although not as intense as the deep blue of Ondrej's eyes. A few minutes later, Ondrej placed a mug of coffee beside him and sat down opposite.

"Eat."

Hudson loved the simple commands from Ondrej and his skin flushed with pleasure. He glanced down at his plate and oh... "You've outdone yourself. This looks amazing." He hadn't been kidding when he said he'd ordered a full English breakfast. It had everything, even black pudding, although it was all fancier than any breakfast he'd ever had before.

"Try it."

Hudson ate and flavour exploded on his tongue. "The sausage is incredible." Fuck, he was so repetitive, everything was incredible. But seriously... it was a lot.

"I'm glad you like it."

"What are you eating?"

"Porridge with fruit."

"No English breakfast for you?"

"No. I have a higher protein meal for lunch, after my endurance training session."

Hudson frowned. "Your what?"

"I run or cycle for two hours every morning when I'm not racing. Amy will be here in forty-five minutes. You'll need to entertain yourself—"

"I brought my work. Besides, I need to be at the airport by lunch time."

Ondrej's head jerked upwards. "You are leaving?"

"You invited me to dinner. I booked a flight home today. I do have to work, you know." Even though Ondrej had paid for the flights, Hudson had ensured he wasn't going to overstay his welcome. He knew how it felt to be in a space where he wasn't wanted.

"Work here. Stay with me for a few days."

Hudson couldn't breathe. "What?"

"Last night was … nice. Stay." Ondrej cast his gaze downwards, as if he was embarrassed to be asking. No, that didn't make sense. The man before him was always so certain about everything. Hudson must have imagined it.

"I don't have any clothes." Hudson cursed his mouth as soon as he said that. No clothes. What a ridiculous reason not to stay, but he couldn't say what he really wanted to say. *Please invite me to stay for longer. Ask me to be with you. Take me to your bed.*

"Buy some."

Hudson cringed, unable to enjoy Ondrej's invitation when it came with such a reminder of their economic differences. "Um…"

"Fine. I will buy you some. I want you to stay. If clothes will keep you here, then we can sort that out."

That made it worse. "But—" Hudson didn't want to be beholden to Ondrej like that.

"It will make me happy." The tips of Ondrej's ears were pink.

"Okay." Because what else could he say? He liked making people happy, and if he was honest, from the moment Ondrej had invited him to dinner here and told him to book flights on his account, he'd dreamed of being asked to stay longer. "Yes. I'll stay."

"Okay. Now eat up. I will run and you can do whatever, then we will shop."

Hudson eased out a long slow breath. "Alright. I'll do some work while you run."

Ondrej finished his breakfast, dumped his dishes in the kitchen, slipped on his running shoes and left. Hopefully the gorgeous sun would help Hudson find something that wasn't another useless dead-end in his hunt for the missing Bugatti. Something that made him feel like he wasn't outclassed and pointless and that he didn't belong here. One thing he'd taken from the Trew family was that hard work was the key to changing his future. Whatever happened in life, he'd always have his ability to work—even the crappiest job—and get himself out of a hole. He'd learned since then that the saying itself was quite ableist as not everyone had that option. The saying still resonated with him because it made him feel like he could change whatever crap was sent his way. Being able to work had power, especially when he didn't feel powerful. It mattered now, because he didn't need to feel like he didn't belong in Ondrej's fancy world. He had a job to do and damned if he wasn't going to find this missing car. It would be easy to feel down about it, after so much work had yielded nothing to date. He'd changed his laptop background to a photo of the car, but the inspiration wasn't helping. Every line of questioning he tried ended up with nothing. Determination and persistence would prevail—he truly believed that.

The time passed quickly as he hunted around the internet, reading old newspapers. Using online translations to read newspapers in French and German wasn't perfect, and he was probably missing nuance in the stories, yet it gave him much more local information than he'd had before. He'd shifted inside away from the sun. As nice and warm as it was, it would be hell on his skin. With his red-hair, his colouring wasn't exactly designed for long sunny days, and he had too many freckles as it was. By the time Ondrej walked back through the door, Hudson hadn't discovered anything, except to plot the whereabouts of the car from the moment it was manufactured to when Grover-Williams had left France. Historically interesting, and Mackenzie would make the timeline look amazing, but completely pointless for actually finding the car now.

"Come." Ondrej waved towards his bedroom and Hudson leaped to his feet. He'd explored the whole apartment while Ondrej had been running, and there was only the one bed. Slowly over the past couple of hours, the feeling that he didn't belong had ebbed away and he realised that Ondrej had invited him to stay. With him. Here. In his apartment that had only one bed. It must mean that Ondrej felt the same connection that he did. Why else would he ask? Hudson found it hard to believe that Ondrej wanted him, yet the evidence was strong that it was a fact.

"Hey, did you sleep on the couch last night? I'm sorry."

Hudson followed Ondrej into his bedroom. It wasn't the question he wanted to ask, but he had to start somewhere.

"Yes. It's no bother." Ondrej started to strip out of his soaked running gear and Hudson had to lean against the doorframe to stop his head spinning. Ondrej walked through to the bathroom and turned on the shower, giving Hudson a glorious view of his naked back and ass. Should he follow?

"Are you coming?" Ondrej stepped into the shower and tipped his face back under the water. Hudson's brain caught up.

"Hold on. Something has changed. Last time we kissed, you pushed me away and said you shouldn't do this."

"Maybe I want this more than any other consideration." Ondrej turned, giving Hudson a full-frontal view, including Ondrej's firm cock.

"Ahh..." What were they talking about? "Like your career and your fans and your sponsors?"

Ondrej scrubbed his hands through his hair. Every muscle on his lean body rippled. This wasn't the easiest way to have a conversation. He hoped Ondrej didn't expect Hudson to be able to think enough to communicate; not with that view distracting him.

"JP reminded me that there is more to life than living up to other people's expectations. Maybe I want a try and have what he has."

"A world championship?"

Ondrej nodded, perhaps involuntarily at the notion of being the world champion. "Yes, definitely that. But also, he has a partner who adores him. I would like that."

"And that's me?"

"I don't know. Hopefully? It's likely too early to know, and if you don't get in this shower now, we'll never know if we are compatible."

"And you think I'll just obey you?" Hudson's knees weakened.

Ondrej simply raised one eyebrow, then turned to wash himself. "Your choice."

It was no choice at all. How could he walk away from a beautiful man who wanted him? Even if it made no sense, Hudson wasn't going to not leap at this chance. His fingers trembled as he removed his glasses and placed them on the shelf above the sink. He pulled his shirt over his head, and kept his gaze focused on Ondrej. Being short sighted, he had to step closer to the waterfall shower, so he could peer through the open shower door. At this distance everything was still clear enough for him to notice all the details about Ondrej. The way his wet brown hair darkened and clung to his temples and forehead, the ripples of muscles as he moved and the perfect amount of hair on his chest—as if it'd been sculpted in a studio—trailing down his stomach to his cock. Hudson stripped off the rest of his clothes and joined Ondrej in the—quite frankly incredible—shower. None of the surroundings mattered when Ondrej reached up and pulled him close for a kiss. Steaming water splashed off Ondrej's head and bounced onto Hudson. It was awkward and amazing, and ... Ondrej was kissing him.

Hudson wrapped his arms around Ondrej's waist, spreading his hands greedily over Ondrej's back. He wanted to touch all of him at once, every muscle and bone and every inch of his skin. Hudson reached out for the bar of soap—citrus-scented—and began to wash Ondrej's back. It was completely natural to slowly sink to his knees, brushing his mouth down Ondrej's throat and over his chest and stomach, tasting the last remnants of sweat from his run. The little hints of salt were almost washed away by the water. Hudson knelt, wanting to bow his head and let the water run over his hair, but he kept at his task, washing Ondrej with the soap. Washing his ass and thighs and calves and feet, down the back and up the front, and was rewarded with Ondrej's fingers grasping at his hair. The little tugs on his scalp were everything and Hudson couldn't hold back a groan of need. He washed the insides of Ondrej's lean thighs, then cupped his balls. Ondrej's fingers tightened, and Hudson took his time to lather up the soap and wash Ondrej's cock thoroughly.

"Stop."

Hudson removed his hands from Ondrej's cock and rested them on Ondrej's knees instead. The water rinsed off the soap, with the citrus scent lingering in the air.

"Your mouth. Please."

Fuck yes. Hudson gripped the outside of Ondrej's thighs and licked all the way up Ondrej's cock. The clean skin tasted like simple perfection—a little bit of soap washed away by the fresh water, and mostly Ondrej's skin— and he savoured the whole length. He would never get another first time doing this and he wanted to be perfect for Ondrej; which meant it would be perfect for himself too. His own cock ached, ignored and happy that way because if Ondrej so much as moved his foot to touch him, Hudson would explode.

"More."

Hudson's skin came alight at the command and he

covered the end of Ondrej's cock with his mouth. A light teasing hold that allowed him to lick the top of Ondrej's cock until he moaned. Yes. Only then did Hudson flatten his tongue and sink down on Ondrej's length. Water ran in rivulets down Ondrej's stomach and into the edges of Hudson's mouth. He slid up and down, using all his skill to pull satisfying noises from Ondrej. Over and over, he moved his head and mouth, full of glorious cock.

"Up." Ondrej pulled hard on Hudson's hair and Hudson sucked hard as he started to rise up. His mouth released with a pop, which was apparently enough for Ondrej to come.

"Fuck." Ondrej cried out, with his head thrown back, as he came onto Hudson's throat and chest. He was painted with it, and he fucking loved it. "Holy shit."

Hudson stayed on his knees, his cock hard and needy, and yet already satisfied by Ondrej's joy.

"Come here." Ondrej beckoned him with a gentle gesture and Hudson staggered to his feet. The rush of blood back into his ankles and feet added another sensation to the already overwhelming situation and he swayed a little. Ondrej kissed him gently. Little kisses along his bottom lip, and then, just as Hudson was in a hazy heaven of being cared for, Ondrej wrapped one hand around Hudson's cock and stroked.

"Now come for me." Ondrej's voice was soft, a lazier command than before, but so much better. Hudson obeyed, coming so hard that his eyes rolled back, and he leaned into Ondrej's hold. If life could be distilled down to this moment, this was the best time of his life and he never wanted to leave. He rested his head on Ondrej's shoulder.

Slowly the real world filtered back into his sated haze, and he realised what he'd thought. Okay, that was probably overstating it a little. Just because he hadn't been with anyone for a while, didn't mean he had to make a big deal of it.

"Let me wash you." Hudson bent down to grab the bar of soap from the floor of the shower—he must have dropped it at some point—and began to wash his mess off Ondrej's belly. Caring for his partner like this was one of his favourite things; it added depth to the act of sex. Sex wasn't finished for him when he came; he needed to provide care and he adored the way it extended the sense of connection and intimacy. A fine-toothed comb sat on the shelf in the shower and he grabbed it, gently combing through Ondrej's chest hair, then down his belly, and lastly through his pubic hair, removing all traces of come, until Ondrej was tidy and clean. He stood up and kissed him, showing Ondrej his thanks for this time together with every relaxed stroke of his tongue. Ondrej cradled his head and kissed him back, urgent and almost... competitive. Just like him.

"Okay, I'm done." Ondrej suddenly pushed him away and stepped out of the shower.

"Hey, you rude asshole." Hudson grinned as Ondrej turned with a smirk on his lips.

"You can wash yourself, yeah? You are good at it." Ondrej raked him with his gaze and Hudson started to grow hard again. "Look at you." Ondrej's grin grew, then he turned away to grab a towel and casually dried himself while staring at Hudson.

Hudson squared his shoulders, then gave Ondrej a good show as he washed himself. He turned around and soaped his backside, spreading his legs as he washed his hole, listening carefully for Ondrej's gasp, then he turned around and soaped his cock until Ondrej's nostrils flared and his chest rose and fell. For someone who'd just returned from a two hour run, Ondrej panted hard. Gratification mixed with heat and Hudson cursed aloud as he came again.

"Look at you." Ondrej whispered. "Fucking just look at you."

CHAPTER 7

A month later, Ondrej was back in his apartment at Monaco with the race at France less than a week away. Spending a week with Hudson before the race at Monaco had been one of the best weeks of his life. They'd gone clothes shopping together in Milan, staying there for a couple of nights. They'd discussed safe sex and shared their test results, then spent hours in bed together. Ondrej didn't feel an ounce of guilt at using sex to keep them both away from the press. He hadn't exactly planned it that way; but the need to keep his life private was ever-present. Going shopping with a friend might get a few nibbles on social media—S1 fans were everywhere in Europe and they tagged him whenever they saw him—but eating dinner in public was a step too far. Room service and sex was a wonderful way to avoid the press and spend time with Hudson. He'd even let Hudson drive his Maserati GranCabrio on the way home again. Hudson has surprised him with his excellent driving skills, and Hudson had showered him with kisses in the basement garage, excited to have driven a sports car. The day kept improving when Hudson had lain spreadeagled on his bed, while Ondrej had fucked him thoroughly.

Contrarily, the race in Monaco had been shit; a slow pit stop had wrecked his chance of points and he'd finished in twelfth. Victor and Socrates had put the pit crew through intense training sessions after that, so the team had been on point in Canada. Not that it had mattered. It'd been a dull race; he'd started in P11 and improved his placing by one, picking up one measly point for tenth place. Hudson had refused his offer to stay at his apartment while Ondrej was in Canada—stubborn man—and gone back to England. Ondrej wished he was here; remembering their week together had helped him through the boredom of long hours of travel and the empty nights in hotels between work. From tomorrow, he had four whole days at home before he needed to be in France for a sponsor's dinner, then the race.

Ondrej: Come He smiled as he sent Hudson a commanding text, imagining how Hudson would blush so nicely when he read it. He needed to kiss his freckles again.

Hudson: Now? I'm having dinner with my sister and her family.

Ondrej: Tomorrow. I will email tickets

Hudson: Where are you?

Ondrej: Monaco until next Wed

His phone rang and he answered. "I take it that's a yes." He didn't want to ask if Hudson would come, knowing Hudson loved to be told what to do. And he was gloriously good at it. Ondrej especially loved the times when Hudson obeyed with a hazy look in his gaze and his cheeks flustered and pink.

"You can't just expect me to drop my whole life and be with you for a few days." Just like that. Hudson had a way of saying yes while protesting against Ondrej's command. Hudson liked to be given an order then make his own decision about obedience. Ondrej never pushed, just suggested, then waited, leaving it in Hudson's hands to make his own choices. Consent was always in Hudson's court.

"I can." He couldn't expect that, not really, but he wanted to hear Hudson protest.

"What?" Just like that. Hudson's breathy annoyance shouldn't please Ondrej this much. "You've been away for—"

"Less than a month. I went to Canada to race, and now I'm back." He'd arrived back on Tuesday morning, having raced on the Sunday, flown out late on Monday, and then he'd rested—slept—until now to recover from the race and the travel. The time zone change was a bitch and he was glad for the extra week between races with the leap to Canada, then back to Europe. "It's not like we didn't communicate for a month."

"A text or two to remind me of my duty to your father doesn't count as communication." Oh, Hudson was properly annoyed now. Ondrej grinned, wishing he could see Hudson's expression now. Would he glare at him? Or perhaps Hudson would do that nervous little thing where he licked his bottom lip with the tip of his tongue.

"What do you want me to say?"

"Normal things. How are you? I miss you. Instead, you mostly ignore me, then summon me back to you?"

"Yes, like a demon who haunts my bed." Ondrej hadn't known what to text. They'd shared a few days together with a lot of sex. It was an extended hook up, not a relationship. And he dared not ask for more yet, not when he longed for it so much and his job wouldn't allow it. His phone was private, but there was always a risk some nosy reporter might hack it. He knew better than to text anything he didn't want the world to see.

"What?" Hudson spluttered.

"I'll pick you up from the airport." Ondrej had had a taste of what it would be like to have a partner to share his life with, and honestly sex with Hudson was the best he'd ever had. Better than random late night hook ups where he pretended to be his own doppelganger. He wanted more with Hudson. More sex. More shared breakfasts on the balcony. More lying in bed together at night watching Hudson read a book, wearing only his glasses. He couldn't have Hudson as his partner at work dinners, or out in public, but he could have these small private moments.

"I haven't said yes yet."

"But you will."

"Argh." Hudson growled at him, then laughed. "Damn you, I want to say yes, but I can't. I need to go to France to visit the old Bugatti factory. There's a small museum in the township that might have some information that isn't online."

Ondrej grinned. "The next race is in France. Stay with me, then travel with me." He couldn't ask Hudson to be with him at the race, but he could have the few days before. They could drive together to wherever Hudson needed to be, then Ondrej could continue to his race alone.

"France?"

"Yes. You can check my racing schedule on the S1 website."

"I suppose I could." Hudson's lack of interest in S1 amused Ondrej. Too many people spent time with him because he was one of only twenty S1 drivers in the world. It appealed to him that Hudson didn't place any great importance on his fame, although they still bickered about Ondrej spending money on Hudson. He must know, by now, that it gave Ondrej great pleasure to do that. Hudson was so giving, especially in bed, that it seemed unfair that all he could give back to him was money; something that he had plenty of. He'd do more, give more, if Hudson would let him. After all, Ondrej couldn't give Hudson time or a proper public relationship. Money was the only gift he could bestow on his stubborn beautiful man. Ondrej rubbed his hands through his hair. After such a short time, he was already besotted with Hudson. This wasn't going to end well. One day, Hudson would see that Ondrej couldn't offer him a completely open and free relationship and he'd leave.

"Don't come then." Ondrej had spent eight years as an S1 driver with only his training routine to fill the time between races. He didn't need the distraction of Hudson in his bed. He closed his eyes and the memory of Hudson's red hair sliding over his stomach as he sucked Ondrej's cock had him blinking.

"Make up your mind."

"Are you teasing me?"

"Yes. Hold on a second. Yes, Mackenzie, I won't be long. No, it's not my boyfriend. ..."

Ondrej wanted to argue with that. He would be happy with that tag, if it didn't mean Hudson might expect to be seen in public with him. Hudson's red hair was distinctive and if they were seen together again, then rumours might start to fly. S1 loved a good rumour; many fans said the politics were more interesting than the racing. One day someone was going to realise that Ondrej had abruptly left a championship team and been scooped up by the only openly gay man in S1—Socrates. They'd put that together with other details and come to the only conclusion possible. At least now he knew JP would stand by him, even if the other drivers and most of the fans did not.

"Hey, swear jar." Hudson laughed. "Sorry about that, Ondrej. Yes, send the tickets but book them against the job I'm doing. I need to finalise a few things before I go to France, but I can do that at your place as easily as from mine."

"So pragmatic."

"Well, I promised I wouldn't disappoint your father and he's still my client."

"No, you promised you would be gentle with him when you finally admit the car can't be found."

"I'm not admitting that just yet, but yes. I promised and I'll keep my promise."

"Stubborn. Get on a plane tomorrow." Ondrej couldn't quite admit his feelings, not when they were so new and uncertain. He could admit that it was nice to have someone to chat to like this. Everyone else wanted to talk S1; Papa was his agent and dealt with all contractual issues, his team was all about work, and his best friend, JP, was a rival driver. Hudson allowed him to get away from work for a few precious days. Even Amy, his trainer, was focused on keeping him fit and strong for work. Her and her partner, Mei, were Olympic level triathletes, and he couldn't imagine anyone better placed than her to keep his body ready for work. Women's sport was a lot more openly accepting of queer relationships, and while he'd never mentioned being gay to Amy, he liked working with someone queer who wouldn't judge him if he was ever brave enough to talk about himself.

"Fine."

"Don't sound so reluctant. You know you want this."

"Yes." Hudson's voice croaked a little.

"How soon will you get on your knees for me?" Ondrej couldn't help pushing Hudson a bit.

"As soon as you want." Hudson paused but Ondrej didn't—couldn't—answer. There were too many people at airports with cameras in their phones. "Maybe you shouldn't pick me up from the airport if public displays of affection bother you so much. I can take a cab." It felt like Hudson read his mind and he tried not to freak out.

"If I bring the SUV, you'll fit on the floor." The obvious response was to pretend it didn't bother him at all, as if he were able to let himself get blown in a public carpark. Hudson cackled.

"I'm six feet tall, Ondrej. Are you that desperate to feel my lips on you?"

Yes. "Take a cab. I can wait." His jaw clenched tight with the lie.

"Okay."

"Check your email later tonight." Ondrej hung up before he blurted out anything else. He was in so much trouble. Ever so slowly, over the first third of the season, Hudson had wormed his way into Ondrej's life, and he wanted more of him than he would be allowed. If they ever found out he was gay, S1 media would turn his life into a circus. Alicia Blasi would be the worst; she swooned over him too much already, although much of that was because she was a fan of Ondrej's mother. Maybe she would surprise him and protect him to protect his mother's legacy? Whatever. He really didn't want the distraction while he was still trying to figure out to keep his new car on the road. If he told himself this often enough, he wouldn't need to admit the possibility that this could be more.

A day later, and just as he'd planned when he bought Hudson's flight tickets, he'd finished up his afternoon strength training session with Amy and showered when his doorbell buzzed. Hudson. He straightened his collar and pushed the button to allow him up.

"Travelling on a Saturday sucks." Hudson walked through the door, a picture of flustered, tired man, and Ondrej wanted to cuddle him. Fuck. No, he wanted to kiss him, then fuck him.

"Are you such a connoisseur of travel now?" Ondrej teased.

Hudson smiled, and suddenly everything was right again in Ondrej's world. "It's your fault."

"Mine?" He smirked.

"Yes. I'd never been on a plane until your father employed me for this ... job." Why had Hudson paused?

Did he regret taking on the impossible puzzle of the missing Bugatti?

"And now you fly so often you've probably started seeing the same movie more than once."

"Yes." Hudson's eyes widened.

"Welcome to my life." Ondrej didn't mean for that to sound quite so important.

"Yeah, yeah, Mr high and mighty, fancy world traveller." Hudson didn't react to Ondrej's statement in the same way that made Ondrej's stomach twist in panic. There was only one possible way to quell the sudden rise of emotion.

"Come." Ondrej didn't wait for Hudson to walk towards him. He strode over and kissed him, pushing him up against the wall of his apartment hard. Hudson gasped into Ondrej's mouth, and Ondrej swallowed down the rush of hot air, taking from him with every stroke of his tongue, lashing Hudson with all the pent-up desire. It'd been a month since he'd tasted Hudson, a month of jerking off in the shower to thoughts of Hudson, and now he was here. Ondrej wanted to touch Hudson everywhere, wanted to kiss the trail of freckles that ran down his spine. He tugged at his shirt.

"Off."

Together their hands pulled at their clothes until both were naked. Ondrej pushed Hudson backwards until he fell onto the couch, his legs spread wide and his cock hard and eager. His red hair—red all the way down—and his freckled pale skin looked great against Ondrej's dark leather couch. He leaned over him, his hands on Hudson's shoulders and almost covered his body with his own, but purposefully leaving a gap between them.

"Hey." Hudson wrapped his arms around Ondrej and pulled, but Ondrej used his strength and balance to stay where he was. He had plans.

"Patience."

"But you said—"

He cut off Hudson's whine with a kiss, kissing him with all the words he couldn't say. It was ridiculous how easily Hudson had burrowed into his life and he wanted him to stay. He wanted things he couldn't want. Instead, he could show Hudson. Not by telling him to get on his knees for him, but by doing it himself. He knelt between Hudson's legs, pushing them wider with his knees, then broke their kiss to lick his throat and neck in long strokes. Hudson lifted his chin, giving him more access, and he couldn't resist. He sucked at his skin, a little too hard, loving the way Hudson's skin felt in his mouth. And just as Hudson whimpered, he stopped, kissing the spot gently until Hudson moaned a little. Yeah, just like that. Hudson lifted his hand and wrapped it around Ondrej's cock. It took all his control not to buck into his hand and for a second, he forgot what he was doing. Pleasure and heat centred in his balls and he nuzzled Hudson's neck, just breathing in his scent for a few breaths as Hudson stroked his cock with his warm hand. He had calloses on his palms—an unexpected texture—and it'd been a month... He sank lower onto the couch, removing Hudson's hand as he shifted, then slowly kissed his way down Hudson's chest. Hudson wasn't as fit as himself—not many people were—but for someone who stared at a computer all day, he was trim and surprisingly strong. Ondrej flicked his gaze up at Hudson's face, whose glasses rested on his nose. His cheeks were flushed, making his freckles stand out more, and Ondrej had to hide his reaction—infatuation —by biting Hudson's nipple. Hudson gasped. His erection brushed against Ondrej's stomach, a teasing touch.

"You like that?" He dipped his body to just touch Hudson's cock again, then moved away again.

"Yes."

"How about this?" Ondrej moved lightning fast, purposefully giving Hudson no time, and sucked Hudson's cock into his mouth. He was already leaking pre-come and it was salty and delicious on his tongue. The reward came with Hudson's strangled yes, followed by moans and breathy pants as Ondrej licked and sucked the hard length. He loved this—there was a power in giving a blowjob that was unique—the control of pace, the taste of skin and pre-come, and best of all the way his mouth and throat was full of Hudson. If he asked for anything right now, Hudson would say yes just to keep this pleasure going, and simply knowing that was enough to push Ondrej to the edge. He cupped Hudson's balls, using one hand, while the other pushed on Hudson's hip to keep him still. He changed his pace, deliberate and slow, then just as Hudson begged for it, he sped up again. He didn't need to look up at Hudson's face to know his eyes would be hooded, almost closed in pleasure. Instead he focused on the way Hudson's stomach muscles clenched and trembled. It wouldn't take much for him to come. Not much at all. Ondrej slid his fingers behind Hudson's balls, and gently circled his hole. Hudson cried out and came hard, his cock hitting the roof of

Ondrej's mouth. Ondrej swallowed, then slid off with a final kiss. Hudson rested back on the couch, his hair all in disarray and his eyes closed. Sunlight glinted off his glasses.

Ondrej rested back on his legs, content to sit and watch Hudson in his post-sex haze for a while. His own cock screamed for attention. Really, it was amazing he hadn't come too. He'd gone right to the edge a couple of times as he'd focused his attention on Hudson. He traced his hands up and down Hudson's thighs, enjoying the feel of his skin under his hands, and to stop himself cuddling against him. He could kneel here, resting his head on Hudson's thigh and just stare at him. No, he really couldn't.

"My turn." He jumped to his feet and grabbed Hudson's hands, pulling him to his feet as well. Hudson's eyes flashed open, a little unsteady as Ondrej interrupted his happy sated space. Good. He liked it when Hudson was off-balance, it made his own uncertainty feel less lonely. Ondrej spread his hands all over Hudson's back, as he pressed close, pushing his cock against Hudson's body. He stood on his tiptoes to get height and kissed Hudson hard. A kiss that said, 'wake up, pay attention to me.' Every action was deliberate, and every touch was a bit harsh as he tried to keep this to fucking and not let himself have feelings for Hudson. This was simply mutual pleasure, nothing more. It couldn't be more. He refused to let himself dream that it might be. Hudson inspired these thoughts of more, not because of who he was, but simply because Ondrej wasn't allowed a loving partner and damned if he wasn't going to accept that anymore. If he told himself that often enough—that it was situational, not about Hudson—then he might believe it. Regardless of all of that, he couldn't have a partner because he needed to drive. He didn't need this distracting wondering about fucking love or something. He humped Hudson—there was no other word for it—dragging his cock against Hudson's body. It was way too dry, rough and awkward, but he was so close. He poured all of his frustration with his cogitating brain into the kiss, and when Hudson cupped the back of his skull and threaded his fingers into Ondrej's hair, he came with a roar.

CHAPTER 8

MOLSHEIM, FRANCE

Hudson wished he'd planned better. A couple of days ago, he'd waved goodbye to Ondrej—without a goodbye kiss because they were in public—and stepped on a plane for the short one and half hour flight to Strasbourg. From there, he'd made his way on a bus to Molsheim, the small town that used to be on the outskirts of Strasbourg but was now absorbed by the larger city. The original Bugatti factory had been in Molsheim on the border of France and Germany. The travel had gone well and his research was even better, but now he was alone and unsure about what to do next. He didn't want to ring Ondrej for anything. Did they even have that type of relationship? No. Ondrej would just throw money at him, and he already felt the weight of the ever-growing debt. Besides, they weren't in a relationship, not really. Mostly they just had a lot of sex in Ondrej's apartment. He rang his sister instead. She was always good for a sensible opinion when he was stuck in his own head.

"How's things?"

"Ah, I'm in a little bit of a pickle."

"Are you safe?" Mackenzie asked, immediately making him feel both loved and foolish for needing help over a simple thing. He could just get on a bus, go to the airport, and book a flight home to England.

"Yes. Just—" He wasn't even sure how to explain this problem. He wanted to be on the other side of France with Ondrej; not going home to be alone. Only yesterday, Mackenzie had emailed him two new clients to research—yet another reason to head home and not contemplate being with Ondrej. Ondrej had stayed in Monaco for the past couple of days because the drive to the French racetrack in Le Castellet was only a couple of hours drive from Monaco. It made zero sense for him to come to Molsheim, eight hours drive across the other side of the country. This was the dilemma; go and watch Ondrej race tomorrow or fly home to England and type up the latest Bugatti report and crack on with his new client's research.

"How did the research go?"

"Oh, brilliant. This place is great. There's a town museum in an old monastery called La Chartreuse and I found a ton of information about the old Bugatti factory. I spent a whole day at Chateau St. Jean. Can you believe it? The family made the Bugatti factory out the back of their stately home. It's the most wild thing you can imagine." Hudson had been in his element these past couple days. He'd gathered information and found out all sorts of useful information in their archives. Most importantly, he'd discovered that the car hadn't arrived here at any point after 1937. The property here in Molsheim had been confiscated by the government during WWII, thanks to French anti-

Italian sentiment, although it was restored into the Bugatti family's ownership soon afterwards in 1947. Hudson quickly realised that the Bugatti family's Italian origins and this ownership drama meant that Chateau St. Jean would not have been a safe place to take the missing Bugatti Atlantic, even without the risk of being bombed. Being so close to Germany, during WWII, was reason enough not to take the car there, and Hudson didn't think anyone related to Ondrej would be so unthinking as to head towards war with a rare vehicle.

"What exactly is the problem?"

"Apart from having not found the car and just having ruled out a place it might have been?"

"Yes. All knowledge is useful and it'll make a good report for our client."

"I should come home and write that up…"

"But you want to spend time with your famous boyfriend?"

He's not my boyfriend. Hudson held back a sigh. "Yes."

"Seriously, Hudson? That's the dilemma you rang me for?"

"Yes. I could do with some advice."

"Life is for living and enjoying. If you want to see him, go and see him. It's simple."

It wasn't simple. He knew Ondrej didn't want their relationship known at his work. He couldn't just turn up to watch him race, could he?

Mackenzie sighed, loud and exasperated in his ear. "Stop overthinking it. Isn't our client your boyfriend's father?" Which was kind of the point. This was a mess and he needed to walk away before it mattered. Before it was going to hurt. Being with Ondrej was still new and fresh and exciting, and he had never had sex quite like it with anyone else. Ondrej's intensity and the way he made Hudson melt was special. If he wasn't careful, this would easily become more than just sex for him. Ondrej was rich and famous; people like that didn't care for people like him. Not in the long term. Not ever.

"Yes?" He gulped, weighed down by the negativity of his thoughts.

"Bloody hell, Hudson. If you need to justify going to see your boyfriend, tell yourself you are going to see your client. Ring him, make a meeting, and bonus..." She said that with a sing-song voice that grated at Hudson, "—you get to see your boyfriend too."

"Assuming they are together." Hudson knew they were. Mr D'Grieg was at every one of Ondrej's races, not just for fatherly interest, but because he was Ondrej's agent and dealt with all the legal stuff. Ondrej had explained it one evening last week while they'd been lying together in Ondrej's amazing bed. They'd just had incredible sex—again—and Hudson was curled up next to Ondrej, cuddled against him as he chatted to his dad on the phone about some sponsorship deal.

"It's a race this weekend. They'll be together." Mackenzie probably understood their client's schedule and whole life much more than Hudson did. She always researched the heck out of their clients before they took them on, because she wanted to understand that they'd get paid. He was more interested in the client's ancestry and family stories than what they did now.

"Just go. Hudson. Enjoy this while it lasts, and if it turns to shit, I'm here for you."

"Fine."

"And all the best. Send me an email with everything you found, and I'll make up the latest report. Tell Mr D'Grieg it'll be ready next week after Austria." Her pragmatism pulled him back to the world and he let himself be okay with heading to see Ondrej.

"Austria?"

"The next race. It's only a week after this one. The S1 schedule is tight this month with three races in three weeks." Trust Mackenzie to have it memorised. Hudson had been avoiding knowing the racing schedule, even though it was easily searchable online, because he didn't want Ondrej to think he only cared about his fame. Being accused of being mercenary—even as a joke—had made him cautious. Oh... Huh, that's why he didn't want to ring Ondrej and ask for a plane ticket.

"Go. Have some fun. You've worked hard for this." Mackenzie didn't just mean the research on the Bugatti. Overcoming their childhood had been—still was—lots of work. He was highly conscious of power differentials and this situation with Ondrej pushed all those buttons. Mackenzie would probably tell him it was good for him to confront that, or as she actually said, have some fun.

"Okay, I'll let him know." Hudson changed the subject to ask about the twins and Brian, and he listened to Mackenzie happily chat about her family and the latest naughty-cute things the twins had been doing. Eventually they hung up and he immediately rang Mr D'Grieg who told him not to worry and just ring his PA to book a flight to the race.

Sixth! Ondrej had finished the race in France in sixth place. It'd been nail-biting stuff with another car right on his tail for the last few laps, and Ondrej defending his position all the way to the finish line. Hudson had sent a text to Ondrej, congratulating him, and letting him know he was here. That was over three hours ago. He checked his phone again. Nothing. This was a mistake. He shouldn't have come here. His phone dinged.

Ondrej: Come to my room. 1340

Hudson's fingers trembled as he tried to type an answer. The relief in getting the command overrode the instinct to be annoyed at Ondrej for ignoring him. What, no. Ondrej had been busy doing his job, not ignoring Hudson who just needed to stop overthinking whether he deserved being with Ondrej. In the end, all he managed was a thumbs up emoji. He brushed his hair, cleaned his teeth, and carefully locked his hotel room, taking only his entry card and phone with him. By the time he knocked on Ondrej's door, the nerves—adrenalin—had calmed down.

Ondrej opened the door, looking incredible with damp hair and a plain white t-shirt over loose sweat pants. "Inside, quick."

Hudson rushed inside. "What's the matter?"

The door clicked shut. Ondrej pushed Hudson against the wall and kissed him. Urgently. It was an overwhelming experience; Ondrej used his tongue and teeth and lips to kiss Hudson with passion and energy. Hudson adored it. He wrapped one leg around Ondrej's ankle and melted between him and the wall. He kissed Ondrej back with the same intensity; a kiss that said, 'congratulations and I miss you.' There was a familiarity in this kiss now, and it made it even better. Hudson clung onto Ondrej's hips. Ondrej reached up and cupped Hudson's cheek. Holy. His knees softened. He needed more, needed to get his mouth on Ondrej's cock. Now. He started to slide down the wall.

"Come with me." Ondrej stepped backward and Hudson wobbled a little, thankful the wall was holding him up. Ondrej held Hudson's hands. Damn him for being so perfect… Hudson swallowed… so, so perfectly fuckable. Hudson followed Ondrej into his hotel room.

"Congratulations. Sixth is awesome." Hudson's voice cracked.

"Thanks." Ondrej sat in a high-backed leather chair, still holding Hudson's hands, leaving him to stand between Ondrej's bare feet. Hudson glanced up. They'd turned around, so Hudson stared at the hotel room's entry door, and Ondrej would have a view out of the main windows, if Hudson wasn't in the way.

"Are you going to congratulate me properly?"

Hudson's face flushed with heat. "On my knees?" His cock rubbed against his underwear, pushing hard on his jeans.

"Only if you want. It's always your choice, Hudson." *Way to say the perfect thing, Ondrej.* Hudson swallowed, slowly collapsing to the floor. He tugged his hands free from Ondrej's grip and waited as Ondrej leaned back in the chair.

"Take off your shirt." Hudson needed to see him. "Please."

Ondrej pulled his shirt over his head and flung it aside. He tucked his hands behind his head, elbows wide, giving Hudson an incredible view of his torso. Hudson stroked his hands up Ondrej's legs, caressing his thighs, deliberately skirting around his cock. His cock that strained against his sweatpants. Hudson hooked his fingers into Ondrej's sweatpants and pulled them down. His cock stood tall and beautiful, and Hudson didn't want to wait, or tease, anymore. He leaned forward and covered it with his mouth, taking him in as far as he could in one long motion. It'd only been a few days since he'd done this and he missed it, missed Ondrej, especially the way his fingers threaded into Hudson's hair. Not to control him or his pace as he slid up and down Ondrej's cock. Ondrej's fingers were just there, almost as though he needed to touch Hudson and have more connection than just his mouth on his cock. Hudson licked the tip of Ondrej's cock, savouring him until he drew out a salty taste of pre-come. He sank down again, this time, using his hand to cup Ondrej's tight balls, loving the way Ondrej groaned.

"Up." Ondrej tugged on his hair a little and Hudson released Ondrej. He used one hand for balance on the chair, leaving the other wrapped around Ondrej's cock. He slid up Ondrej's body, kissing as he went, and when he used his teeth to nibble at Ondrej's nipple, Ondrej came suddenly with one hand cradled around Hudson's cheek. Oh God. Hudson was so close too. Ondrej brushed his lips against Hudson's forehead. The intimate kiss sent Hudson over the edge and he came without Ondrej even touching his cock.

"Fuck. I'm sorry." It'd only been a few days. He should've been able to last longer. He collapsed against Ondrej, coating his clothes in Ondrej's mess, uncaring.

"Why are you sorry? You are wonderful." Ondrej kissed his forehead again and Hudson rested his head on Ondrej's shoulder. He was pretty sure he had the world's sappiest expression on his face.

An odd noise had Ondrej shifting underneath him.

"Ondrej." Shit, Mr D'Grieg was here. The noise must have been the hotel door opening. Mr D'Grieg must have his own key to Ondrej's room since there had been no knock.

"Fuck." Ondrej whispered. This had to be the worst moment of Hudson's life. He couldn't move; just stayed there, lying on his client's son, covered in come. Shit. He couldn't even breathe.

"Papa, would you mind giving me a moment? Just step out into the hallway for a bit, thanks." How could Ondrej even think enough to request something like that right now? The door clicked again, the noise really loud in the deathly silence hovering in the room.

"What now?"

"It's okay. Papa knows I'm gay."

"Yeah, but—" Hudson jumped to his feet, staggering a little. His shirt was a disaster. His jeans were wet with his own come. This was a fucking disaster.

"Let's get cleaned up and then we can talk. It'll be fine."

Hudson stared at the floor. "If you say so."

"Come." The command was soft and gentle. Ondrej stood up in a fluid easy motion and walked to the bathroom, beckoning Hudson to follow. He did. Because there was no other option.

"Take off your clothes. You can wear some of mine." Ondrej helped Hudson undress. One day he was going to look back at this moment and adore the care that Ondrej was giving him, but right now, he struggled for breath. He felt like he'd fucked up everything.

"I shouldn't have come here."

"Yes. You should. It'll be okay. It's only Papa. No one else knows." Was Ondrej asking him to trust him? Could he? He took off his jeans and threw them onto his shirt in the corner of the bathroom. Ondrej removed his own sweatpants and stood there naked.

"Your underwear too." Ondrej wet a cloth and cleaned up Hudson's cock. He leaned backwards, gripping the sink for balance, then watched as Ondrej cleaned his own chest and stomach too. Ondrej leaned in and kissed Hudson on the lips, a gentle quick press of lips.

"Come on. Let's get dressed. Papa will have opinions on this." Ondrej walked, naked, out of the bathroom. Opinions. Yes, that was what Hudson was freaked out about. He'd just been caught with his client's son, in flagrante delicto. He'd fucked up. He was certain of it. He followed Ondrej, his legs trembling with each stride.

"He saw us."

"Yes. It doesn't matter. Stop panicking. Get dressed." Ondrej threw a pair of clean sweatpants and a Gamble t-shirt in his direction and Hudson mechanically put them on. He let himself be led by Ondrej to the couch and sat down. As soon as Ondrej walked towards the hotel door... and his father... Hudson buried his face in his hands.

"Papa, come in. You remember Hudson."

"Yes." Mr D'Grieg's voice was tight. Hudson hoped the floor would swallow him up, or he could hide under this very nice hotel couch, or anything, really. "I understand that you are an adult, Ondrej, but really? Here. At a race? You know what happened last time."

Hudson sat up straight. Last time? Ondrej had his head bowed.

"You can't put your career at risk like this."

"I know, Papa. Trust me, I know."

"And yet, I walk into your hotel room and see you... like that with him."

Hudson expected Ondrej to protest. It was hardly like anyone in the world could just walk in and see them. But he didn't, he just bowed his head and accepted what his father was saying.

"This can't leave this room." Mr D'Grieg glared at him, and Hudson stood up.

"Mr D'Grieg. This is a matter between your son and myself. I don't see—"

"No. You don't see. He nearly destroyed his career last time he kissed a man at a race. And he isn't allowed to fall in love. It's not safe."

Ondrej finally looked up. "Thankfully, JP talked to Socrates and found me a seat."

"And now you put it all at risk again."

"I hardly think—"

Mr D'Grieg cut his son off. "Yes, you hardly think. This ends now. Go home, Mr Lockley."

"No. It is Ondrej's decision."

"How dare you? Don't you understand what is at risk here?"

"I do. Believe it or not, Ondrej and I have talked about this. I understand his need to stay—" Hudson cleared his throat, "—closeted. We risked nothing today by celebrating his success." His face was burning with shame for the way Mr D'Grieg spoke to his son, and for causing such upset between them when they clearly had a lovely relationship most of the time. He was the worst person in the world for creating tension between them; here he was literally wrecking a good family.

"Hudson. You don't need to..." Ondrej walked across the room, turning away from Hudson.

"What? Defend you? Stand up for you against your own father? We've done nothing wrong." Hudson wanted to stamp his foot and dig this hole deeper. How dare Mr D'Grieg talk to Ondrej like this; Ondrej who went out of his way to protect his father's emotions? Why couldn't Mr D'Grieg respect Ondrej's feelings in the same way? But mostly, it was a lot easier to get angry on Ondrej's behalf than to let himself become overwhelmed with shame at having caused tension in a family. Hudson breathed in and out slowly, his blood rushing loudly in his ears.

"I know you have done nothing wrong. I'm not against my son being gay. I'm against him being gay at work." Mr D'Grieg's expression softened, and Hudson almost apologised for his outburst.

"Papa supported me when my old team sacked me for kissing a mechanic in a storage cupboard. He was there for me when no one else was." Ondrej's whisper echoed in the room. That's what had happened? Hudson's stomach churned. He wanted to say that this wasn't like that. He cared about Ondrej and his career and well... him. But he couldn't say that because he wasn't Ondrej's boyfriend. Not officially or anything. It wasn't his place to stand beside Ondrej. He was just the next guy that Ondrej was fucking at work when he shouldn't be. He was the guy ruining Ondrej's good relationship with his father.

"I don't want him to fall in love."

As if that were a risk right now. "Okay. I will leave now." Hudson left and it wasn't until the door clicked behind him that he realised his phone and hotel room card were in the jeans he'd left on Ondrej's bathroom floor. He stood in the hallway, his heart pounding as the entirety of the conversation sunk in. What should he do now? He could hardly knock and ask for his phone. Yes he could. It wouldn't be any more fucking weird than the rest of this mess. He already burned with shame. What was a little more? With another couple of deep breaths, he knocked on the door. After a long tense moment, Mr D'Grieg opened the door.

"I left my phone behind."

Mr D'Grieg stared at him in an eerily similar way to Ondrej's intense annoyed glare. On Ondrej it was hot as fuck, on his father, it just intimidated him. Hudson was about to abandon his need to get his phone and just bolt, when Mr D'Grieg waved at him to come in. He walked directly to bathroom and grabbed his phone from his pants. Should he take the pants too?

"I'll get them washed for you."

He spun around. Ondrej stood right there, far too

close. Hudson stopped breathing. He managed to nod in thanks at Ondrej's comment.

"I wish this were different. Papa is right. I can't do this at work." Ondrej looked so … sad. Hudson's arms twitched, but he didn't reach out and hug him like he desperately wanted to.

"I understand." He didn't want to. "Thanks for everything."

"This doesn't mean we are over." The anguish in Ondrej's voice nearly broke him.

Hudson shook his head. "I think it does." He gripped his phone and hotel key card tight, then brushed past Ondrej and fled from the room, wearing Ondrej's clothes.

CHAPTER 9
SILVERSTONE, UK

Ondrej had shut everything out for two weeks to focus on work. A fucking podium in Austria—his first in two years—had been bittersweet. He'd only achieved it because he had thrown himself into work, so he didn't have to think about the way Hudson's voice growled and cracked when he said, 'I think it does.' It was over before it had really started. And now he pulled onto the weigh bridge after finishing in seventh at Silverstone. His teammate, Paulo, had beaten him for the first time this season, finishing in fifth. He climbed out of the car, and went through the usual post-race processes, before walking towards the whole team. They crowded around him.

"Another cracking drive, Ondrej." Socrates slapped him on the back.

"Brilliant by Paulo too." He pushed his way through the crowd of mechanics to find his rookie team-mate. He embraced him, then pulled off his helmet.

"Brilliant drive, mate. Well done."

"You aren't mad that I beat you?" For a young driver from a rich shipping family, Paulo often lacked the necessary ego that made the best drivers stand out. He'd have to start believing that he'd earned his seat, not bought it, like many in the media liked to say about young S1 drivers from wealthy families. It was silly since they were all like that, barring a few rare exceptions. Car racing was a rich person's sport.

"Yes, but it won't happen again, so you should enjoy it today." Ondrej made sure he grinned to show his teammate he was teasing.

Paulo gave him a shove. "Thanks. Just wait and see." That was better.

"We should do this for the press. They love this team rivalry shit."

Paulo shook his head. "Nah. I'm a terrible actor."

"They probably got it already. Cameras are everywhere in S1." Ondrej cringed internally. As if he needed the reminder that he'd broken up with Hudson for this reason. Or to be technically correct, Hudson had left him, and he'd done nothing to stop him, even after he'd magically reappeared for a moment to get his phone. It hadn't been magic, of course, it just felt like it for a nasty temporary second. Papa had been gentle after Hudson had left—too gentle— and yet, he'd made him promise to keep the two parts of his life separate. He glanced up, sure that he'd seen a flash of red hair in the crowd. No, he'd just been imagining it. When he was in the car, it was easy to focus. It was only away from the car, or the hours he'd spent in the simulator this week, that he saw red hair everywhere. It made no sense. He'd even looked it up online. Red hair was less than two percent of the global population, although oddly it went up to thirteen percent in Scotland, so he was never going to visit there until he'd figured out a way to stop thinking about Hudson. He should be able to live his life without encountering anyone with red hair at all; yet everywhere he went, bloody red-haired people seemed to pop up and remind him of the wonderful stubborn historian with glasses and a British accent that he couldn't have. Fuck. All week, he'd been here in Hudson's country, listening to British accents all day. At least his pit crew had a huge variety of global accents, but away from them, he couldn't escape snippets of Hudson. He missed him. And he couldn't have him.

"True. I have to hide in my hotel room to get any privacy."

Ondrej shrugged. "It's the unfortunate part of the job. Worth it though, on days like this." He slapped Paulo on the shoulder, then walked towards the rooms out the back of pitlane. He'd rather be in his caravan having a shower and a wank. Today, he wouldn't think of Hudson while he jerked himself off. Not at all. Ha. Not like every other day in the last two weeks. When he was alone in the shower, he allowed himself to think of Hudson with something like freedom.

"Hold up a minute." Socrates walked beside him, away from the crowds, into the private team space behind the pits where no press were allowed. He waited until they were alone. "Ondrej, are you happy?"

"Yes, I'm happy. Third in Austria and now seventh here. We are steadily collecting points."

"I didn't mean that. You are more than a driver to me, Ondrej. You are a good person, and hopefully a friend. I watched you struggle last year, after your last team behaved in such a disgusting fashion."

"Last year's struggle was because of a shit car."

Socrates grimaced. "Yes. And this year you have been inconsistent in a good car. So let me ask again, are you happy?"

"It's complicated." When he was in his car, he was... not exactly happy, but content and balanced. Everything always felt right with the world when he drove. Driving made sense. It made everything else fade away as he pushed hard to the edge of the limits of the car and found the spot where adrenalin and skill blended perfectly. It was just the other times that were hard. Socrates glanced over his shoulder. Even here in the safest, most fucking inclusive S1 team, he still checked. Ondrej held his breath knowing what was coming.

"Are you still seeing that mechanic?"

"Alex? No. He found someone else."

"So you dealt with a romantic breakup and a team breakup. Tough. I'm sorry I didn't take more time to chat to you about this." Socrates was a known thrill seeker. It was weird to see him so interested in anything soft like emotions.

"It was hardly a breakup." Not like with Hudson. "It was just a few hook ups."

"You need someone. Someone to celebrate with after a podium and to hold you when it goes wrong."

Ondrej yearned for that, but he shook his head, hoping Socrates couldn't see through his poker face to the reality underneath. "I can't. You know why. You didn't come out until a long time after your career was finished."

"True." Socrates laughed. "The world was a bit harsher in the eighties. It doesn't mean I was chaste during that time though. There were plenty of opportunities if you knew where to look."

"I..." Ondrej wanted to defend himself. "I have plenty of opportunities in the off season and the mid-season break when no one knows who I am."

"But this thing with Alex? It was exciting, yeah? To do it at work, knowing the risks." Socrates hit the nail on the head. Ondrej just nodded cautiously. Where was Socrates going with this line of questions?

"I understand. A good driver takes risks; we chase the line between absolute speed and disaster knowing that a miniscule error could be catastrophic. You want that thrill all the time, not just in the car." Somehow Socrates made it sound like a statement.

"Is that what you did?"

Socrates spread his hands wide and grinned. "I was a champion, a sex god, every gay man in Europe wanted to be fucked by me. A satisfied driver is a good driver. It's not healthy to go so long without sex. I worry about you."

"Fucking Jesus. That's a bit fucking much." Ondrej blinked.

"In the end, I was lucky."

"Because you didn't get caught?"

"It was the AIDS crisis and the legal situation in most countries was dicey." A sadness filled Socrates eyes for a moment. "I didn't get the virus. That's what made me lucky."

Ondrej gulped. It made Ondrej's problems seem miniscule by comparison. "Did you lose many friends?"

"Yes." Socrates paused and Ondrej waited. "Different times. We drove without halos, without all the safety regulations. Drivers died more often. Friends died too. Tough times." Socrates shrugged, even though his eyes were shiny.

"Are you trying to give me advice?"

"Yes. You are driving inconsistently. It's my job to think about all the reasons why that might be. Get regular sex, Ondrej. Keep it private if you must, but honestly, I don't care if you invite a different man to every race. You are an athlete, and you have physical needs. Leave dealing with the sponsors to me. Times are different now. The media would welcome a gay driver. They welcome me."

"Um, okay." Ondrej just stared at his boss. One thing was true. He was driving inconsistently this year. He should get someone in Victor's team to go through the data with him and see if he could figure out why. Ondrej pushed away the voice that wanted to scream that it had anything to do with the confusing way he felt around Hudson.

Socrates thumped him on the back. "Good." He walked off, leaving Ondrej stunned. The mixed messages between Papa and Socrates had him totally confused. Papa always said the sponsors would be upset if he was out as gay, but Socrates... Did Socrates just imply that all their sponsors knew about Socrates and his husband Mike and gave them money anyway? His whole world felt like it had shifted off its axle.

Ondrej: What's your address?
Hudson: Why?
Ondrej: I have your clothes. It was just an excuse. After

the weird discussion with Socrates, he needed to see Hudson. He growled. Even thinking that was a lie. He'd packed Hudson's jeans and t-shirt in his suitcase for this trip to Silverstone just in case he saw him. Hudson was still working for Papa. He knew that because he'd received the latest report on his trip to the original Bugatti factory in Molsheim. For a few minutes, his phone sat silently with Hudson ignoring his text. What he deserved was Hudson texting him to say keep them, keep the clothes, he didn't want to see him anymore. Instead, his phone rang.

"Hudson?"

"You should just keep the clothes. You bought them for me anyway."

"I did?"

"In Milan."

Ondrej closed his eyes. His heart raced as he remembered the joy on Hudson's face as they'd gone shopping in Milan, and the way his skin flushed when they'd gone back to their hotel room and removed all his new clothes.

"Ondrej? Are you okay?"

"Yeah, why?"

"You made an odd noise."

Shit, an odd noise, like a groan at the memory of Hudson's touch? "I need to see you."

"I don't think that's wise."

"Fuck wise. I miss you."

Hudson made a weird, strangled noise and Ondrej wished he could see his expression and know what that meant.

"I don't need to be in Germany for ten days. Please."

Ondrej wasn't above begging right now. He should be ashamed of needing Hudson so much.

"What about your father? What about your career? S1?"

"Socrates said it was okay."

"Who?"

"He owns Gamble Racing. I would think his opinion overrides Papa's on this matter."

Hudson growled. "I won't get between you and your father."

"You aren't."

"That's not how I remember that conversation, Ondrej." How could Hudson say his name like that? Like a scold. It shouldn't be so hot to hear it. What a fucking mess.

"It's complicated."

"People always say that when they want something they can't have." Hudson's intake of breath was loud in Ondrej's ear. "Not that I'm arrogant enough to think you want me, but—"

"You should be. Arrogant. I do want you."

"But not enough to risk your job."

"I can have both."

"What? Me and your job and a good relationship with your father? Family is more important than sex, Ondrej."

All of Ondrej's blood fell to his feet and he felt woozy. "Sex?"

"Isn't that what this is for you? Sex with someone who will come when you call?"

"Socrates says I need someone. I'm driving inconsistently."

Hudson gasped. "I don't even know what that means, but it feels like you are saying that I'm only useful when other people say it's okay for you to fuck me."

"Hudson. Are you mad at me?" Ondrej felt like he'd been kicked in the balls by this conversation.

"No." Hudson breathed loudly again. "I'm not mad that you have a good relationship with your father, and you prioritise that. It's what you should be doing."

"Please can we meet? At least let me give you your clothes."

"Fine. I'll text you my address." Hudson hung up and Ondrej sank down, crouching on his feet with his head pressed against the wall. His phone dinged with a message. Hudson had sent an address. He needed to get out of his sweaty driving suit and shower, then get a cab to take him to wherever the fuck Hudson lived. He punched the address into a map app—the outskirts of Manchester was three hours drive away. Shit. He was too tired to figure out what to do; he was always exhausted after a race. Two hours of high-speed racing was physically draining. Maybe he could pay someone to drive him that far, and just sleep the whole time, but he'd arrive late in the evening. That would certainly give Hudson the wrong impression.

A couple of hours later, Ondrej knocked on the very ordinary cottage front door on a very ordinary suburban street. An Asian guy answered the door.

"I'm sorry, I must have the wrong address."

"Ondrej D'Grieg?" The man had a British accent.

People always recognised him, and since the man looked nothing like Hudson, it was probably the wrong place.

"Yes." He expected to be asked for his autograph, then he'd leave, and double check the address Hudson had sent. It would serve him right if Hudson had deliberately sent him to the wrong place. Fuck, Hudson would never be so cruel.

"Hudson lives out the back. Come through."

"Okay." He hoped his relief at being in the correct place didn't show on his face as he took off his shoes and added them to the rack in the hallway, then followed this man through the house.

"Hudson. Your boyfriend is here." The man called out.

"How many times do I have to tell you? He's not my boyfriend."

"Right, whatever. Anyway, he's here."

They walked into an open plan kitchen and living area with glass doors that opened out into a small back yard. A little cabin was situated at the back of the yard, and a couple of toddlers were playing in a tiny blow-up pool with a red-haired woman sitting beside them, laughing. The mid-summer sun wouldn't set for a few hours this far north. It was a picture-perfect version of family life.

"Already?"

He turned to see Hudson standing at the stove, stirring a small pot. His shirt sleeves were rolled up and his bare feet sticking out of the bottom of tight jeans. He looked so good. Kissable. Fuckable, if Ondrej was completely honest.

"I flew here."

"Of course you did." Hudson rolled his eyes. "I suppose you've met Brian, he's my sister's husband."

"Hi," Brian said. "What do you mean you flew here?"

"On a plane." Hudson's sarcasm made Brian roll his eyes and laugh. Ondrej felt like an intruder in their family.

"Yeah, but didn't we saw you on telly only a few hours ago? Hudson was glued to the screen."

Ondrej adored the way Hudson's cheeks flushed at Brian's teasing. He suddenly understood how Hudson felt when he'd walked into JP's apartment in Monaco. These people had such a lovely ordinary existence, how could he explain his life to them without sounding like an absolute fuckwit?

"The race finished around five this afternoon. My team boss offered to fly me here. He has his own plane." And now he was here in time for dinner, without being invited to eat with them... It was unsettling and not just because they were so welcoming and nice.

"Like a private jet?" Brian asked.

"No, more like a two-seater Cessna. Socrates has his pilot's licence. He lives near Silverstone, so it didn't take long to get up in the air and then we basically landed in some farmer's grass landing strip not far from here..."

"Mackenzie, did you hear this?" Brian walked outside and sat next to the red-haired woman, leaving him alone with Hudson.

"Are you hungry?" Hudson kept stirring the pot.

"Yes." His stomach grumbled loudly and Hudson raised one eyebrow. "I had a post-race snack, but then we've been flying and stuff."

"Stay for dinner. There is plenty."

"What are you making?"

"Nothing special. Bangers and mash with peas and gravy. The twins love it."

"It smells great. I'd love some if there is enough." Ondrej didn't want to impose. "I didn't mean to end up here at dinner time."

"It's fine."

"Okay. I have your clothes too." He held up the bag.

"Thanks. Just chuck it on a chair." Hudson waved vaguely.

"Can I help?" Ondrej hadn't expected to end up in a family dinner, and now he was here in the same room as Hudson, he realised that he was exhausted. Usually after a race, he showered, ate, and then slept.

"Sure. Set the table." Hudson pointed in the direction of a cupboard, so Ondrej opened it to see plates. He grabbed some and laid them on the table.

"For a rich guy, you are good at that."

"It was just me and Papa growing up, so we both shared the tasks around the house." He didn't mention that they had a cleaner. Hudson served up the dinner while Ondrej added cutlery. Being domestic with him was nice. Hudson called everyone inside and they sat down to eat. It was loud and fun and the toddlers were messy.

"Is that your normal life? Like you just want to go somewhere and you fly there?" Brian asked.

"Yes." He shrugged one shoulder. "Socrates loves his planes, so he's always offering to take anyone up. He'd probably take you up if you wanted."

"Seriously? That'd be awesome." Brian smiled. "I like your boyfriend, Hudson."

"Not my boyfriend."

"It's complicated." Ondrej spoke at the same time as Hudson. Awkward. He focused on the food. He was starving and the simple fare was exactly what he needed after a race day.

"Speaking of complicated..." Hudson's sister, Mackenzie, spoke. "What is with the weird names during the race?"

"Like?" Ondrej was happy to explain S1 to people; much easier than trying to explain why he was here when Hudson kept saying he wasn't his boyfriend.

"Maggots in buckets. Does that mean something is wrong with the car? Make it make sense." Mackenzie bit her bottom lip in the exact same way Hudson did when he was nervous about something. The siblings shared the same striking red hair and freckles, but it was the little gestures that truly painted them as family.

"Maggots and Becketts. It's the name of a corner on the track. Most of the S1 tracks have names for nearly all the corners; like Aqua Minerali at Imola or Eu Rouge at Spa." Ondrej could recite them all, not just their names, but also the feel of them as the car moved past the apex.

"But maggots? Like the grub?"

Hudson laughed. "It's named after Maggot Moor which is next to the track. And Becketts is named after St Thomas à Beckett. There used to be a medieval church there, that's why the next corner is called the chapel corner."

"Look at you, knowing stuff about S1." Mackenzie laughed, then turned back to one of the twins who was using their spoon to splat the mashed potatoes.

"It's nothing. I heard Maggots in Buckets too and was curious."

Ondrej shoved another mouthful of mashed potato into his mouth, so he didn't say something technical about how he loved the way he had to have a precise driving line through Maggots and Becketts, hitting all the apexes at exactly the right angles, otherwise he'd end up in the grass and spinning. He stayed quiet for the rest of dinner, just listening to them all chat together as they ate. The twins joined in too with cute little things. It was all so charmingly domestic.

"I'll clean up," Brian said. "Hudson; take your guest away. It's obvious the two of you need to talk."

Hudson, who had hardly spoken to him all dinner, nodded. "Okay. Come along then." He walked outside and into the little cabin in the backyard. Ondrej followed, smothering a yawn as he stepped inside Hudson's tiny home.

"Are you tired?" Hudson asked.

"Not too tired to talk to you."

Hudson shook his head. "I think you are. Didn't you just drive in a race today?"

"Yes."

"At what speed?"

"Silverstone track average is 153 kilometres per hour." JP's average speed was slightly higher since he'd finished 36 seconds ahead of him, but Hudson probably didn't need that level of precision.

"For how long?"

"Not counting out laps; one hour, fifty-nine minutes, and one point three five seconds."

"And you think you aren't tired? You've just driven for

two hours at intense concentration at speeds that normal people never go at. Like, what was your top speed today?"

"Just a tick over 304 kph. You'll have to convert that if you want it in miles. I'm used to using kilometres. It's a European standard."

"It's fine. Fucking fast is enough for me. We can talk tomorrow. Hop in bed and sleep."

Ondrej nodded and followed Hudson through a door into his bedroom. He quickly stripped off and fell into bed. He wanted to be the one looking after Hudson. After the last time they'd been together, Ondrej didn't deserve this kindness. Just before he fell asleep, he felt Hudson's lips brush over his forehead.

"Sleep well, champion."

"Not a champion. Yet." One day. He fell asleep dreaming of a cute red-haired British man waving at him as he stood on a podium holding a trophy.

CHAPTER 10

Hudson woke up beside Ondrej and ignored the guilty twist in his stomach. They had so much to talk about and he probably shouldn't have slipped into bed with him before they'd resolved anything. But as he lay on his side and stared at Ondrej's sleeping form, he found it impossible to regret his choice to be physically close to him. Ondrej slept on his back with one hand slung behind his head. His lean muscles were relaxed; everything about him was relaxed, and Hudson realised he never saw him like this. When Hudson had stayed at his home in Monaco, Ondrej had been the first one up. A reasonable feat given Hudson's habit of getting up with the sunrise. Something about Ondrej's home and luxurious bed had led to him sleeping in more than usual; probably all the sex they'd had. Fuck, he missed Ondrej. Missed his touch, his kisses, and the way he made Hudson feel like he was someone who mattered. Someone important. Without Ondrej's gaze boring into him, Hudson could take his time to look at this beautiful intense conflicted man in his bed.

"Good morning." Ondrej rolled on his side and whispered with his lips so close to Hudson.

"Morning." If Hudson moved an inch, they'd be kissing, but Ondrej moved away.

"Thank you for letting me stay." Ondrej got out of bed. "Where's your bathroom?"

"Through there." Hudson pointed, then closed his eyes. He was so confused. A few minutes later, Ondrej slid back under the blanket and pulled Hudson's body close, searing him with his body heat.

"What happened?"

"Plenty has happened in the last two weeks. Celebrate with me." Ondrej rolled onto Hudson and kissed him. Hudson couldn't resist and kissed him back. It felt like home, this raw, desperate, needy kiss that screamed hungrily for the two weeks they'd been apart. Hudson wished he could shut up all the questions in his head and just enjoy the way Ondrej pressed his hard cock against Hudson's own aching cock. He bucked his hips a little, pushing back, hinting at what he wanted.

"Why are you so hard to give up?" Ondrej whispered against Hudson's ear lobe, then nibbled at it, tugging until Hudson gasped. He slid his hands down Ondrej's back and grabbed that lean ass with both hands.

"Do you want to give me up?"

"No." Ondrej kissed his neck, slowly making his way down Hudson's throat and across his left shoulder. He followed his lips with his hands, with such a light touch it tickled. Hudson pressed his mouth against Ondrej's hair, needing to do something with his mouth, so he didn't beg Ondrej for more. The very idea that this man—this gorgeous famous man who could have anyone—couldn't give up Hudson blew his mind, except he'd been there when Ondrej had chosen his job over Hudson; and so he should. It was ridiculous for any other choice to be made.

"But you should? Because of S1 or because of your father?"

"Later." Ondrej rolled them both sideways and wrapped his hand around both their cocks. He stroked a couple of times—dry and rough—but it didn't matter. Two weeks without Ondrej's touch and Hudson was already leaking and ready.

"Fuck me. Condoms are in the drawer." Hudson threw his arm out in that direction, and Ondrej crawled up his body until his cock hovered near Hudson's mouth. He lifted his head to lick the tip, then sucked his length in as far as he could from this awkward angle. Ondrej knelt with one leg either side of Hudson's chest. Hudson focused on Ondrej's cock, using his mouth with all the skill he'd learned in various hook ups over the last decade.

"Stop." Ondrej pulled out and rolled on a condom so competently that Hudson almost came on the spot. Wow, how ridiculous to be so overcome from such a small swift motion. That'd never happened to Hudson before. He swallowed as he watched the decadent way Ondrej covered himself in lube, those intense dark blue eyes never leaving Hudson's face.

"You want this?" Ondrej asked.

"Yes please." Hudson rocked his hips up and the tip of his cock brushed against Ondrej's ass. Back in Monaco, they'd shared topping each other. Today, Hudson wanted to be filled with Ondrej. If this was going to be their last time together, he wanted to feel Ondrej for days. "As hard as you can."

Ondrej growled as he swung his leg across Hudson's chest, then flipped him over. He pressed greedy kisses between Hudson's shoulder blades, scraping his skin with his teeth, as he made his way down Hudson's body. Ondrej used his hands to spread Hudson's legs wide. The cool wetness of lube against his hole made Hudson pull his knees under himself so his ass was up in the air for Ondrej. Ondrej took his time, opening up Hudson for himself. All Hudson could hear was Ondrej's heavy breathing, and the roar of building desire in his ears. Just as he was ready to beg in the most undignified fashion, he felt the blunt end of Ondrej's cock against his hole.

"Yes, please."

Ondrej slid in with a slight grunt. "You still want it hard?" His croaky voice sounded wrecked as if Hudson had fucked his mouth and it was almost enough. Hudson had already gone to the edge a couple of times this morning without much of a touch from Ondrej. Just being here in his own bed with him set him on the edge.

"I want to feel you for days." Hudson begged and when Ondrej thrust, Hudson had to grab the sheets with his hands. Ondrej fucked him hard. Just as he wanted. The bed banged against the wall and Hudson pushed his face against the mattress to muffle his cries. Beautiful tension built and built with every stroke against his prostate until Hudson wanted to come. Desperately needed to come. Ondrej reached around him, holding the base of his cock tight, stopping him from coming in the most deliciously agonising way.

He made a strangled noise, a noise that tried to say, 'Hey that's not fair, please let me come.' Ondrej slid his hand up Hudson's cock, then thrust hard three more times. With each one, he pressed his other hand on the back of Hudson's neck, pushing him into the mattress. It was fucking perfect and Hudson cried out as he came. Only a second later, Ondrej came too, collapsing on him and surrounding him with heat. His breath was hot and rapid against Hudson's skin. After a while he pulled himself out and rolled off.

"Let me clean you." Ondrej disappeared for a few moments, returning with a warm cloth, and he gently rolled Hudson over onto his back away from the mess, and cleaned him.

"You are going to ruin me for anyone else." Hudson clamped his hand over his mouth. Oops, he hadn't meant to say that aloud.

"I hope so because I feel the same way." Ondrej kissed him. He placed the damp cloth on the top of Hudson's bedside table, then cuddled in against him. With the sheets being a mess, they stayed together on the cleaner side of the bed and Hudson buried his face against Ondrej's firm chest. He breathed him in, his skin was a little salty and smelled like sex and warmth.

Eventually, Hudson's stomach rumbled. "We should get up and eat something."

"Okay. Shower with me first?"

"Ondrej! You are insatiable today."

"Today. Everyday. Only with you."

Hudson jumped out of bed and stared at him. "Who

are you and what have you done with Mr S1 comes first and I can't do this?"

"Are we at my work now?"

"So that's it?" Hudson shook his head and walked to the bathroom, not wanting Ondrej to see the disappointment that was bound to be showing on his face. He didn't want to be a part time boyfriend, only there for sex when Ondrej had time for him. He wanted to demand that Ondrej share his whole life with him, but he dared not ask. He wasn't worth that kind of commitment from anyone. It wasn't fair to ask Ondrej to be out with him when his job demanded that he couldn't. Hudson turned on the shower, and waited for the water to heat up before stepping in. Ondrej joined him in the tight space.

"There's more to it."

"Okay. I need to eat before we have this conversation." Hudson grabbed his bodywash and quickly washed himself all over. Ondrej tried to help, sliding soap suds covered hands all over Hudson's body too, and Hudson tried not to squirm under the attention. Soon enough he was hard and Ondrej quickly stroked him until he came. Again. Hudson leaned—wilted—against the shower wall and just let Ondrej look after him. It was nice and he was too weak to say no.

"Go and get dressed." Ondrej gave him a little shove and Hudson reluctantly stepped out of the shower and grabbed a towel.

By the time Hudson was dressed and had made some porridge for them both, Ondrej sat at his small table looking fresh and amazing. His damp hair curled at the ends. Hudson stared as he handed him a bowl of porridge and a spoon. An unsettling sense that this would be the last time they'd be together hung around Hudson.

"I didn't have any fruit, so it's not like the porridge you have in Monaco."

"It's fine. Sit down."

Hudson sat.

"We probably should talk." Ondrej ate some of his porridge and Hudson just waited for him. He hadn't brought his own plate of food to the table, and he glanced over at his small kitchenette.

"Get your breakfast. Hell. I'm doing this all wrong."

"Okay." Hudson didn't want to agree, but yeah, this felt really wrong. He grabbed his food and sat down to eat. They ate in silence. Eventually Ondrej put his spoon in his empty bowl and leaned back with his hands linked behind his head.

"After the race yesterday, Socrates pulled me aside for the strangest conversation."

"Okay?"

"He... He was worried that I've been driving inconsistently all season and he thinks I should have sex more often."

"Seriously? Isn't he your boss? That's pretty fucking weird."

"He thinks it will make me a better driver."

"Um, does he know you are gay?"

Ondrej nodded. "He knows. JP went to him when I was dropped by the other team. JP hoped that because Socrates is gay, he might understand my situation and help me."

"Does that mean you are here because your boss says

you should have more sex?" Hudson wasn't sure how that revelation made him feel. Weird as fuck, like his skin was too tight and he wanted to rip it off.

"Yeah, and he said, he wouldn't care if I brought a different man to every race as long as I started to drive more consistently."

"Well, that's…" Hudson's mouth was dry. He didn't want Ondrej to be with a different man each race. Just the one. Him. "That's very different to what your father said."

"I know." Ondrej stared up at the ceiling. "I'm so confused."

"You still came here." Directly after the race, in a plane flown by his boss. Huh.

"I want to be with you and Socrates—"

"Gave you permission and flew you here for a dirty weekend… or whatever." It was Monday morning now, technically. "All so you will drive better?"

Ondrej jumped to his feet and paced around. "It makes no sense. I got a podium finish on the weekend after Papa made you leave."

"I left. It was my choice."

"Why?"

"I didn't want you to have to choose between me and your family." Hudson didn't want that responsibility and he didn't want to risk not being chosen either.

"It's not fair that Papa made you feel like that."

"Sure. It's also not fair that you now have to manage different expectations between your boss and your father."

"Shit. Fuck." Ondrej tugged at his shirt, dragging out the swear word. "I didn't even think about that."

"Family comes first. It's not a hard choice."

Ondrej frowned. "You want me to pick the option that doesn't include you?"

"I can't break up a family, Ondrej. I'm not worth it. Nothing is worth that."

Ondrej stopped pacing to stare wide-eyed. "I think I need to have a long conversation with Papa."

Hudson opened his mouth to agree when Ondrej's phone rang. He waved towards it and Ondrej answered.

"Yes. ... When? ... Yes, can do. ... I'll ask. ... Okay."

Hudson tidied up his kitchen while he eavesdropped shamelessly, not that he gained any clues from Ondrej's short answers.

"Hey, want a ride in a helicopter?"

"I guess so?" Hudson blinked at the sudden switch in conversation.

"Cool. Grab an overnight bag. I'll order a ride share." Ondrej poked at his phone.

"Stop. The twins would love to see a helicopter. I'll get Brian or Mackenzie to give us a ride to wherever we are going."

Ondrej nodded. "Sure."

Hudson jogged across the yard to the main house and walked into the kitchen where Mackenzie was attempting to get the twins to eat toast for breakfast.

"Who wants to come and see a helicopter?" His announcement was met with yells of excitement, and not just from the twins.

"I take it this is something to do with your boyfriend?" Mackenzie asked with an eye roll.

"I have a team meeting in a couple of hours." Ondrej wrapped his arms around Hudson's waist, and he tried to be cool about it, when all he wanted to do was lean against him.

"And this requires a helicopter?"

Ondrej shrugged. "Yes. The team meeting is at headquarters, Pewett Downs in Syresthorpe, near Silverstone."

Hudson spun around. "You are asking me to come to a team meeting?"

"No. You won't be allowed in the meeting..." Ondrej shifted from one foot to the other. "Socrates owns a big estate with a library and I thought you might like to see it."

"Estate like country manor house?"

"Yeah. His grandfather made all this money in liquid packing and bought the place off a bankrupt Duke."

"Liquid packing? Is that like putting juice into bottles?"

Ondrej nodded. "Yeah, he invented machines to do that faster. He's probably responsible for half the plastic in the ocean."

"Only if he was into fishing. The fishing industry creates the most plastic in the ocean," Brian said. "The whole plastic straw debate of a few years ago was the best marketing idea that the fishing industry had to take pressure of their own problems."

Hudson shook his head. "Don't let him get started. Brian works in environment management."

"Somewhat at odds with car racing then," Ondrej said.

"Yes, and don't give me some crap about planting trees to offset your emissions." Brian raised his eyebrows, and Ondrej just hugged Hudson tighter.

"I wouldn't dare. S1 is entertainment. It doesn't pretend to be eco-friendly. If it helps, my team also runs a Series E team."

"Stop. Both of you. Who wants to see a helicopter?" Hudson asked. He stepped away from Ondrej's hug. He really needed to pack a bag and get ready.

"I'm pretty sure we are agreeing with each other?" Ondrej winked.

"We agree that S1 isn't great for the environment. That's not the same as a fundamental agreement; you still contribute by being part of S1. Just understanding the issues doesn't matter if you don't make changes."

"That's fair." Ondrej pulled his phone out of his pocket. "Well, I need to meet the helicopter in ten minutes, so if we aren't going to get moving, I'll have to get a ride share."

"And that's the attitude that is screwing the whole world. Look at me, I'm so important." Brian laughed and Hudson realised he was holding his breath. "Ha, look at your face. Come on, Henry, Harriet, let's get in the car and go and look at a helicopter."

Mackenzie walked over and kissed Brian. "Darling, you shouldn't tease our guests like that."

"But it's such fun."

"One day, I'll get Socrates to take you for a joy ride." Ondrej's eyes sparkled. "You'll have to put aside your environmental concerns for an hour."

"Mummy, he has a big neck," Harriet said. Ondrej crouched down to the same height of the toddler and smiled.

"I need to have a very strong neck for my job."

"Why? Do you carry things on your head?"

Ondrej's smile grew. "Does G-force count? No, I drive very fast around corners and my head would do this if it wasn't strong." Ondrej made his head flop all around and both Henry and Harriet giggled.

"You are silly," Harriet said. Henry reached out and touched Ondrej's neck.

"Come on, you two. Leave Ondrej alone. Let's get in the car and look at a helicopter."

"Helicopter," Henry said slowly. His vocabulary wasn't as good as Harriet's yet.

"Yes. I have to go to work."

"Uncle Huddy with you?" Henry asked.

"Yes. I will keep him safe. I promise."

Henry nodded solemnly, seemingly satisfied, and he ran towards the front door. His rush spurred everyone into action. Hudson realised he needed to pack a few things, and not just stare at the awesome way Ondrej talked to Henry and Harriet. He fled back to his little cabin before he blurted out something cringe-worthy and weird. Seeing Ondrej interact so well with Mackenzie's family twisted something inside that Hudson wasn't ready to confront yet.

CHAPTER 11

The last thing Ondrej had expected when they hovered above Socrates' place ready to land was Hudson making breathy excited noises about there being horses in the paddocks. Horses! Hudson had made vague noises about going to look at them first, and Socrates had told him to ask his niece, Xenia, if he needed anything. Hudson had disappeared with an excited grin on his face, and Ondrej had followed Socrates into the team meeting. Four hours later, Ondrej allowed himself a moment to think about Hudson.

Ondrej: Meeting done. Where are you?

Hudson: Stables.

"Hey, Socrates? Where are the stables?" Ondrej asked.

"Why?"

"Hudson is there. I thought he might want some lunch."

"Take him a sandwich or something. The stables are on the northern side of the driveway." Socrates waved at the grand luncheon that his house staff had put on for the team today. Ondrej grabbed a plate and filled it up with assorted things from the table, making sure he had enough for them both. Cute little cucumber sandwiches, salmon topped fritters, a miniature Banh Mi, and a decadent looking chocolate cupcake. By the time, Ondrej had arrived at the stables, he'd eaten half the food. He walked through into the stone building through an archway to find Hudson standing on the grass beside a big brown horse. He was patting it and looked so happy.

"I didn't know you knew anything about horses." Ondrej kept his distance from the giant animal in case it did something unpredictable.

"Meet Gardening Babe. She's a granddaughter of Rose of Gardenia, who I looked after years ago."

"What?" Ondrej felt like he was meeting Hudson all over again.

"One of my foster families trained racehorses. When I mentioned it to Xenia, she wanted to know if I'd worked with any famous horses. Of course I talked about my Rosie, and then to find out that she has one of her grand-daughters. It's so cool." Hudson stroked the horse's long neck again. "We've just been hanging out while she has a pick."

"A pick?"

"Of grass. How was your meeting?"

"Productive. There's lunch if you want some."

"Sure, just let me put Gardening Babe away." Hudson led the horse towards a half-open stable door, walking beside her in a relaxed fashion that declared how comfortable he was with the giant beast of a creature, then they disappeared through one of the doors. A moment later, Hudson came out alone, and closed the door. He hung up a bunch of leather beside the door, presumably the bridle or whatever was on the horse's head. The horse leaned out over the door and nuzzled him, and Hudson giggled, rubbing the horse's head again. He walked to the end of the stable block, patting horses as he walked along, then washed his hands under a tap at the end of the row. It was obvious Hudson knew his way around a set up like this.

"I'm so impressed."

"By?"

"You. The horse. You are a natural." Ondrej preferred cars and other machines; they didn't have a mind of their own, although arguably Victor's design definitely did under braking.

"Thanks, I guess. I was with the Trews for three years, so I had lots of time to practice horse skills."

"You don't want to do it for a job? You look really good at it."

Hudson barked out a laugh. "Hell no. Horse trainers work very long hours and they almost never get a holiday. Horses have to be fed and exercised every day; it's so much work. I love horses, but no, I couldn't do that lifestyle."

"I should buy you one." Ondrej wanted to see Hudson smile like that again. He loved making Hudson smile, and the relaxed happiness on his face when he'd been standing there with the horse was something Ondrej wanted to see again and again.

Hudson stopped and stared at him. "What? No. You couldn't."

"I could. I earn more money than I know how to spend."

Hudson took off his glasses and polished them on his

shirt. "Leaving out the fact that we aren't really in a relationship, I'd be the worst horse owner."

"We are in a relationship. And why? You look like you adore horses."

"I'd be the worst owner, a total pain in the ass. I know enough to want so many details from a trainer, and I'd want to visit the horse all the time, and I'd have opinions."

"Probably good opinions."

"Maybe. But if I'm not with the horse every day, then my opinions aren't as good as the trainer who sees them every day. And while I'd only ever send my horse to a trainer I trusted, I just know I couldn't help myself."

"That doesn't sound like a pain to me. It sounds like passion." Ondrej knew nothing about horses, but he really wanted to do this for Hudson. "How do you buy a horse?"

"You are not buying me a horse." Hudson poked him in the chest. "No."

Ondrej opened his mouth to agree—fine, he wouldn't do it—when Hudson laughed under his breath.

"Oh my god. I'd love to go to Tattersalls and buy a yearling one day. But no. You can't."

"One day, I will buy you a horse."

Hudson shook his head. "Did you ring your father yet?" The abrupt change in subject was a big enough hint for Ondrej to drop the subject. He knew that his money made Hudson uncomfortable, and he didn't want to push. He just wanted to make Hudson smile like that again.

"He's here."

"You talked? Good."

Ondrej wished it was that simple. "Papa is here to talk to the team's marketing team." Papa was negotiating with a new sports clothing company that were keen to have Ondrej as one of their promotional faces when they launched soon. He'd have to do photo shoots and all that stuff, but he was accustomed to that process, having to do them for his team, for TV rights, and for other sponsors.

"Does Socrates run the car racing team from his mansion?"

"Yes. There is an engineering workshop behind the house." This estate was massive with plenty of room for all the different things that Socrates liked. Planes, his car collection, and his niece Xenia's horses.

"I would say that this place is like nothing I've ever experienced, but it has the same vibe as the old Bugatti factory."

"How so?"

"Fancy house, rich people, engineering shop out the back. I thought that place was unique. Apparently not."

"Socrates would cringe if he thought he wasn't unique."

"Well, the Bugatti homestead didn't have racehorses."

Ondrej laughed. "Stick with me, and I'll show you around the rest of Socrates' mansion. Like the library."

"Are you trying to seduce me with horses and books?" Hudson joined in with Ondrej's laughter.

"Is it working?"

"No." Hudson's expression sobered. "Seduce me with a conversation with your father. Family matters. Solve that first before you think about me."

Ondrej flinched. The flippant way Hudson spoke hit him right in the vulnerable part of his ego. Hudson kept pushing him away and it was probably fair since Ondrej couldn't give him a proper relationship. Unless Hudson was just playing around with the rich guy... He couldn't think that way. It made no sense to wonder about that when Hudson didn't want him to buy him a horse.

"Okay." He couldn't look at him in case he pitied the way Ondrej wanted Hudson a lot more than Hudson seemed to want him. Instead of saying any of that—because it was too raw—he walked back to the house. If talking to Papa was what it would take to get some clarity around this whole situation, he'd do it. The whole conversation with Socrates had been confusing as fuck anyway, so maybe he should drag them into the same room together and figure out what he was and wasn't allowed to do. He hated the way this made him feel like he had no power in his own life. If he wanted to drive, he needed to toe the team line. What-ever that line was.

He handed the plate of food to Hudson and pulled out his phone. He quickly sent a text to both Papa and Socrates requesting a meeting asap with them both.

Socrates: My office in ten minutes.

Ondrej sent a thumbs up and walked faster.

"Hold up a second." Hudson called out. "What's going on?"

"I have a meeting with Socrates and Papa in ten minutes to sort this out."

Hudson raised one eyebrow. "I hope you know what you want."

"Yes." Ondrej wanted Hudson and he wanted to drive. In that order? No. He wanted a championship more than he wanted Hudson. Didn't he? "Come with me."

"Oh no, it's not my business."

Ondrej hid behind a scoff. "I've called a meeting with my boss and my father slash agent to talk about wanting to keep fucking you. That makes it your business." He ignored the way Hudson flinched. If he kept this about the sex, and not about how he wanted to ... well, anyway, he wasn't going to think too hard about this. If he couldn't fuck Hudson, then anything more than that was never going to happen anyway.

"Ondrej. It's important to me that you are safe first. You can't come out for me."

"Who said anything about coming out? This is private; between Papa and my team." Fuck—he wasn't going to tell the world about himself, not if Papa thought it would upset the sponsors. Having Socrates say that he would take care of that only added confusion, and made him doubt Papa's motives. He just wanted to know both Papa and his team were on the same page about him and Hudson.

"Okay. As long as this is what you want." Hudson didn't look at him.

"It is." Ondrej wasn't going to admit that he didn't have all the answers and he was confused as fuck about this situation. His life was simple; all he wanted was to drive and have as normal a relationship as anyone could have while doing his job. Other drivers managed to have a family while they lived and breathed the S1 circuit.

He marched into Socrates' house and up the stairs to Socrates' office without looking back to see if Hudson was following him. He opened the door to see Socrates seated behind his ridiculously large mahogany desk; it'd belonged to one of the Dukes who'd built this estate a few hundred years ago. Papa stood at the window, and for the first time in his life, having Papa here didn't make Ondrej feel better.

"We have some miscommunication to resolve." Ondrej approached this the way he did for any situation where he was uncertain. By leaning into his ego and sounding confident. In his car he was great at split second decision making. He always knew what he wanted when he was behind the wheel. The world made sense when he looked at it through his helmet. If he applied the same principles here, then everything would begin to look clear. At the moment, it felt like he was driving through pouring rain in the middle of the night. He needed the skies to clear and the sun to come out, so he could see past the spray to where he was headed.

"We do?" Socrates looked way too comfortable, as if he knew exactly what Ondrej was going to say and that the whole idea was terribly amusing to him.

"We do. Papa said—"

Hudson interjected. "You said, I'm not against my son being gay. I'm against him being gay at work."

Papa nodded. "That is not quite accurate. I worry about—"

Socrates waved his hands and interrupted. "It's not relevant. I want Ondrej driving to the best of his ability. If getting regular sex is what it takes, then he will get that wherever he wants. Even in the storage cupboards if that's his kink."

Ondrej refused to blush or look away. He raised his eyebrow at Socrates who smirked back at him. His boss was a piece of work.

"No." Papa's voice cut through the room like a sharp blade.

"Why the hell not?" Ondrej stared at Papa. "Socrates says my sexuality is no problem for the sponsors."

"That is true. Look at me. I own this team and all the sponsors clearly support myself and Mike."

"See." Ondrej glared at Papa, unable to form words as his ears rang with frustration. Hudson rubbed his back, gently between his shoulder blades.

"I don't want you to argue with your father," Hudson whispered.

Papa raised his eyebrows. "That's not what I've been hearing."

"Fine. Mr Sanchez won't be happy. I can manage that. He pays for his son to have an S1 seat and I can remind that him that other teams aren't exactly clambering for Paulo. Maybe we will need to keep Paulo separate from Ondrej for a while until Mr Sanchez's bigoted opinions calm down."

"And you think he'll eventually decide not to worry?"

"I can't stop someone being a bigot. I can only remind him of the truth. No other team will give his son a seat."

"He can reduce his sponsorship level, though?"

"Yes. But then his son doesn't get the very best car we can afford. I've already employed the Lead Engineer he wanted, and we are getting results. Mr Sanchez has many faults relating to his religious ideas, but he has one weakness."

"And that is?"

"He wants his son to be a champion and this team is currently the only place who is willing to—"

"—put up with his crap." Ondrej was tired of this argument. If Socrates said he could manage it, then he could.

He'd been in S1 his whole life and he understood the game better than anyone.

"Let me deal with the sponsors. If Ondrej wants to come out, it's a non-issue as far as Gamble Racing is concerned." Socrates waved. Why did everyone assume he wanted to come out to everyone? He wasn't ready for that much fuss just yet. Just his team was enough for now.

"I have more to think about than just the team sponsors..." Papa's reticence sent a cold chill over Ondrej's neck. So much for wanting Ondrej to be...

"Don't you want me to be happy?" Ondrej tried to keep his voice level, even though Papa's continual questioning of his decision to come out felt like betrayal.

"I want you to be safe." Safe. Papa echoed what Hudson had said too.

Socrates laughed, in a really loud and irritating way, and Ondrej glared at him instead of his father. He had to swivel his head to glare at each of them in turn. This meeting was turning to shit. Hudson was right, he didn't want to be arguing with Papa, and his boss was being an obnoxious fuckwit.

"If you wanted that, you shouldn't have encouraged your son to drive race cars for a career," Socrates sneered.

"It was his mother's dream." Papa's quiet voice echoed around the room and Ondrej wanted to hug his father. The dizzying switch in emotions forced him to stand tall and stiff. He knew this. He'd been told it every day since he first stepped into a kart as a small child. Papa had been dedicated to Ondrej's kart racing for as long as Ondrej could remember. He'd never known his mother; she was a champion rally driver who'd died in a racing accident just after he was born. It'd always just been him and Papa. And Ma's dream was that he would follow in her path. He would honour her memory by becoming a racing champion too. She would be proud of the way his career had gone; well, until the last two years anyway. Oh. He closed his eyes. Had his thrown away Ma's dream by kissing Alex? And now he was making it worse by arguing with Papa about Hudson. His selfishness two seasons ago had put everything Papa and himself had built at risk, and now he was still doing it.

"Lovely. What has this got to do with Ondrej being gay?" Socrates asked.

"Nothing. It has everything to do with love." Papa stood straighter, his spine stiff, and his face drawn and old. Love? Ondrej frowned. Papa had mentioned that back in Australia and on the day Ondrej had first met Hudson, but he'd dismissed it as irrelevant. Just another confusing comment about his desires that he didn't have any context for.

"First safety and now love. All I want is a driver who is focused," Socrates said.

"Then you can't let him fall in love. It's a distraction."

Ondrej had had enough of this. "I'm right here. And this bickering between you two is more of a distraction than love would ever be." Whatever the fuck that might mean. Sometimes Papa's ideas had no grounding in reality; this nonsense was the same crap as his continual chasing of the missing Bugatti. All Ondrej wanted was to be a success like his mother, to honour her. Love had nothing to do with that. He wasn't even in love with Hudson—Ondrej ignored the cool whisper over the back of his neck—he just liked fucking him and having him around between races. He wanted that without having to worry all the time that he was going to sacked again. There was a long silence, and all Ondrej could hear was the rushing thud of his pulse. He almost rubbed his tattoo—the one on his shoulder blade honouring his mother—but stopped himself by shoving his hands into his pockets.

"Okay. This is clear to me." Socrates stood up. "You don't want Ondrej to fall in love because it will be distracting to his racing. Leaving aside the lack of logic in that, let's accept it as a statement. I want Ondrej to be himself off the track so he can focus. He's been inconsistent this season in a fast car. We finally have a fast car and I need him to drive the car like it deserves. We want the same outcome."

Ondrej realised they were all being silly. "It's even more simple than that. I am the star. I will get what I want. Right now, I don't need to be out in public. All I want is to win and to have Hudson." He just couldn't look in Hudson's direction in case his face was too ... sappy. Hudson's hand stilled in the middle of his shoulder blades, too close to his tattoo, and even though they'd never talked about it, Ondrej suddenly wished that he had.

"Your mother died because of love," Papa said. "She returned to racing too soon after you were born, and she was distracted."

"I promise you I won't be distracted by the birth of my child." Ondrej snorted. Sarcasm shielded him from the churn in his gut. He couldn't believe her death was his fault.

"She told me on her death bed in the hospital that she regretted racing that day. She'd felt the pressure from her team to return to the car after your birth. She didn't want to disappear from the racing world. The pressure on her as a woman driver was huge and she needed to get back behind the wheel to prove herself against the men. She returned to the car too early. All she'd wanted to do was spend more time with her true loves. Me and you. She was distracted by wanting us and it killed her." Papa wiped his face with the back of his hand.

Ondrej hid his own emotions the only way he knew—with sarcasm. "It's fine. I only want to fuck Hudson. I'm not going to fall in love with him."

Hudson's touch disappeared. Ondrej didn't need to look to know that Hudson was hurt by his statement. His stomach sank.

"Perfect. Meeting over. Let's get winning." Socrates waved his arms. "And Mr D'Grieg, perhaps you should read some of the gay fan fiction that gets written about your son. There are lots of fans who will love this announcement."

Ondrej stormed out of the room. He'd just fucked up everything with Hudson and all his boss could say was some fucking throwaway bullshit. Papa and Socrates still didn't agree on his sex life—even after this meeting—and now he'd told Hudson the harsh truth. His breath hitched. It wasn't the truth—not really—he just wanted it to be that way. If he worked hard enough at it, then he would force it to be. He wasn't going to fall in love with Hudson. This ... thing between them was merely Ondrej's need to be himself with someone. Anyone. Hudson could be anyone.

"What the fuck was that?" Hudson pushed him up against the wall in the hallway. He hit the wall with a thump that stole all his breath.

"This." Ondrej did the only thing he could and kissed Hudson to shut him up. From now on, he would take charge of this. It was just sex, and nothing would distract him from racing. No amount of bickering between his boss and his agent could compete with Ondrej's desperation to win races and to fuck Hudson. Hudson kissed him like he understood; like this was why they did this. This connection of two bodies that needed release with each other and even though Ondrej didn't want to say anything, he could communicate how much he wanted Hudson with this desperate kiss. He plundered Hudson's mouth, using the wall to push upwards and regain the one-inch height advantage Hudson had over him. With one hand he gripped Hudson's hip, and he wrapped the other around the back of Hudson's neck, threading his fingers through his bright hair.

"Why do I keep doing this?" Hudson wrenched himself away from Ondrej's tight grip.

"For the same reason I do. Because I can't resist you."

"Me?"

"You have no idea what you do for me, do you?" Ondrej had known from the first time they'd touched in Bahrain that he would end up desperate for this man. So much for just fucking. He bolted before he said too much.

CHAPTER 12

Three weeks later, Hudson sat alone in his cabin staring at his laptop. He'd virtually given up on the Bugatti project, unable to focus on it, because every time he opened the files, all he could think about was the argument at Socrates' mansion and the incredibly confusing kiss afterwards. Ondrej had sounded so hurt when he'd said that he couldn't resist him. And when he'd wrenched himself away from Hudson and marched down the hallway, Hudson had stood there unable to chase him. Socrates had flown Hudson home with a smirk that kept Hudson silent.

He'd barely left the house since, except for when Mackenzie got annoyed at his sulking and forced him to do the grocery shopping. He knew he shouldn't just mope, but it was hard to think of himself as worthy when Ondrej reacted in such conflicted ways to being near him. It made sense that Mackenzie was mad at him for behaving like this; she knew how rejection felt having had almost as many foster homes as him and she had tried her best to pull him out of this resignation to being rejected again. His phone dinged with a message.

Ondrej: Come outside.

Hudson: Outside?

Ondrej: Yes.

Hudson saved the client's file he'd been working on and walked out into the yard. He had achieved a lot in the last few weeks, hiding his feelings in hard work. The Trew methodology might not have helped his emotional state, but it did give him the satisfaction that he'd achieved something concrete in all the turmoil.

Hudson: I'm outside.

Ondrej: All the way out the front. On the road.

"Fine." Hudson muttered as he walked around the outside of Mackenzie and Brian's house to the road out the front. A bright red car, maybe a Ferrari or something flash like that, sat double parked on the road.

"Ondrej?"

Ondrej opened the window and leaned his forearm on the sill. It was a great look on him, with his linen shirt rolled up and his lean forearms exposed. How dare he look so good? Ondrej belonged in a car like that. Suddenly Hudson could see the appeal of a red sports car driven by a smoking hot man, and he knew from experience that Ondrej wasn't compensating for anything in having a car like this. After the last time they saw each other, Hudson really shouldn't be thinking about Ondrej's cock. He breathed out slowly.

"Why are you here?"

"You know why." Ondrej gazed at him with his intense dark blue eyes. Too many competing reactions flooded his body, and his skin was too tight, and his stomach churned.

Did he want to growl at him or fuck him or tell him to fuck all the way off? Ondrej couldn't just say things like, '*I only want to fuck Hudson. Not fall in love.*' And then turn up assuming Hudson would jump in his flash car with him and head straight back into Ondrej's bed. He hated the little voice inside that told him sex was all he was worth. But it wasn't as dreadful as the loud voice screaming at him—sex with Ondrej is incredible. Do it. Now. If he couldn't have all of Ondrej, maybe he could live with only having some of him. It was better than feeling cast aside and rejected completely.

"I have four weeks off. Stay with me."

"What? Since when do you have four weeks between races?"

Ondrej grinned. "When are you going to read the S1 schedule online? It's the mid-season break. We have four weeks before the next race in Belgium. Stay with me in Monaco and we can be together."

"I thought you only wanted—" Hudson folded his arms across his chest, unwilling to say the word sex while standing outside the twin's bedroom.

"Stay with me." Ondrej didn't answer the question, except... Hudson squinted. Was Ondrej blushing? It could just be the reflection of the red painted car on his cheeks. Yeah, because that made no logical sense. Hudson wished he understood what Ondrej was asking.

"You want me to stay with you for four weeks? I just pack my bag and go with you with no warning at all." As he said it, his whole body leaned towards Ondrej, yearning to do exactly that.

"What else are you planning to do?" The little shrug

pushed Hudson back towards being irritated as fuck with Ondrej.

"My job." Hudson couldn't believe his audacity. "How dare you assume that I am available for you whenever you need."

"Last time you did your job at my place. What does it matter where you are when your business is all online?"

Hudson swallowed. "Fine. Use my own logic against me."

Ondrej laughed, throwing his head back against the head rest in the car. "You see. It will be fun."

"Okay." Hudson suspected—from the moment he'd seen Ondrej parked here—that he was always going to go with Ondrej. He couldn't resist him; from the way he leaned his delicious forearm on the car door to the flash of power in his dark blue eyes. The argument was performative, really. He'd never been able to resist Ondrej's version of commands.

"But I'll need time to get ready, so park that ridiculous car somewhere and come inside for a while." Hudson spun on his heels and marched back to his cabin. Ondrej stared at his ass the whole way; or at least that's what Hudson wanted to imagine, since he didn't hear the car start until he turned into the back yard.

The car, a 2019 Ferrari 488 Pista, was from Socrates' collection—because of course he had a collection of expensive cars—so they'd driven it down the freeway to Socrates' estate, then flown to Monaco. Hudson wasn't quite sure how this had become his life, and yet somehow along the way he'd become comfortable with this level of rich person nonsense. If countries bothered to stamp passports anymore, he'd have collected more this year than he could ever have imagined.

"Let's fuck." Hudson had spent the whole trip wondering what the hell he was doing coming here to be with Ondrej. Ondrej had made it clear he only wanted sex and only on his terms. It shouldn't be a problem, like, it was hardly a hardship to have sex with Ondrej multiple times. The man was gorgeous, fit, and amazingly talented in bed. He could undo Hudson with a kiss. So Hudson figured he may as well set that boundary himself to prevent Ondrej keeping him in the sexy part time boyfriend bucket, or whatever this was. If he put himself in that bucket, maybe he'd be able to guard his heart for when Ondrej decided he was bored and wanted someone more in his own class.

"Are you still mad because I told Papa it was just fucking and I wasn't going to fall in love?"

Hudson cursed his skin as his cheeks burned with heat. He almost lied and said no. "I'm here, aren't I?"

"You are. I would like to take you apart. But first, let's wash off the travel dust." Ondrej dumped his bag in the hallway and walked towards the bathroom. He left the door wide open and stripped off, gifting Hudson with the perfect view of his lean fit body, from the tattoo on his shoulder blade, to his narrow hips and perfectly sculpted ass. In for a penny, in for a pound. There was no point standing here aimlessly when he could be in the shower with Ondrej, wrapping his lips around Ondrej's beautiful cock. He shed his clothes quickly, pulling them off and leaving them where they fell, uncaring for anything except joining Ondrej under the stream of his impressive waterfall shower. There were some perks to being with someone who was absurdly wealthy.

"Look at you." Ondrej's gaze travelled over Hudson slowly, lingering on Hudson's hard cock. "Red all the way down."

"It's just hair."

"Don't be bashful. Come here to me." And with that command, everything was alright. All the worries and circular conversations about what the hell they were doing stop mattering. Hudson stepped into the shower and placed his hands on Ondrej's chest. Water ran in rivulets over his shoulders and bounced off Hudson's hands.

"I'm glad you came." Ondrej reached up and cupped Hudson's face.

"Haven't come yet." Hudson meant it to be a joke, but it came out all sullen, so when Ondrej laughed, it didn't surprise him. He cut off Ondrej's laugh with a kiss, using his slight height advantage to angle down over Ondrej. Ondrej lashed his mouth with his tongue until Hudson's knees weakened under the onslaught. This dance was familiar, and Hudson loved it. He sank down, dragging his hands down Ondrej's body as he deliberately collapsed to the floor of the shower. From here it was easy to lick Ondrej's cock, to watch the way it twitched against his stomach, and see the water from the shower wash away the leaking pre-come from the tip. Hudson wanted to do that. He gripped Ondrej's thighs with his hands and opened his mouth over the end of the Ondrej's cock. Wet hot skin and Ondrej's hard length filled his mouth as he slid up and down, sucking hard. Ondrej's fingers threaded through Hudson's hair, creating little pinpricks of pain as he clutched on tight. Hudson flattened his tongue and took in Ondrej as deep as he could. He hummed around his length, encouraging Ondrej to fuck his mouth. He loved this. This devastatingly simple gift that he could give Ondrej, and one that was returned to him in spades with every groan from Ondrej.

"Stop. You are too good at that."

Hudson kissed the leaking end of Ondrej's cock. "Are you sure? I could swallow you down."

"Fuck." Ondrej's hips bucked and Hudson opened his mouth to receive his thrusting cock. He would've cried out, 'yes, more' except his mouth was full. He used his mouth with all the skill he had to draw all the pleasure from Ondrej. There was something incredible about being able to take someone who had so much control and reduce them to the blathering desperate noises currently being emitted by Ondrej. Hudson slid his hands up the insides of Ondrej's thighs until he was able to cup Ondrej's tight balls with one hand and use his fingers on his other hand to ease inside Ondrej's hole. Ondrej's muttered swearing intensified and his grip on Hudson's hair tightened so much that Hudson briefly wondered if he was going to be bald after this encounter. He spluttered slightly, then dragged his mouth up and down Ondrej's length slowly. Ondrej thrust hard enough for Hudson to nearly gag; his eyes filled with tears as heat speared him. Then Ondrej came.

"Hudson. Holy fuck."

Hudson's mouth filled with salty heat and he swallowed. He pulled his mouth off slowly, giving Ondrej's softening cock a long luxurious lick as he released him. Ondrej's grip on his hair relaxed and Hudson opened his eyes to see Ondrej kneeling in the shower before him.

"You are..." Ondrej closed his eyes for a long terrible moment, leaving Hudson to wonder what the heck he was. Great or terrible. Logically it was unlikely that Ondrej would say terrible given that he'd just come.

"You are stunning. Come to me." Ondrej stood up and pulled on Hudson's hands. Hudson slowly rose, his legs trembling as they prickled with pins and needles. His hard cock grazed against Ondrej's stomach.

"Absolutely stunning." Ondrej wrapped his hand around Hudson's cock and stroked him. Too roughly but also exactly as Hudson needed. His head fell backwards and he let himself get lost in the sensation. It was over too quickly as Ondrej pressed his lips to Hudson's neck and sucked. Hudson's release was quick and left him feeling soft and sated.

"Stunning. And mine." Ondrej slung one arm possessively around Hudson's waist to match his comment. Hudson wished it were true, and not just the aftermath of a good orgasm. With his other hand, Ondrej washed Hudson's stomach and chest. Hudson could barely stand, his legs had turned to jelly, and he let Ondrej guide him out of the shower. Soon enough he found himself efficiently dried and marched into Ondrej's bedroom.

"Sleep." Ondrej pushed him down on the bed and pulled the covers over him. Hudson almost protested at the treatment, but as soon as his body hit the high thread count sheets, he let the softness surround him. Completely sated and relaxed. It wasn't long until Ondrej joined him in bed and pulled his body closer under Hudson was tucked against him.

"It's not even bedtime."

"Who says it needs to be. Have a rest and then we can do this again."

"Promises, promises." Hudson muttered as he waggled his ass against Ondrej. Ondrej chuckled and gently stroked Hudson's hair until he drifted off into a satisfied sleep.

Hudson, once again, found himself sitting in Ondrej's lounge staring at his laptop while Ondrej went running with Amy. It made sense that his mid-season break didn't include a break in his fitness regime. No amount of Hudson wanting to spend all day relaxing with Ondrej was going to change that. It was better this way anyway, since Hudson still had a job to do. He had a business to run, although technically Mackenzie did most of the running part. He had client's ancestors to research and reports to write. Hudson had slept in again; what was it about Monaco? He chuckled under his breath. The mammoth sex session last night was probably the reason. His phone rang and he gulped some water before answering.

"Mackenzie. How are you?"

"I'm fine. It's been two days since you left. How are you?"

"I texted you when we arrived." Hudson had been a little busy since then.

"I didn't ask that. How are you?"

Hudson breathed in. "I'm good."

"Why the big breath?"

"What?"

"Hudson. I'm your big sister. I know when you are hiding something from me."

Hudson rolled his eyes. "Mackenzie." He used the same tone as she had.

"Out with it."

"Don't get your back up. The problem I have is nothing to do with Ondrej. That's all good."

"Then what?"

"It's this case."

"For the Jones family in Stratford? I thought your research was excellent."

Hudson wished he could fling the phone across the room. "No, all our new clients are going well. I've hit a dead-end in the Bugatti case for Ondrej's father."

Mackenzie scoffed. "Maybe Ondrej is right, and it can't be found. It was always going to be a big ask. To find a rare car that hasn't been seen since World War Two."

"Maybe. I just feel like I'm missing something."

"Want to brainstorm?" Mackenzie had read all his reports, so she knew exactly where the research had gone and ended.

"I'm open to all ideas."

"Cool." Mackenzie's end of the phone went silent for a few minutes. "I've got nothing. Let me read all your reports again and get back to you."

"Okay. I should have the Agnesto report done by the end of today too." Hudson could bury himself in working on that instead. Tonight, they were going to dinner at JP and Sofia's place again, but until then he could work on something productive. He opened his laptop to the

Agnesto files and started to hunt through immigration documents to fill in the blanks on their family tree. After working steadily on this for a while, a tendril of an idea almost formed in the back of his brain, but as soon as he stopped working to try and grab it, it disappeared again. Damn it. His phone dinged with a text. It was an image from Mackenzie of the original letter.

Hudson: And?

Mackenzie: What is the core of our business? Family heritage.

Hudson clicked on a confused emoji and almost sent it when he gasped. Of course. He rang and she answered immediately.

"I need to do the D'Grieg's family tree."

"Yes. If there is this letter, there will be others, and they won't be with the sender. They'll be with whoever Mr D'Grieg's grandfather sent them to."

Hudson stared at the ceiling. It was so fucking obvious. "Why didn't I figure this out ages ago? I need to know everyone he might have corresponded with and find them. If he wrote letters—"

"—maybe they'll have clues in them." Mackenzie's voice rose, echoing the excitement building in Hudson's chest.

"Yes." Oh God. How had he missed this? People wrote letters all the time back then, although in the war letters often got lost. No. No more negativity. He was going to find letters written by Mr D'Grieg's grandfather about this car and he was going to find out what happened to it.

"Good luck. And hey, call me when you find something."

"When? Not if?"

"Abso-fucking-lutely. When. Hudson. You are going to find this car."

"Okay." He didn't really believe it, but he finally—finally—had a pathway forward. The poor Agnesto file was about to get abandoned for a while. He bent over his laptop and began to set up a new family tree file for the D'Grieg family.

CHAPTER 13

Ondrej opened the door to his apartment after his strength training session with Amy. His arms and neck were dead after she'd pushed him hard today. His plans were simple; drag Hudson into the shower with him and enjoy the way his red hair looked with water flowing over it as Hudson sucked his cock. Let the water flow over his aching muscles and let Hudson's mouth finish the job nicely.

His plans changed from the moment he walked in the door. Seeing Hudson hunched over his laptop with his fingers flying on the keyboard was hot and his half-hard cock sprung to life. He stared for a while until he realised there was no way he wanted to interrupt Hudson's concentration, so he quietly snuck to the bathroom, and closed the door to shower alone. Once clean, he threw on some shorts and walked into the lounge. Hudson hadn't moved, apart from his fingers, and the occasional huff of breath. Ondrej put some iced water in a glass.

"Drink this." He placed the glass of water beside Hudson's keyboard.

"What?" Hudson glanced up, blinking rapidly behind his glasses.

"When did you last move?"

"Um, a while ago?" Hudson drank some of the water. "Thanks for this." He took off his glasses and rubbed his eyes. "I should probably look at the distance for a while, or something."

"What are you working on?"

"Your family tree."

"Why?"

Hudson stood up and walked out onto the balcony. He tipped his head up towards the sky, then slowly turned around. "You aren't dressed."

"I had a shower after my session and it's hot today."

Hudson blushed. "It is." He shook his head a little. "Um, I'm putting together your family tree on your father's side to try and figure out who your great-grandfather would've written letters to."

"Okay?"

"Right. I should've made this connection ages ago." Hudson blew out a breathy exasperated laugh. "If he wrote to anyone about the car, he wouldn't have the letters ... the people he sent them to would. And if those people kept those letters, then hopefully I'll be able to read them and maybe, just maybe, the letters might include a clue."

"Family tree it is then."

"And a chart of friendships mentioned by Grover-Williams, and a list of all the people who drove in the same races as your great-grandfather. And then I'm going to track down their living relatives and see if I can find new information."

"Wow. That's extensive." Ondrej was glad he hadn't interrupted Hudson before. The amount of time and effort Hudson was putting into finding the Bugatti was impressive. For the first time in ages, Ondrej hoped that the bloody missing car was actually able to be found. He'd spent years feeling cynical about the mystery, especially after so many historians had failed to find it, and every time Papa paid someone else to try, the cynicism deepened. Thinking about it caused a twinge of guilt in Ondrej's gut; he shouldn't be fighting with Papa about Hudson or how he lived his life as an S1 driver. Papa had his best interests at heart.

"Yeah. How was the training or whatever?" Hudson's casual comment pulled Ondrej out of his head.

He shrugged. "Fine."

"I should join you sometime. It's probably not good for me to sit here all day." Hudson stretched out his shoulders.

"Tomorrow is reflex training. Come along. Amy and Mei can make you up a program if you want."

"They don't have to do that." Hudson frowned. "What is reflex training?"

Ondrej winked. "I'll show you."

"Now?"

He couldn't resist. Ondrej pounced, wrapping his arms around Hudson and drawing him in for a kiss. He pressed kisses all along Hudson's bottom lip. "Reflex training keeps my reaction times quick. Like this?" He pushed his hands up under Hudson's shirt.

"Stop."

Ondrej froze. "What's the matter?"

"Are you making a joke?"

"Yes. Talking about training is boring. Touching you is not."

Hudson breathed out slowly, and his mouth stretched into a shy smile. "Okay."

"Okay, I can keep touching you now?"

"Yes." Thank fuck. Ondrej pressed his mouth against Hudson's neck so he could cover up the relieved sigh and spread his hands all over Hudson's skin.

"Take off your shirt." There was too much fabric between them, and Ondrej was already mostly naked. He needed Hudson to join him.

"Bossy." Hudson pulled his shirt off, his wink disappearing under a rush of cloth. The shirt was flung aside on the floor of his balcony, and Ondrej drank in the sight of Hudson. His freckled pale skin and all that red hair across his chest and down his stomach, showing him a pathway down to Hudson's glorious cock. If Ondrej was the type of person who might write, he would write sonnets about Hudson's cock. Jesus, fuck. Having Hudson here, with his hands all over him, was turning Ondrej's brain into sappy mush. Luckily no one could read his mind. He buried his face against Hudson's neck, nipping at his ear lobe, then sucked on the skin covering Hudson's pulse—pleased to feel it racing like his own was —all to hide his expression in case the—stuff—in his head was written on his face for Hudson to see. He pressed his thumbs into the tight muscles at the base of Hudson's neck.

"All that typing isn't good for you." He'd rather admonish Hudson, than admit how hot it had been to watch Hudson's focus when he'd arrived back from training this afternoon.

"I should stretch more."

"Yes. Let me stretch you."

Hudson's breath hitched, and it made Ondrej glow inside. "What?"

Ondrej slid his hands down Hudson's spine. Slowly. Hudson arched his back at the feather light touches, which made his chest press against Ondrej's torso. He teased him by doing it again and again until Hudson growled at him.

"Stop tickling me."

"You would prefer this?" Ondrej slipped one hand into Hudson's shorts, down between his legs until he brushed his finger over Hudson's hole. Hudson let out a shuddery breath that sounded like a yes, and when Ondrej did it again, Hudson let out the most perfect moan.

"Let me fuck you over the table while you look at the view." Ondrej knew no one would see them up on his balcony, high above Monaco.

"Yes please." Hudson's nostrils flared and he stood absolutely still as Ondrej toyed with his ass. "Please."

Ondrej removed his hand from inside Hudson's shorts and slapped him playfully on the ass. "Go. Get yourself ready for me." He turned away, knowing Hudson would obey, and he almost tripped over his own fucking feet in his rush to grab lube and a condom from his bedroom. When he came back, Hudson was completely naked. He'd draped himself over the table on Ondrej's balcony, his legs spread and his ass in the air. A blatant invitation waiting for Ondrej's cock.

"You are fucking perfect." Ondrej ran his fingers down

Hudson's spine—this time hard enough to leave a red mark from his clipped short fingernails—then grabbed Hudson's ass and spread his legs even wider.

Hudson groaned. "Please."

Ondrej stripped off his own shorts, and quickly rolled on the condom while he could still think properly. He knelt on the balcony between Hudson's legs and gently pressed his face between his ass muscles. Hudson trembled, and Ondrej removed his face for a second.

"Wriggle towards me a little." Ondrej used his hands to guide Hudson's hard cock away from the edge of the table. He needed to give him enough space so he would not get hurt later. "Yes, just there." Ondrej licked up the inside of one of Hudson's thighs, savouring the taste of his skin against his tongue. He had to tuck himself into a ball, and it wasn't that comfortable, but from here, he could tilt his head back and suck Hudson's balls into his mouth. He wrapped one hand around Hudson's cock, and slowly stroked him.

"More."

"No. I will come first." It was harsh but from the way Hudson's thighs shook and he groaned, he loved it. "Inside you."

"Fuck. Please." The hint of a whine in Hudson's voice was perfect. Ondrej grinned and kept up teasing Hudson with touches that were too light, with licks that made Hudson moan, playing and playing until Hudson cried out.

"Please. I can't wait anymore."

Ondrej stood up, keeping one hand tight around the base of Hudson's cock, and with the other, he grabbed the lube and poured it over Hudson's hole. He used his fingers to slick the area, pushing one finger then another inside him.

"Ondrej." Hudson's cry made him sound like he was in pain.

"Are you okay?"

"Will ... be ... if ... you ... fuck ... me." Each word was clipped, and Hudson's breath was ragged and loud.

"Ahh." It was that type of anguished pain. The neediness and agony of desperation. Ondrej removed his fingers and placed his hand in the middle of Hudson's back. He needed both hands for this, so he released Hudson's cock and guided himself slowly in. Hudson let out a soft exhalation and spread his arms wide across the table. Everything in Ondrej's brain went blank. All that existed was Hudson and his gloriously spread-eagled body and the absolutely perfect way he accepted Ondrej in. Ondrej took his time, savouring Hudson's tightness, as he thrust in and out slowly.

"More."

"So greedy."

"Only for you." Hudson reached behind him with his arm and grabbed Ondrej's hand. "Harder."

Ondrej couldn't tear his gaze away from how Hudson's hand covered his own. It was somehow more intimate than watching his cock slid in and out of Hudson's body. He stared at their hands as he thrust, and when Hudson's fingers tightened, he closed his eyes and let pleasure take over. He came hard; a bright orgasm with sparkling stars flashing on his eyelids. The warm sun on his skin multiplied the heat surrounding him. Hudson cried out too, and then his hand softened. Ondrej pulled out carefully and pressed a hard kiss to the base of Hudson's spine.

"Stay. I'll clean you up."

"I should come inside. All this sun isn't great for my skin." Hudson's whisper was a little hoarse. Ondrej traced his hands up Hudson's back, then helped him stand. Hudson leaned on him as they walked inside, both of them ending up flopped on the couch.

"I really should clean up."

"Yeah." Hudson brushed his hands down Ondrej's arm. "Thanks." It would so easy to just relax here against him.

"I'll be back soon." Ondrej forced himself towards the bathroom where he quickly disposed of the condom and then ran a cloth under warm water. So many times after they had sex, Hudson was the one who cleaned Ondrej, he wanted to return the gesture this time. Afterwards, they lay entangled on the couch for ages, just resting against each other. Hudson held his hand, tracing slow circles on his wrist, and the touch added sleepiness to his sated body. Ondrej let himself drift off.

"Is your tattoo about your mother?" Hudson asked. The question came from nowhere, punching into Ondrej's sated happy state of bliss.

"Yeah."

"I was curious, and I looked her up online. I'm sorry if that is invasive."

Ondrej shrugged. From what Hudson had said earlier, he'd spent the last few hours researching Ondrej's family tree as part of the job he was doing for Papa.

"It's no secret. I'm surprised it took you so long."

"I don't know much about my birth parents; except

they weren't capable of looking after Mackenzie and me." Hudson traced his fingers around Ondrej's nipples, as if he were doodling on Ondrej's skin absentmindedly. "But your family is all over old newspapers."

"I take it you've read all about her crash then. There are photos, apparently."

"Apparently?"

"I don't want to see them. I'd rather think of her as the smiling person in the photos Papa has on display at home." He'd seen photos when he was younger, and he wished he hadn't. Now he pretended that he had never been curious. At least the photos weren't of her; just her rally car twisted around a tree.

Hudson nodded. "That makes total sense. Don't look up her crash online. There are photos."

"I've been thinking about what Papa said..." Ondrej trailed off. It was more accurate to say that he'd been trying NOT to think about Papa had said.

"About her going back to racing too soon and being distracted?"

"Yes."

"I can't imagine it being true."

Ondrej jumped to his feet. "You didn't know her."

"No." Hudson held out his hands and Ondrej let himself be pulled back down into Hudson's arms. "No, I didn't know her. But I know you, and I've read all about her. Someone should write her story properly; the snippets I read in different newspaper articles are extraordinary."

"Media quotes don't tell you about the real person. Just look at mine." Ondrej scoffed. He presented only part of himself to the press—obviously.

"She had a lovely sense of humour." Was Hudson deliberately ignoring Ondrej's comment? "And I can see a lot of the same stubborn drive for success in the way she talked to the press."

"Same?"

"The same as you. It's uncanny reading her quotes, reading the way she put words together, because it's so familiar to the way you talk about driving to the press."

"Really?" Ondrej yearned for Hudson's comment to be true. He'd always assumed that he got his driving ability from Ma, and perhaps from Papa's grandfather, but to know that he shared some of the same personality traits with Ma felt like someone was hugging his heart. He'd been a baby when she died.

"Yes. I should put some quotes together for you." Hudson leaned in and kissed Ondrej on the cheek. "Unless that would be weird."

"I don't know." Ondrej wanted to know everything about Ma, and he didn't know he could've done this. Apart from that one time he'd seen her accident when he was fourteen—regretfully—he'd always avoided looking at Ma's career online. Hudson didn't say anything, just let Ondrej mull it over in silence, although he still trailed his fingers across Ondrej's chest.

"Thirty-six was her racing number," Ondrej said eventually. "I picked thirty-seven because it's her number plus one. Whenever I get in a car, I know she's there with me."

"There is some amazing footage of her from the 1980s."

Ondrej laughed. "Believe me, I've seen all her races except the last one. Papa has them all. She was tough, one of the few women who drove in the Group B class rally until it was banned. Our cars are so much safer than the ones she drove." The spectators back then were wild too; standing all over the course and jumping out of the way as the cars came flying past. Rally cars drove along public roads and back then, there had been almost no attempt by the organisers to manage the crowds at all.

"I'm glad to hear it. Everything I've read about motorsport makes it sound incredibly dangerous."

"When you watch the footage of Group B, it's pretty amazing that only three spectators were ever killed." The drivers... well, that was a different story. He knew the risks when he climbed into his car—all drivers did—and he trusted his skill to keep himself out of trouble. Crashes happened to everyone. The big awful crashes were rare now, and engineering and safety standards had improved enough that Ondrej didn't worry about it. He couldn't think about it, because as soon as he let those thoughts in his head, he'd never push hard enough towards the limit.

"I—" Hudson stopped.

"You what?"

"Do you think your father is right? That being with me is a distraction?"

"No. He's wrong. I'm never distracted when I get in my car. The whole world disappears—even you—and all I think about is my job."

"Good. I... I really like you."

Ondrej swallowed. "Besides, I only have eight more years left in my career." He'd never told anyone about this superstition. Eight years should be plenty of time to win a championship.

"Is that in the S1 rules? You have to retire at a certain age?"

"No." Ondrej rubbed his jaw to try and unclench the muscles that had suddenly cramped. "Um, Ma was thirty-six when she died."

"Her racing number was also thirty-six." Hudson's eyes widened with each word. "And ... because your number is thirty-seven, you think you'll die in a crash when you reach the same age as your racing number?"

"Yes." It felt ... nice to not have to explain it to Hudson. Even before Ondrej signed his first S1 contract, six years ago, he'd known he had an end date to his career. If he was lucky enough to make it into S1—and be one of the twenty best drivers in the world—he would retire the day before he turned thirty-seven. Back then, thirty-seven had seemed so far away that he thought he'd never reach it. It hadn't mattered that it had a time limit; and besides, almost no drivers had careers that long.

"That makes sense."

"It does?"

"Superstitions don't have to be logical. I'm sure most people would tell you that it's illogical to worry that you'll die at the same age as your racing number, just because that happened to your mother."

Ondrej nodded—that was exactly what he expected from people—and it was the reason he'd never told anyone. Not even Papa. He held his breath. Especially not Papa.

"I hope you drive safely until your thirty-seventh birthday, and you can make your own choice about your retirement date," Hudson said. Ondrej wished he was brave enough to tell Hudson what a special gift he'd given him by believing his very private superstition.

"Not many drivers are still in S1 in their late thirties, so it probably doesn't matter anyway." Ondrej shrugged off Hudson's comment, ignoring the way he worried about Ondrej's safety. Ondrej never worried about crashing because he believed he wouldn't die in a racing accident until he reached the age of his racing number. Until then, it was utterly irrelevant to even think about dying. He crashed occasionally—too many times this season—because everyone crashed. It happened when pushing a car to the limits. But he could keep pushing hard and risk a crash because he knew he wasn't going to die. And once he got to thirty-seven, he had a plan. It was all under control and his plan allowed him to throw everything into every race, knowing that he'd be fine. He late braked and took gaps between cars, and loved the thrill of acceleration, all the time pushing the car to the edge of control.

"It matters to you, so it matters to me." Hudson pulled him into a hug and Ondrej let himself be held by Hudson. There were much bigger problems in his life right now than worrying about something that wasn't going to happen. The ongoing discussion between Socrates and Papa about Ondrej's sexuality dominated his thoughts when he wasn't in his car. He released all the air in his lungs on a slow exhale. For the next four weeks, Ondrej was going to enjoy this time with Hudson as much as he could before the real world beckoned again.

CHAPTER 14

BELGIUM

The crowd at Spa was raucous. Now the race was over, the sky filled with brightly coloured smoke from flares let off by spectators. Ondrej loved it here, the atmosphere was always wild. The Belgium fans knew how to party, and Spa would be rocking tonight when the party moved from the track—Circuit de Spa-Francorchamps, colloquially known as Spa—to the small town of the same name nearby. He finished his in-lap after finishing in P6, listening to Jaxxon congratulate him over the radio. When he was racing, he never noticed the crowd, all his focus was on his job; the track, his car, and the other nineteen drivers. Now he'd finished and was cruising back to the pits, the wildness surrounded him. His helmet and ear buds reduced the engine noise by about forty percent; enough so he could hear the team radio while still being able to listen to the engine. At speed, the wind was the loudest noise. Doing his in-lap at a low cruising speed meant he could hear people cheering. The grandstands heaved with movement as the crowds jumped in unison, and so many flags were being waved that they blurred into a giant mass of colour and fabric. He was back! The mid-season break had been good for him. Good for the team too with Paulo finishing behind him in seventh; like a proper midfield team.

"Victor. You've built a fucking great car." There was only so much he could say on the radio. During the race, the only channel he heard was the one between his race engineer Jaxxon and himself, but technically, all the radios were open channels, and every team had people who listened to all the different team chatter in the hope of picking up something useful for their own race strategies. The broadcaster beeped out any swearing, although they kept it in for that streaming show that aired all the behind the scenes politics and made S1 seem even more dramatic than it was.

He drove into the pits, onto the weighbridge, and went through his usual end of race routine. Last time he'd done this—a month ago—he'd imagined glimpses of red hair in the crowd. Hudson. This time, he didn't need to look to know that Hudson was in the pitlane with Papa and the rest of the Gamble team. No one had blinked when they'd turned up together today. No one would, unless Ondrej kissed him in full view, as S1 was dominated by men and Hudson was just another bloke among many in the Gamble team. While they were keeping things quiet as much as they could, it was so relaxing to know Hudson could be part of today. He knew his team would react positively if he mentioned Hudson was his boyfriend. Boyfriend? Yes. After the last month living together, that's definitely how he saw Hudson.

Socrates clapped him on the back. "Great drive. It'll really inject motivation into the team for the second half of the season."

"Thanks." But Socrates had already walked off to talk to Paulo.

Papa pulled him into a hug. "Well done son."

"Thanks Papa. I know this isn't the team you wanted me to drive for—"

"This isn't a time for doubts. We can make the most of the opportunities given to us. I've set up an exclusive interview with Ms Blasi." Papa waved towards the private rooms at the back of the pit garage and Ondrej followed him.

"When?"

"About an hour. She'll be fair to you. She always has been."

"She's a fan of Ma's, that's why." Alicia drove rally cars when she wasn't working as a journalist on the S1 circuit.

Papa nodded. "I know. That's why I requested her for this interview."

Ondrej held his breath. "Hold on. What is this interview about?" Holy shit, surely Papa didn't want him to come out yet. It would be a fucking circus. "I need more time to figure out what I want to say about that."

"You are not to mention Hudson." Papa's face tightened.

"So it's not about being ..." Ondrej didn't need to say 'gay' as Papa's nostrils flared.

"Not yet. We will talk about that at the right time."

Ondrej shouldn't feel this relieved. Now that Hudson was here with him, it was only a matter of time before they were outed. Maybe he should get it done and stop worrying about hiding himself.

"The interview is about the team's changed fortunes from last season. It's for that streaming channel series."

"Okay." Ondrej relaxed. The show followed all the drivers through the season and was always pulling them aside for interviews. He'd done so many of them over the past few years that he stopped worrying about the process. The fans loved the show because it gave them all insight into the complicated politics of S1. "Where is Hudson?"

"He'll be around somewhere. Be careful, Ondrej. We need to think carefully about controlling this message on our terms."

"Does that mean you are starting to agree with Socrates on this?"

"Agree with me on what?" Socrates appeared.

"I have been doing a lot of research on other sports, and I think there is no need to ask Ondrej to continue to hide such a large part of his life." Papa sighed. "It's really no one's business how Ondrej spends his time away from the racetrack or who he spends his time with, but looking at other sports, having a—" Papa glanced around even though they were only people in the room, then lowered his voice. "—gay athlete is a big deal."

"Representation matters." Ondrej used the platitude because this was awkward as fuck. He just wanted to be himself without knowing that it was going to be such a huge fucking big deal. "This is frustrating. I'm not even the first gay S1 driver."

Socrates laughed. "Yeah, there's been a few of us. Unless

you count Lucien who didn't care who knew, you'll be the first one to be out while you are driving."

Lucien Grenville was gay? "Lucien?"

"You should look at his social media sometime. He doesn't bother to hide himself, but he's never made a public statement either. Doing one of those is a little more intense."

"If you choose to do that," Papa said. For the first time, Ondrej couldn't be sure where Papa stood on the issue. There was something in his tone that suggested he was okay with the potential mess.

"Choose to do what?" Hudson walked through the back door into the room and Ondrej knew exactly what he wanted. "Mr D'Grieg, here is the brochure you wanted from your car."

"Papa. Did you send Hudson on an errand to keep him out of pitlane at the end of the race?"

"Yes. I know you, Ondrej, and I didn't want an impulse to—"

"—to what? Ruin the narrative of my story?"

"Ondrej." Hudson laid his hand on Ondrej's forearm. "Please don't argue with your father."

"Well, this is a nice happy family thing you guys have going on. Tell me what you plan about this, and I'll say something supportive for the press." Socrates shook Papa's hand and left the room.

"Ondrej. Please," Papa said.

"Please, what?"

"As your father, I only want what will make you happy. I love you, son. I still worry that falling in love is a distraction for your safety. But ... as your agent, I have a duty to protect your career, your reputation, and your mother's legacy. Sometimes those things are in opposition to each other."

He wasn't a fucking child, he understood enough about life and S1 politics that he didn't need Papa to explain. Ondrej breathed in and out slowly until the flash of rage reduced. Slowly, he noticed Hudson's palm in the centre of his back, grounding him and supporting him. "I understand that, Papa. It's always just been the two of us, and you do a good job as my agent. I know this situation is complex."

"Yes. I've spent years worrying about what might happen if you get accidentally outed and I have several different strategies that we could employ in that case. Obviously every single strategy includes my support of you. If you want to be more deliberate about controlling this story, then we need to discuss a strategy for the revelation and make the most of it."

Ondrej wished he'd had the courage to talk to Papa about this before now. To learn that Papa had created plans for how to deal with the media fall out if he'd been outed shouldn't be a surprise. Papa was good as his job and good at protecting him. But it still hurt that Papa hadn't talked to him about it. Hudson was right, they shouldn't have let this hang unspoken between them for so long.

"Mostly, Ondrej, I'm your father and I don't want to disappoint you. I think I've done that a lot lately around this issue and I'm sorry." Oh. Ondrej's chest hurt as Papa apologised.

"Hey. Papa." Ondrej hugged his father. "I'm not disappointed in you. Just frustrated by all of this. It's not your fault."

"Perhaps I made it harder for you though."

Ondrej tried not to glance at Hudson, but failed, and yes, Hudson's expression was exactly the disbelief he'd expected to see. "It's your job to think about how the press see me."

"Speaking of which, you'd better shower before your interview with Ms Blasi."

It was a couple of hours before Ondrej finally walked into his hotel room. Hudson sat at the table, typing away on his laptop. He looked so sexy, but more than that, having him here was comforting in a way that Ondrej wasn't ready to accept. Or perhaps he was more than ready to accept it, if only the rest of his life would catch up to that desire. Hudson's red hair was all in disarray as if he'd been pushing his hands through it occasionally.

"Hey."

Hudson turned, blinking rapidly. "How was the interview?"

"Good. Alicia, that's the journalist, wanted to do a piece about Ma and how her legacy impacted on my driving career."

"Are you okay? Talking about some of that stuff must be hard."

Ondrej shrugged. "Yes and no. I never really knew Ma. Sometimes it just feels like I'm reciting facts about her without knowing her, if you know what I mean."

"You must be exhausted."

Ondrej was. He nodded slowly. "Yeah." He was glad that Hudson didn't bring up the conversation with Papa. He didn't have the capacity to talk about anything anymore.

"It seems rude to ask you to do an emotional interview right after a race."

"Alicia probably thought she'd get a less practiced response, by surprising me with an interview right after a race."

"How cynical."

"Of me?"

"No, of her."

Ondrej shrugged. "Journalists, you know. Getting the story matters more than—" He stifled a yawn, and Hudson jumped to his feet.

"Come with me. Did you eat?"

"A little. We can order something." Ondrej grabbed the room service menu and picked his favourite; steak with mashed celeriac and a summer salad on the side. He leaned against the wall as Hudson rang through their order.

"Should be about twenty minutes." Hudson hovered, standing on one foot, then the other. Ondrej pushed off the wall. He wasn't that tired.

"The perfect amount of time for you to blow me."

Hudson's cheeks flushed and then slowly, he licked his bottom lip. Fuck, did he know what that did for Ondrej? He'd been half-hard when he'd seen Hudson crouched over his laptop, but now, his cock ached. Ramrod hard.

"Come here."

Hudson almost smiled, the corners of his mouth twitching, and then he took three strides and was in

Ondrej's arms. They kissed. Hungrily at first, as if they hadn't spent the last three nights together during the whole race weekend, and a whole fucking month together before that. It wasn't enough. Ondrej would never tire of this man's kiss and the way he openly desired him. Okay, a lot of men had desired Ondrej over the years, and most of them had no idea who he was. He'd always pretended not to be himself during the mid-season and off-season breaks. Hudson knew who he was, and even better, he didn't treat him as special because he was famous. His level-headed approach to the world helped Ondrej feel normal when he was away from his job, away from the media focus.

"Stop thinking." Hudson sucked Ondrej's ear lobe, and just as Ondrej was about to protest—even though it was true that he'd been thinking too much—Hudson traced his fingers over Ondrej's face. The touch wasn't soft or gentle, but it did caress his soul. Shit. This overreaction had to be simply due to his excellent race result and the remnants of trying to hide his emotions during the interview about Ma. He swallowed.

"On your knees." There was one way he knew how to stop his brain thinking, and it was to have this man on his knees before him. Hudson licked Ondrej's neck, a long decadent stroke of his tongue. A promise of things to come. And then Hudson did Ondrej's favourite thing. He softened his body against his. Even with the wall at Ondrej's back, the way Hudson melted against him was everything. Ondrej pushed his thigh between Hudson's legs and nudged them apart. Hudson moaned against Ondrej's neck, then slowly sank to his knees. The trail of Hudson's body shifting down his, and the way Hudson used his hands for balance as he knelt, was everything. Ondrej's skin felt too hot, and he wanted to rip off his clothes. There was way too much fabric between them both. He needed...

Hudson undid Ondrej's jeans and made a show of slowly unzipping his fly. His fingers were too careful and Ondrej wanted to buck his hips against Hudson's hand. Just as he thought he'd finally get Hudson's skin against his bare cock, Hudson spread his hands wider, holding Ondrej's hips as he pealed his jeans down. Ondrej bit his lip to stop himself crying out when Hudson licked his cock from the base to the tip; the exact same way he'd licked his throat only a few moments before. Hudson's mouth was hot around his cock; each lick and suck sending heat spiralling through Ondrej's body with it all collecting in his balls. Fuck. Usually he could last longer than this, but the way Hudson used his mouth, with his tongue flat taking him deep into his throat was a lot. Hudson kept one hand gripped tight on Ondrej's hip and with the other, he was making light circular caresses around Ondrej's balls, thighs, and yes... further back towards his hole. Ondrej pushed his ass hard against the wall so he didn't fuck Hudson's mouth too hard. He realised he had both hands spread out on the wall with his fingertips splayed out. It was awkward and he forced his muscles to relax enough that he could drop one hand onto Hudson's head. The strands of his hair against Ondrej's hand felt so good; too good. Hudson didn't let up. His finger slid inside Ondrej's hole, and he couldn't contain himself anymore. He yelled out, clutching onto Hudson's hair. Hudson didn't stop, he just took it all, and when Ondrej braved glancing down, Hudson looked up at the same time. His hazel eyes were all glassy and filled with lust and that single glance was all it took to drive Ondrej over the edge. He came, just as Hudson released his cock, and Ondrej spilled himself all over Hudson's chin and neck.

"Fuck." The necklace of come was the fucking hottest thing he'd ever seen, and for the first time in his life, he understood why men bought diamond necklaces for their girlfriends. Would Hudson want one? He closed his eyes and sagged against the wall.

"Don't fall asleep there." Hudson kissed him, a peck on the lips, then held his hands and walked with him to the table. Ondrej pulled up his jeans with shaking hands, not bothering to do up his fly again, and sat down.

"What about you?"

Hudson smiled. "I'm fine." His voice was all croaky, a well-fucked throat. Ondrej wanted to say something, but he was suddenly very tired. Hudson handed him a glass of water, then disappeared.

"Hey."

"I'm not going anywhere, just to get cleaned up a bit."

Ondrej nodded. He didn't have the energy to protest that he liked seeing Hudson messy like that. Maybe tomorrow. Instead, he drank the water and then rested his head on his hands, elbows on the table.

"Wake up. Dinner's here." Hudson shook his shoulder gently, then placed a plate before him. Ondrej's stomach growled, and his mouth filled with saliva as he saw the succulent steak before him.

"Eat up. Then sleep. We can talk tomorrow." Hudson slid into the seat opposite him and started to eat. Having someone who quietly just cared for him after a race was incredible. He used to stuff food in his face, then collapse into bed. Ondrej could barely believe that this was his life. He'd always assumed he'd have to wait until after his career was finished before he could find companionship like this. He didn't want to wait. Hudson belonged here with him. All the pieces of his life were coming together and he wanted to tell the world who he was, and more importantly, all about this special man who was quickly becoming an important part of Ondrej's life.

CHAPTER 15

ITALY

To get the fastest lap at Monza was a career highlight for Ondrej. It was more than the extra point he'd earned for the achievement. Monza was one of the oldest S1 tracks and it was a sacred place for many drivers. Legendary. In his old team, he'd achieved several fastest laps at various circuits, but never here. This was also his first fastest lap for Gamble, and after the work the team had put into making this car produce its best, it was particularly satisfying to achieve this today. He found himself mobbed by media after the race.

"You've been driving well since the mid-season break. What is your secret?"

"It looks like both the Gamble drivers have finally started to understand the new car."

Ondrej nodded at that one. It wasn't really a question.

"This is the second time this season that your team-mate has finished higher than you. How does that feel?"

Ondrej turned towards the reporter holding a TV Japan microphone. "This is a team sport. I'm thrilled to see Paulo get his first podium for Gamble Racing. And perhaps he beat me today, but I got my first podium much earlier in my debut season." He grinned so the media would report it as happy banter. This time, the smile came easily with no pretence. The loneliness that'd weighed heavily on him after Australia had gone. With only a week between Spa and Monza, Hudson had stayed with Ondrej and worked remotely using his laptop hooked into the hotel's wifi. It was so domestic and lovely to have him to come home to every day. They'd left Spa on the Monday and gone directly to Monza so Ondrej could do some testing on the simulator with Victor while the pit lanes were set up by the team, ready for practice on Friday.

"What did you think of the incident between Jean-Pierre and his teammate, Grigor, on lap ten?" Of course it was the French media who wanted to know all about their star driver Jean-Pierre!

"It's not my place to comment on the performance of other teams." Ondrej replied in French.

"But you used to be Jean-Pierre's teammate. You must have some insight."

Ondrej shrugged. "Jean-Pierre is a professional. You should ask him for his opinion." Ondrej didn't mention that they had planned to have a drink together tonight; himself and Hudson with JP and Sofia, although that looked unlikely now that JP might be kept in hospital overnight for observation. The crash, caused by JP's teammate Grigor Anthony being reckless, was a nasty one with both drivers being airlifted to hospital. He'd been waiting in the pit lane, thanks to the red flag, when he'd heard the update that both drivers were conscious. The accident had happened at the perfect time for him to take advantage of the compulsory pit stop with a tyre change and that was how the team had leapfrogged into second and fourth, holding those positions until the end of the race.

"Come on Ondrej. This is the team that dumped you with no warning two years ago. You must have some comment on the mess. No petty feelings?"

Ondrej blinked slowly so he didn't roll his eyes. "JP is a good friend of mine. He is okay after the crash and that's what matters to me."

"So the rumours that he didn't want you in the team because you were a threat aren't true?"

Ondrej grinned to cover his surprise. Well, most people would hardly guess at the truth—being dumped for his sexuality wasn't going to be on many people's radar—S1 never expected anyone to be gay. Everyone happily assumed that Socrates was the only one, even though it made no sense for everyone to be straight in a sport with so many people involved. Twenty teams, and each with at least five hundred staff, not to mention the media, marshals, FIA staff, and everyone else who worked to put races on each weekend. Statistically there had to be plenty of queer people in the paddock.

"I have no comment on that old situation, except to clarify that JP had nothing to do with the decision. Even when we were teammates and rivals, he was my friend, and we remain friends."

"I have it on good authority—"

"Let me stop you there. JP is not so easily threatened by his teammate's success that he would need to stoop to such tactics. The reason behind my move to Gamble Racing is confidential and you should probably focus on the current season, not old boring news like that." It was the most Ondrej had ever said on the subject and as he spoke he knew he was going to be quoted for months about it. He'd never signed any confidentiality agreement with his old team, so technically he was free to say what he wanted on the ugly situation. But to say anything now would make him sound bitter; not to mention that he'd need to out himself to the media. He wasn't ready for that drama yet. It would distract from his results.

"Who has any more questions about today's race?" he asked with a wink. There were a few more technical questions before the press moved on to speak to another driver.

He opened his hotel room and was swamped by Hudson, who hugged him tight.

"I'm so glad you are okay." Hudson must have seen JP and Gregor's crash because he was clinging onto Ondrej and stroking his hands up and down Ondrej's spine, as if to reassure himself that Ondrej was really here.

"I'm better than okay. Fourth and fastest lap."

"I didn't watch the race."

"What?" Ondrej had given Hudson ticketed access to the pitlane and had assumed he'd been there all day. He figured this reaction was because he'd seen the crash and was worried. Non-drivers tended to worry about stuff like that more than they needed to. "Did you spend all day here working?"

Hudson cringed a little. "Not exactly working. Did you know that Monza is the third oldest S1 track and it's the also one of the most dangerous. Fifty-two drivers and thirty-five spectators have been killed there."

"Relax Hudson. You really need to stop reading ancient history. No one has been..." Ondrej nearly said hurt, but JP was in hospital right now. "... um, killed for decades."

"Okay." Hudson breathed slowly. "Okay. I read that too, but I was worried about you."

Ondrej probably shouldn't feel glad to hear Hudson was worried about him. He held back a snide comment because Hudson deserved better if he was upset.

"I'm fine. We have good safety equipment now." Ondrej was able to breath now that Hudson relaxed his grip a little. "If it helps, I could take show you the car and all the safety stuff?"

"Now?"

Ondrej gulped. "Um, not now. Everything is locked away for the night and will be packed tomorrow for shipping to Singapore."

"I think that would help. I went down a bit of a rabbit hole of research this afternoon and watched way too many crashes on Youtube. Some of them are so scary, like the big one with the giant explosion a few seasons ago."

"Brutjan at Bahrain." Yeah, that'd been the worst crash Ondrej had ever seen. He'd been at the front of the field and had known nothing except for hearing the red flag message on the radio. It'd only been once he'd parked his car in pitlane that he'd seen the footage of Brutjan walking out of the flaming wreck.

"Scary as fuck. I can't believe he walked away. Imagine his family waiting for him to emerge from the flames like that."

"Hudson!" Ondrej kissed him gently on the forehead. "Brutjan survived because of our good safety equipment. Besides, you of all people should know better than to scare yourself with historical research."

"Yeah. Ever since we talked about your mother's crash, I can't stop thinking about it." Hudson let out a shaky breath. "How do you do it? Knowing the risks and with your mother and everything?"

Ondrej shrugged. "It's part of the job. I don't think about it. When a driver starts to worry about the risks, they stop riding that edge of success, and that's the end of their racing career. I love the challenge of pushing my car to the limits of its engineering."

"You make it sound so..." Hudson sighed. "I don't know, clinical or something."

"Yeah, I suppose it is." Ondrej cupped Hudson's cheeks so he could kiss him properly. "Congratulate me on today's success." He kissed him thoroughly. "Promise me you'll stop worrying about me. I'm protected until I turn thirty-seven."

Hudson scoffed. "I don't think it works like that."

"It does. Trust me." Ondrej didn't need to explain his superstition and how right it had always felt.

"Alrighty, then." Hudson huffed out a breath. "You are right about one thing though."

"Only one?" Finally, he managed to tease a fragile smile out of Hudson.

"Um, yeah."

Ondrej kissed him again. "You've forgotten your point, haven't you?"

"No." Hudson stiffened in Ondrej's arms, then after a moment, he relaxed again. "You are teasing me, aren't you?"

"Yes. Now tell me. What am I right about? I love hearing how good I am."

"Such an ego." Hudson's grin widened. "Fine. You are right that I shouldn't scare myself by looking at S1 history. Show me your car and I'll feel even better about you going out into danger."

"Is that a euphemism?"

"What?" Hudson's eyes widened for a second, then he laughed. "Is everything about sex for you?"

Ondrej heard himself bark with laughter. He narrowed his vision, then stared at Hudson with as much lust as he could summon. "Yes. At this very second, all my thoughts are about sex." He paused dramatically. "With you."

Hudson softened and it was everything Ondrej wished for. He kissed him again. Hudson's mouth was a little rough today, surrounded by red stubble, and the texture was fucking perfect. This man held so much power to undo Ondrej and the best part was that Ondrej wanted it. He wanted to command him and see him succumb to desire until it was Ondrej who was overcome too. The kiss went on and on, and Ondrej savoured every stroke of Hudson's tongue.

"Shall we go to bed?" Hudson whispered in his ear.

"Are you tired?" Ondrej teased, suddenly realising that he was shattered, just like after every race. He fought to keep his eyes open.

"A little. It's stressful spending all afternoon imagining you in awful car crashes."

Ondrej snorted. "Fucking hell. Should I be worried about you?"

"No. I'm the one worrying about you." Hudson look so affronted that Ondrej had to try hard not to grin.

"If I command you to stop worrying, will it work?"

"I wish."

"Stop worrying about me. I'm not going to die in a car crash until I'm—"

"Thirty-seven." Hudson raised both eyebrows.

Ondrej shrugged. "It's fate. Don't argue with that. And I'm going to change the future by being retired by then."

"And you'll never drive a car ever again?" Hudson lifted his chin a little.

"What? No. The issue is racing, not boring road driving. Why are we even discussing this? I want you in my bed."

"You started it." Hudson poked him in the chest and Ondrej laughed.

"Are you a child now?"

"No."

"No. You definitely are not a child." Ondrej raked his gaze over Hudson's body, loving the way he blushed. All of Hudson's freckles stood out against his blush, so Ondrej kissed him again, and not just to prove his point. He loved it when Hudson teased him, loved it when Hudson relaxed around him. He especially loved it when Hudson kissed him back, like he was going to drown in him. The kiss of a man dying of thirst who'd just stumbled across a well of water, and it was all he could to stop himself immersing himself in the water and maybe even drown in his desperation to drink his fill.

"To bed."

"It's a bit early for sleep." Hudson extracted himself from Ondrej's hug, stepped away, then grinned. "Should we?" And with a not very subtle lustful glance, Hudson turned and walked towards the hotel bed that dominated the room. He threw himself across the bed, sprawled for Ondrej to enjoy.

"You little hussy." Ondrej tapped him on the ass with an open palm and Hudson waggled his ass in the air, so Ondrej did it again. "You have too many clothes on."

"Then do something about it." Hudson wanted to play it that way, did he? Ondrej's ears roared with anticipation. He rolled Hudson over, handling his body slightly roughly, and from the way Hudson's mouth gaped and his face was flushed, he liked it.

"Do you want this?" Ondrej stripped off his jeans, then knelt on the edge of the bed, looming over Hudson, and stroked his hard cock.

"Yes."

"Then earn it. Get naked." Ondrej ignored the fact that Hudson had told him to undress him only a moment earlier. The shock on Hudson's face was amazing, and when he obeyed with a slight tremor in his fingers, Ondrej knew Hudson was already close. Hudson pulled his shirt over his head, giving Ondrej a full view of his soft belly and masculine chest covered in hair. Hudson didn't have the defined abs that came with an S1 exercise regime. He was trim in a more natural way without the definition and Ondrej loved the contrast between their bodies. Hudson discarded the shirt, then lifted his hips to slide his shorts down his legs.

"Were you bare for me all afternoon?"

Hudson's skin flushed pink all over. "No. I just took my undies off at the same time."

"What a shame. I rather like the idea of you wearing nothing, just for me."

"Okay?" Hudson kicked off his shorts—and undies—and flopped back on the bed, wearing nothing but his glasses.

"You are more than okay." Ondrej spread Hudson's legs wider on the bed, then knelt between them. He loved the contrast of having Hudson completely naked while he was still dressed. He took his time, exploring Hudson's body with his hands and tongue, skirting around his cock until Hudson grabbed himself with his hand. Ondrej clicked his tongue.

"Well, I wouldn't have to if you didn't ignore me."

"You like it."

Hudson scrunched his nose. "No. Yes. Fuck you."

"No, I will fuck you if you remove your hand."

Hudson's arm muscles trembled but he obeyed slowly with a defiant glare. Fucking perfect. Ondrej leaned forward and sucked one of Hudson's nipples hard and was rewarded with Hudson's groan.

"Please. Ondrej."

"You want me to fuck you. Like this?"

"Yes." Hudson extended the word into a long hiss. Fuck. For all that Ondrej loved to tease Hudson like this, it came at a price, and now Ondrej was so close to coming that he needed some space. He leaped off the bed.

"Stay." He finished taking off his clothes, then opened his suitcase and took his time locating a condom and the small bottle of lube he'd packed. With every breath, he gained more control over his body, and it wasn't long before he was able to walk back towards the bed and Hudson. Hudson who was sprawled for him. Hell. Hudson propped himself up on his elbow and watched intently as Ondrej rolled on the condom. He made a show of covering the latex in lube; it was more show than actual stroking of his hard cock because he wanted to come inside Hudson, not now. Not yet.

He grabbed Hudson's ankles and dragged him towards the edge of the bed. Hudson swallowed a squeak and the way the sound escaped a little sent a shiver all over Ondrej's skin. This man was going to destroy him. And he wanted every piece of it.

"You want this?"

"This being what?" Hudson winked and Ondrej was tempted to leap onto him, crush him, and kiss the smirk off his face.

"Do you want to be fucked with my cock?" His voice sounded like it'd been dragged over broken glass.

"Yes please."

Ondrej didn't need anything else. He tugged Hudson again, positioning his ass on the edge of the bed, and slowly pushed his way inside. Hudson was too tight, unprepared, and he let out a ragged breath. The way he tried so hard for Ondrej, tried to relax for him, was fucking hot and Ondrej's muscles shook with the effort of making sure he impaled Hudson slowly. The lube covering his own cock helped him slide inside.

"You know what would be hot?" Ondrej stopped moving.

"What?" Hudson whispered. "What could be hotter than this?"

A bright burning hot flash spread all over Ondrej's skin and he forgot what he'd intended to say.

"Fill me." Hudson lifted his knees to his chest. "Now."

The change of angle opened Hudson up and Ondrej slid all the way in. Heaven. Hudson was so tight around him, and he was so close to coming. Fuck. With every thrust, he recited the track at Monza to help him delay the inevitable and make this good for Hudson. The first chicane, Variante de Rettifilo. Turn two, Curva Grande. Chicane della Roggia. Turns four and five, di Lesmo. Lactic acid built in his muscles as he thrust in and out. Hudson moaned under him and hooked his legs around Ondrej's waist. Fucking hell. Hudson's cock was hard between them, bouncing a little with each thrust, leaking and untouched. Turn six, del Serraglio. Only two turns until he could come. Sweat dripped into his eyes, stinging a little. The Ascari chicane. And now he was flying towards Parabolica and the finish line.

"You." Ondrej stroked Hudson's cock until Hudson closed his eyes and came all over his stomach and chest in long spurts. That was all it took for Ondrej to follow. He collapsed on top of Hudson.

"Fucking hell. That was ... You are amazing." Hudson shifted his legs and now Ondrej was even more comfortable. He buried his face against Hudson's neck. Hudson kissed his temple with a raspy brush of his stubble surrounded lips. Ondrej probably should roll off Hudson and get cleaned up, but he really couldn't be bothered. He lay there absorbing the way Hudson's skin smelled like salt, sex, and the freshness of grass after rain. After a while, Hudson shifted a little under him.

"Am I too heavy?" Ondrej didn't want to move.

"A little."

Ondrej braced his arms on the bed either side of Hudson and pushed off him. He made sure he took care with the condom as he eased his slackening cock out, then walked to the bathroom to tidy up. When Hudson wrapped his arms around Ondrej's waist, he nearly jerked in surprise.

"Let me clean you up."

"I can do it."

Hudson pressed an open-mouthed kiss between Ondrej's shoulder blades. "I know. But I like doing it."

"Thank you."

"Go on. Lie down. You raced today. You'll be tired."

He was surprised to realise that Hudson was correct. "Okay, but we have a team dinner at eight to celebrate Paulo's first podium."

"I'll wake you." Hudson gave him a little shove and Ondrej gladly walked back to the bed, a huge smile splitting his face. He collapsed on top of the covers, burying his face in the pillow so Hudson wouldn't see. He was only vaguely aware of Hudson cleaning him with a warm cloth before everything went dark.

CHAPTER 16

Hudson followed Ondrej through the large stone building towards the team dinner. The setting was quintessentially Italian winery; from the stone farmhouse with flagstone floors, to the way the pergola sat on the edge of the hill overlooking a steep valley covered in grape vines. Being here was like being on the food channel on television. With every step, his pulse sped up. What was he doing here? Wouldn't it be obvious that he was with Ondrej? They probably should've talked about this.

"Here is our next champion." Socrates stood up at the long table and waved at Ondrej. They were outside under a pergola on the back porch of a local winery's main building, and a large group of people were seated around two long tables. Each table was covered in large platters of food. Several types of bread with olive oil and balsamic dips, sun-dried tomatoes, fresh salads filled with colourful vegetables, and a lot of cheese. Bottles of wine were placed along the middle of the table, whites in ice buckets, and reds in tall bottles. It was casual and sumptuous. Lemon trees grew up the edges of the pergola creating a rich citrus summer scent in the air, one that inconveniently reminded Hudson of the soap Ondrej used in his apartment in Monaco.

"I hope you greeted Paulo in the same way. He's the one with the podium today." Ondrej waved at his rookie teammate who waved back. Hudson hung back, unsure on what the etiquette would be tonight.

"Have a seat." Socrates picked up his wine glass and walked to the side of the pergola. Ondrej sat down and turned to the handsome plump Black man beside him. Was everyone in S1 ridiculously sexy?

"Hey, good race today."

"Yes."

"This is Hudson Lockley. He's working on a project for Papa." The bland introduction shouldn't disappoint. Ondrej was hardly going to call him his boyfriend at a team dinner. The man reached around Ondrej's back and shook Hudson's hand.

"Welcome. I'm Jaxxon Loharani-Jones, Ondrej's race engineer."

Hudson tucked away the question about the difference between a race engineer and a team engineer to ask later. "Hi, nice to meet you."

"What is the project?"

Ondrej leaned forward and poured wine for them both, as if it were perfectly normal to bring someone who worked for him to a team dinner.

"I'm doing some historical family research for the D'Grieg family."

"And this is part of your research?"

Hudson glanced at Ondrej. They really—really—should have discussed why he was here with Ondrej because now he was forced to say something that wasn't the whole truth, and he'd probably sound like he was lying. He was going to overthink this and make a damned mess, wasn't he?

"The D'Grieg family has a long history in car racing. Ondrej's great grandfather drove in the Le Mans, and obviously everyone knows his mother was a champion rally driver. Ondrej and his father thought it would help my research if I spent some time with them at the races, and then Ondrej invited me along tonight. I presume it's so I can get an insider's view of how the team works."

"Makes sense." Jaxxon leaned back in his chair. "Hey, Socrates, I thought you had a no media policy at team dinners."

"I'm not media. This is private—" Hudson gulped as Socrates waved away Jaxxon's comment. "Ah, family research."

"Cool. How do you get into something like that?" Jaxxon turned his attention back to Hudson who tried not to shrink under the attention. He was doing nothing wrong being here, even as a secret boyfriend. Was he the only partner here? Hudson mentally shook off the thought; if it were true, this would be weird, and he didn't want to think too hard about that.

Ondrej laughed. "Fuck, Jaxxon, stop being nosy."

"I'm interested. It's not often I get to meet a real-life historian." Jaxxon winked at Ondrej.

"Be prepared to be bored." Ondrej tapped Hudson's foot under the table with his own, and Hudson grinned.

"Hey, history isn't boring. Engineering is boring." Half the table spluttered and protested, which had been Hudson's intent, and he sipped the wine that Ondrej had poured for him.

"You know what we should do?" Jaxxon waved at Socrates. "Socrates. We should get Ondrej's historian to write the history of Gamble Racing for the website."

"Let me finish this job first, then maybe we can talk about it."

"Are you kidding, Jaxxon?" Socrates' voice boomed across both tables and Hudson wasn't that keen for all this attention. "We aren't going to do anything like that until one of these lads wins a championship for us. Victor's car will get us there in the next year or two."

Enthusiastic conversation exploded across both tables and Hudson let the discussion flow around him. He occupied himself by eating some of the food, and just listened to everything.

"History, huh. Sounds like a rich person's type of degree."

Hudson hated that assumption, and he stiffened. "Not for me. I worked hard to get a scholarship to university."

"Oh?" Jaxxon's eyebrows raised.

"Not everyone who studies history has a wealthy background. It was the subject I was best at, and that allowed me to get a scholarship. I had intended to teach afterwards."

"But now you do family research for rich people? How does that work?" The initial judgement in Jaxxon's voice had disappeared and been replaced with curiosity. Hudson tried to relax and put aside the odd tension around being here with Ondrej without being with him.

"My sister and I run a business that does family trees and related research for people. The trend for people to run DNA tests and find out about their ancestors created a niche market for this type of research."

"That's cool. Have you done your own DNA?"

Hudson knew Jaxxon wasn't asking about his fucked-up parents. *Thanks anxiety.* He focused on the question. "Yes. As you'd expect from this—" He waved at his red hair, "I'm mostly Scottish with a little bit of English thrown in."

"Good for you. Walking the talk and all that. I take it you are okay with giving your DNA to a random company?"

"Yes, although I understand the concerns that people have with doing that."

"Fuck yeah. I'm not letting some company use my DNA for profit or whatever."

Hudson nodded. He didn't need to tell Jaxxon about the way Black people had been historically abused by the medical system. The scandalous way doctors and scientists had treated Henrietta Lacks' cancer cells was only the tip of that ugly iceberg.

"It's not for everyone, that's for sure."

Jaxxon laughed. "Yeah, just white people wanting to find something exotic in their DNA."

Hudson nodded, biting back a surprised laugh. He'd never heard anyone articulate it quite like that. "We do get a lot of clients with that aim, yes."

"I bet you do."

"Most of our clients come to us after they've done a DNA test, but it's not something we require. And we don't offer DNA tests. It's not part of our service."

"What exactly do you offer? Sell it to me." Jaxxon leaned around the back of Ondrej, who was chatting to someone across the table.

"Really?"

"Yes. I'm interested."

Hudson didn't like the gleam in Jaxxon's eye. Hopefully he was just imagining it because he was nervous about being here. Fuck, that explained the twist in his stomach. He was worried he'd do or say something, and everyone would know the truth about him and Ondrej. He had no qualms being out, but he didn't want to be the one who accidentally outed Ondrej when he wasn't ready.

"Are you teasing me?"

"I like business. You have a business. Sell it to me."

"Okay. We specialise in helping ordinary families find their extraordinary stories."

Jaxxon elbowed Ondrej. "I can see why you hired this guy. That's a great elevator pitch. I especially like how he's called your family ordinary, Ondrej."

"Hudson's research has been valuable to the family so far." Ondrej didn't react to Jaxxon's teasing with anything more than a flicker of one eyebrow.

"Wow, and a compliment to boot! Well, Hudson, where would you start with my family?"

Hudson still wondered if this was a trap. Jaxxon had a cleverness about him that put Hudson on edge. The sharp intense look in Jaxxon's dark brown eyes should be familiar; many people in the Gamble Racing team had the same look. Socrates obviously hired people with the same intelligent drive for success.

Hudson cleared his throat. "We have a simple questionnaire on our website. You fill in as many details as you know, and it populates family tree software that we use in the back end. It's all confidential and private and if, for example, you know your grandparent but not your parent, it still works. We've tested it on many different families with different structures, even polyamorous families."

"Queer friendly. I like that too. And for someone like me?"

Hudson smiled, even though he felt anything but relaxed. "Now that question sounds like you are trying to trap the white guy into saying something inappropriate."

"Me?" Jaxxon pressed his palm on his chest and laughed. Then his face went blank. "Yes, that's exactly what I was doing."

"Really?"

Jaxxon laughed again. "No. You walked right into that one!"

"Yeah, I guess I did. The honest answer is that we had our questionnaire extensively tested before we launched it to make sure it was fully inclusive of all types of families across the world. And we continually make adjustments based on feedback."

"Excellent answer. I might do this questionnaire sometime."

"The questionnaire is free to complete with no obligation to use our services."

Jaxxon nodded. "That's good business. Hook people in with a need fulfilment, then keep them by increasing their curiosity."

"My sister runs that side of things. I'm just the historian."

Ondrej scoffed. "There's no 'just' about it." The quick outburst surprised Hudson. He hadn't realised Ondrej was listening to his discussion with Jaxxon. "Stop underselling yourself. Don't you have a degree in history?"

"A Masters, yes. I was invited to do a PhD, however, I declined." He succumbed to the need to prove he belonged in this group of quick thinkers.

"Why?" Jaxxon asked. "That's not an invitation I imagine you turned down easily."

"No. It was tempting. When my sister proposed our business as a concept and an alternative to continuing my studies, I realised that I wasn't cut out to be an academic and I would only be accepting the offer because someone offered it to me. The business is a better fit for my strengths and interests." Once again, Mackenzie had known what he needed before he did. He loved being validated, and the offer to do a PhD hit that sweet spot. The highly structured cutthroat academic environment would've destroyed him eventually and he was better off being away from that.

Jaxxon tilted his head. "I'm curious. If you were invited to a doctorate, what was your thesis in? Car racing history? Why haven't I heard of you?"

Hudson smiled. "I didn't study car racing history. I'm learning that as part of the project I'm doing for Ondrej's family."

"Then what?"

"Fuck, Jaxxon, stop being so bloody nosy." Ondrej growled at Jaxxon and Hudson almost rested his hand on Ondrej's forearm to reassure him that he was okay with Jaxxon's interesting style of grilling him. The more that Jaxxon talked, the more Hudson realised that Jaxxon loved knowing about people and talking about business. He had an insatiable curiosity that relaxed Hudson, teasing aside. He unclenched his fingers from around the stem of his wine glass.

"What's the problem, Ondrej? I'm merely being interested in someone who, like myself, won a scholarship to study."

"You did?"

Jaxxon nodded. "Full ride scholarship to Oxford University. Double degree in Mechanical Engineering and Commerce Studies."

"Wow. That's very impressive."

"So is a master's degree in history."

"It wasn't Oxford, but thank you." Hudson figured he may as well tell them his thesis topic. He knew that Ondrej and Socrates wouldn't be rude about it, and from the way Jaxxon had reacted to his mention of polyamorous families on their website, then he'd probably be okay too. "I wrote my thesis on lavender marriages in the Victorian era."

"What?" Ondrej and Jaxxon spoke simultaneously.

Hudson laughed. "I assume you've heard of the Victorian era. A lavender marriage is when four queer people marry as two sets of straight couples as a cover for their identity."

"Clever. So two gay guys in love find a lesbian couple and one man marries one of the women and the other man marries the other woman and they all live together?" Jaxxon's face softened.

"Yes. That's absolutely how it works. It has been used throughout history as a way for queer people to navigate an unfriendly society, to protect themselves through the sanctity of marriage. It worked well because it kept queer people safe during their lifetimes. Unfortunately for historians, it also erased them from public records by making them look straight."

"And you studied this?" Ondrej asked.

"And you hired him without knowing what his speciality was? Do you regret it now?"

Ondrej's cheeks flushed. "No regrets."

"Good. Because I'd be disappointed if my driver was a bigot." Jaxxon's tone didn't need any volume to communicate that this mattered deeply to him.

"Okay boys. Settle it down now." Socrates spoke loudly. "Let's toast Paulo. Everyone charge your glasses and raise a toast to our podium super star."

Everyone shouted, "P2 Paulo." Cheers and laughter filled the air.

Hudson took a taxi back to the hotel alone, making an excuse to leave the party early, so that it wouldn't be obvious that Ondrej and him were together. He spent the next couple of hours working on his laptop. Better that than overthink the whole evening and worry that he'd said something wrong. Anxiety was a bitch at times like this.

"Hey. Why are you working? It's late." Ondrej stripped off his clothes. "Come on. Bedtime."

Hudson grinned. "How drunk are you?"

"Not at all. Why would you assume that?"

"Team party. Some of the people there were drinking a lot."

"Not me." Ondrej rolled his eyes. "Fucking Socrates

was off his face though. Mike and Jaxxon had to carry him into their limo."

Hudson had met Socrates' partner Mike a few times now. He was a very sensible man of Indian descent, a complete contrast to Socrates' wild enthusiasm for life.

"I'm not sure why Mike puts up with it. Socrates is a bit of a fucking alcoholic sometimes."

"I don't think someone can be a part time alcoholic."

Ondrej sneered. "True. He's a fucking adrenalin junkie too. I have no idea how he became an S1 Champion…" Ondrej ran his hands through his hair and Hudson almost asked, again, how much he'd had to drink. Something was bothering him about the party.

"It makes sense to me. Adrenalin junkie. He used to drive cars ridiculously fast, and now he's retired, he's chasing the same highs he used to get from racing."

"No, that is a common misunderstanding of how a driver's brain works." Ondrej stopped moving. "The lack of control he shows doesn't align with being a good driver."

Hudson shrugged. "You'd know better than me. Apart from that, how was the rest of the dinner?"

"Yeah. Really good. Gamble is a great team of people."

"Jaxxon seemed to take pride in teasing me. Do you think he guessed about us? He asked me a lot of questions."

"No. No one guessed. Jaxxon quizzes everyone like that. He wants to be CEO one day."

"Of Gamble?"

"Of anything. He's highly driven, career focused, and he knows that any success I get as a driver, he gets a lot of credit for because he is my strategist."

"I thought he was the race engineer?"

"Yes. He is."

"Okay. Do you mind explaining? I know it's late. It can wait."

Ondrej winked at him. "If you get naked and into bed, then I'll explain."

Hudson laughed. "Sure you will. You'll get distracted like always."

"You say that like it's a bad thing. Fine. A race engineer looks at the live data during the race and decides on the best racing strategy for the way the race is unfolding. Obviously we discuss the base strategy beforehand and we have different plans for different scenarios, but Jaxxon is the one who makes the final call in the heat of the moment. And then he radios it to me."

"And you just do as he says."

"Most of the time. He can see more data than me."

"What happens when you disagree?"

"Fucking hell, Hudson. So many questions. It's not a dictatorship. We are all trying to win. Sometimes my experience and racing instincts matter more than data. Sometimes the data tells Jaxxon a story that I can't see while driving."

"Understood. You two must know each other pretty well then."

Ondrej shrugged. "We've been working together for a season and a half now, so yeah."

"I reckon he knows about us. He asked me a lot of questions tonight."

"Nah. All he cares about is business."

"I didn't get that impression."

"He's a strategist. You'd get whatever impression he wants you to have."

"So cynical, Ondrej."

Ondrej jumped under the covers. "Get in here."

"Now?" Hudson realised he was still dressed.

"One dinner with other people and you've forgotten how to be with me. Get undressed, get in bed, and kiss me. Stop worrying."

"I'm good at worrying."

"I know. And I'm bored of waiting for you." Ondrej patted the pillow beside him. If there was anything guaranteed to get Hudson out of his own head, it was being wanted by someone. Ondrej's dark blue eyes blazed with lust. The impatient tone of his command and the lateness of the evening with nothing to do tomorrow gave Hudson a cheeky idea. If anything could get him to stop worrying, it was this. He took off his glasses and made a show of slowly folding them and placing them on the bedside table. Ondrej's hand twitched and his nostrils flared but he didn't reach out and grab Hudson. Hudson walked to the base of the bed, and with each step, Ondrej sat up straighter until his whole torso was exposed. Hudson nearly stumbled— he'd never get tired of that view.

"Tonight was fun."

"It'd be more fun if you stopped fucking around and got naked."

Hudson traced his hands down his torso, then hooked his thumbs into the belt loops on his jeans.

"Off. I don't want any of this slow bullshit. Just you."

"Patience." Hudson pulled off his jeans and tossed

them aside, leaving on his underwear. He took his time lifting his shirt over his head, enjoying the way Ondrej's breath got louder. As soon as he finished removing his shirt, he crawled up the bed, his knees either side of Ondrej's legs.

"Still too many clothes, Mr show boy." Ondrej raised one eyebrow.

"Show boy?"

"Yeah. What is this performance? Surely you aren't bored in bed already." Ondrej spoke with the ego of someone who knew no one would dare say they were bored with him. Hudson grinned. "I don't know. Tonight was weird. So I thought may as well keep being weird."

"You." Ondrej pulled him close and kissed him, until Hudson was breathless and he collapsed against Ondrej's warm, firm body. All the worries about accidentally outing Ondrej tonight fled, because this was right. It was the only place he wanted to be.

"I want to tell the world about us." Hudson immediately wished he hadn't said that out loud. He held his breath.

"So do I." Ondrej's admission caused Hudson's breath to rush out of his lungs with a whistle. "I'm sorry that it was weird for you tonight."

Hudson kissed Ondrej's forehead. "We probably should've talked about a plan before we went."

"I was being selfish. I wanted you with me."

Hudson smiled. "When Jaxxon asked me all those questions, it was so stressful. I didn't want to fuck up. I know you aren't ready to tell everyone yet—"

"Stop." Ondrej rested his forehead against Hudson's

forehead and they breathed slowly together. The rolling waves in Hudson's stomach calmed. "I am ready to tell people. I know that Socrates will support me. Papa is concerned about sponsors, but I think he's wrong."

"I think Jaxxon will support you too. He seemed pretty happy that my business questionnaire is queer friendly."

"He's a good guy. I know he's curious to the point of annoyance, but his heart is good."

Hudson agreed. "The fans will support you too."

"Some of them."

"The others don't matter." As soon as he spoke, Hudson found himself flipped onto his back and being thoroughly kissed by Ondrej.

After a while Ondrej lifted his head. "They don't matter. This matters. Let me show you."

Hudson didn't have time to smile before Ondrej kissed him again. It was a greedy kiss. Ondrej shoved his tongue into Hudson's mouth, stroking and exploring, and all Hudson could do was respond to the heat being built by Ondrej. Ondrej grabbed Hudson's hands and placed his hands outstretched. Ondrej balanced on Hudson's chest, the weight pushing him into the bed, and Hudson loved it. When Ondrej caressed Hudson's arms, slowly taunting him with long strokes of his hands along Hudson's arms, Hudson pulled in short breaths through his nostrils. His skin was alight and smothered in the best way by Ondrej. If he thrust his hips, their cocks would rub against each other, but he didn't move. He let Ondrej set the pace, let Ondrej touch him all over, and when Ondrej slowly made his way down Hudson's body, Hudson let himself be loud.

"Yes. Make all the noise." Ondrej stripped off Hudson's

underwear, and cupped Hudson's balls, then sank his mouth onto Hudson's cock. The warm wetness of his mouth had Hudson crying out for more, and with every suck and pull, tension built and built until he was sure he was going to come down Ondrej's throat.

"I'm coming." He managed to warn Ondrej who only moved faster. Hudson came with bright lights in his vision. "Thank you. Sorry."

"Why are you sorry?" Ondrej sat at the end of the bed and wiped his mouth with the back of his hand.

"I don't know." It was a little embarrassing to apologise.

"You already know I like the taste of you. We've done this before." Ondrej's pragmatic tone seeped through the haziness of Hudson's release, and he dragged himself up into a seated position.

"Did I do something wrong?"

"Not unless you count ignoring me." Ondrej pointed towards his ramrod stiff cock, then gave Hudson a look that made Hudson want to dive under the sheets.

"I'm sorry."

"I'm teasing. Now roll over."

"Like this?" Hudson rolled onto his stomach.

"Yes. And grab the headboard."

Hudson reached up and held the top of the headboard. It was an awkward position with his arms outstretched. His face and some of his chest raised up off the bed.

"Perfect. The bend in your spine is delightful." Ondrej dragged his fingers down Hudson's back, over the taut muscles, and Hudson was glad he'd already come because this would be torture without that earlier release. Sensation ruled as Ondrej traced circles on his skin. No, not circles. Other shapes.

"The next race is Singapore. It's a street circuit. A long straight from the start into the first corner under the Benjamin Shears Bridge, then turn one, two, three—" Ondrej was tracing the circuit on Hudson's skin. Hudson closed his eyes and listened to Ondrej talk through the course as his fingers followed the path of the race. He sank into a sated zone where the only thing that existed was Ondrej's voice and the touch of his fingers.

"Heading into turn 21, get close to the wall—" Ondrej spanked Hudson on the ass and he yelped in shock at the sudden pain. "—too close. I crashed there in my second season." Ondrej kissed Hudson's ass. Hudson moaned as Ondrej soothed the area.

"Want more?"

"Yes please."

Ondrej spanked him again, and Hudson jerked as bright pain and pleasure rushed over his skin. He'd never thought he'd like that, but damn, he loved it. It reminded him of the way Ondrej clutched at his hair whenever he sucked Ondrej's cock, the prickles of pain, and... He cried out again as Ondrej spanked him again. Hudson was hard again, his cock pressing into the bed cover.

"More?"

Hudson couldn't make words. The combination of Ondrej's soothing mouth and the impact of his hand had him gasping for breath. He tried to say yes, but nothing came out.

"Maybe I should fuck you now?"

"Yes." Hudson found his words. "Please."

The bed shifted as Ondrej moved behind him and Hudson was tempted to drop his hands from the headboard and roll over to see what he was doing. Soon enough, he heard the familiar foil of a condom, and then Ondrej applied cool lube on the cheeks of his ass. He gasped at the sudden change in temperature.

"Too cold? It won't be cold for long."

"Promises." Hudson's arms started to burn with lactic acid and he tightened his grip. He wanted Ondrej to touch him and opened his mouth to beg, when Ondrej spread Hudson's legs wider.

"Fuck, you look amazing like this. Spread for me." Ondrej stroked his hands up Hudson's legs, his touch almost too light, almost ticklish, but firm enough to create shivers instead. Hudson spread his legs wider, stretching his thigh muscles, and he arched his spine even more so his ass was in the air. A wetness shocked him and he realised that Ondrej had kissed him right on his hole. He groaned.

"You want this?"

Hudson shook his head. "Need your cock."

"Precious Hudson. So desperate for me."

Hudson groaned as Ondrej licked up Hudson's crack then kissed the small of his back.

"Yes." He hissed. Ondrej spread the lube from Hudson's ass cheeks, down towards his hole, then Ondrej held Hudson's hips, and slowly slid inside. The lube, as promised, had warmed up and Hudson's whole body was so relaxed that Ondrej's entry was smooth and perfect. Hudson loved this. He closed his eyes and clung on as Ondrej pounded into him. Ondrej's hands on Hudson's hips gripped tight; he'd probably leave bruises, and Hudson wanted that too. With every stroke of Ondrej's cock, he felt like he was floating on pure pleasure. Every thrust jolted him on the bed, adding the texture of the bed cover against his stomach to the overwhelming sensations.

"Now come for me."

"Again?" Hudson knew it wouldn't be difficult. He'd been hard since the moment Ondrej had commanded him to hold the bed.

"Yes. Now." Ondrej buried himself deep inside Hudson and stopped moving. The control he had over his body and his general athleticism continued to wow Hudson, but that thought alone wasn't enough. It was when Ondrej stroked one hand up Hudson's spine and gripped the back of his neck that Hudson shouted out and came. He sagged in the aftermath, head bowed, and absorbed everything as Ondrej began to move again. A soft moan sounded in the room. Him. And then Ondrej came and flopped forward onto Hudson's back. Hudson let go of the headboard and sank into the bed with Ondrej's perfect weight covering him. After a while, Ondrej lifted himself off.

"I should get cleaned up."

"It's quite late." Hudson rolled onto his back and tried to drag himself up to his feet.

"Yes. A long day with a race, then a team party." Ondrej had shadows under his eyes.

"Especially for you. Let me clean you up." Hudson liked to do that part, and energy flooded back into his sated limbs. He stood up and helped Ondrej clean up.

"Come and sleep." Hudson patted the bed, then looked back over at Ondrej who had a strange expression on his face. "What's the matter?" Had he done something wrong?

"Tonight when we put Socrates in his limo, Jaxxon said something odd about him."

"What did he say?" Hudson had to scramble to shift his thoughts from his own anxiety to Ondrej's work. He wanted to slap his own forehead. Of course, Ondrej was worried about something work related, not the crap rolling around in Hudson's head.

"He reminded me that he'd predicted that Socrates was going to unravel, and he wanted my support when he applied for the Team Principal role."

Hudson blinked. "He planned this? That sounds very mercenary."

"I know. He's ambitious. I've always known that, but this sounded like more than that."

"There is nothing wrong with ambition. Perhaps the stress of the moment meant he misspoke."

Ondrej winced. "That's the thing. Jaxxon is so careful about every word."

"If it bothers you, talk to him. You two have a close working relationship. You shouldn't let a potential miscommunication upset that." Hudson flicked back the bed covers. "Now get in and sleep."

Ondrej grinned. "Good point."

"About the sleep?"

"No, about Jaxxon. He's a good guy, he wouldn't actively plot someone's downfall."

Hudson nodded. It struck him that perhaps Jaxxon wouldn't create the situation with Socrates, but he'd certainly take advantage of it. Hudson had only talked to him for a short time at the team party tonight, but he'd gained an impression of someone who knew exactly what he wanted and wasn't afraid to chase after it.

"You can deal with that tomorrow." Hudson patted the bed again, and finally, Ondrej got in. Hudson slid in beside him and tucked the blanket around them both. Ondrej fell asleep with one arm slung over Hudson's chest.

CHAPTER 17
SINGAPORE

The glare from the lights made everything look unreal as Ondrej took off his cap and wiped his forehead again with the little towel one of the team had given him after the race. Night racing was great for fans, and he usually loved the challenge of it. Not tonight.

"What happened tonight, Ondrej?" Alicia shoved her microphone in his face. P15 was a crap result. His worst since the mid-season break. Singapore—one of only three races run at night—was always intense with the naturally high heat and humidity and being a street circuit, the surface was inconsistent and rough. His car hadn't coped with the surface, struggling for grip in each corner and he'd had to back off the pace to stay on within track limits too many times. Victor had gambled with the front wing but they'd ended up with too much understeer, and on this car, which was twitchy at the best of times, it'd been too risky to push it.

"Nothing much. Just one of those days where little

things go against you." Ondrej wiped his forehead. Damn this humidity. Sweat still dripped down his temples. He'd only lost two point one kilos during the race. Not too bad. Two years ago, when he'd finished third, he'd lost three kilos, so he'd obviously not sweated as much tonight. He took a long drink from his specially formulated sports drink.

"Are you worried about your contract? I heard that Gamble aren't going to sign you again for the upcoming season?"

Seriously? That's what Alicia wanted to talk about? Ondrej rolled his eyes. The rumour mill was in overdrive at this time of year. "I signed a three-year deal when I joined Gamble. Let's have this discussion next year when I'm a free agent again." If Victor's car kept improving, he'd be keen to stay at Gamble. Not that he'd let anyone know that just yet; that was the type of thing he discussed with his agent and no one else.

"People are hearing things about you... And after the last time, we all know that contracts can be broken at any time."

"Do you have a question?"

"If it's not contracts, then why are there whispers about you?" Alicia leaned in closer.

Ondrej shrugged. "There are always whispers about all the drivers all the time. It means nothing." He pushed away the panic that threatened. Had someone overheard the many recent discussions about whether he should come out? He needed to sit down with Papa and work out a strategy. Tonight.

"Perhaps people have seen how inconsistent your results have been this year and—"

"They've done what they usually do. Add one and one and end up with six hundred? It's the nature of S1 that everyone thinks they know the story."

"And what is the story, Ondrej?"

"There's no story. Gamble is a team on the rise. This year's car is fast, and we are starting to get the results we have been expecting. A few factors didn't suit the car tonight, but that's racing. We are on track for a season midfield result." Ondrej almost said something about previous years, but media training had taught him to stop talking. It wasn't seen as good sport to diss his own team, even if he was referring to his own previous performances.

"A midfield result would be impressive given where the team was this time last season." Alicia did her job as a journalist and reminded the fans of the things he couldn't say. "Are you happy with the way you've settled into the team?"

"I've been there for nearly two seasons now. If I haven't settled in yet, perhaps the rumours have some truth in them." Ondrej grinned at Alicia, and they both knew his comment was going to be a headline grab for her.

"I suppose if I mention Gamble's owner Socrates Drayton you'll clam up too?"

"Yes. Team orders." He shrugged.

"Team orders. The most hated words in all of Series One."

Ondrej nodded. "Are we done here?"

"Yes. Thank you for your time. Good luck at the next race." Alicia pulled the microphone away and Ondrej turned to walk away from the media area. As much as he knew Papa would want a heads up on Alicia's comment about rumours flying about him, the last thing he wanted to do after a night race was attend a business meeting. He sent Papa a text and as soon as possible, he fled to his hotel room for a shower, room service, and a sleep.

When he woke the next day, Papa was sitting in a chair in the lounge part of his suite. It wasn't unusual to see Papa in his hotel room. For every race, Papa had a spare room card and full access to everything because of their working relationship. Ondrej threw on the hotel dressing gown and sat down with him.

"Shall I order breakfast, son?"

"Yes." Ondrej waited while Papa order room service. It was nice, just the two of them—like it had been for most of Ondrej's life—and knowing that Papa understood his requirements without him needing to select anything or think too hard. He'd woken up thinking about how he was going to talk to Victor about the front wing issue. It was obvious the strategy hadn't worked as Victor had wanted. Having Papa here reminded him there was a bigger problem to resolve, one that he'd fallen asleep feeling certain about, and now he was ... He breathed in slowly. Yes, he was still certain.

"You wanted a meeting?"

"Yeah. Alicia Blasi mentioned yesterday that there a lot of rumours flying around about me, but the only one she would talk about was that Gamble were thinking of breaking my contract."

"Gossip. Don't listen. Besides, you have a year to go

with them, and Socrates seems happy with you. Do you want me to talk to him?"

"No. Just leave it. The two of you talk often enough that I trust you to know what he's planning with the team." The point of having an agent was that Ondrej could focus on the job of driving and not have to expend any thought on contractual matters or financial negotiations, and most importantly media. He turned up when he was needed and for the rest of the time, he worked on staying fit and ready to drive.

Papa nodded. "Besides, if Socrates has any faults, it's that he's too loyal. Look at the way he kept his old Head Engineer for years after his cars were slow and outdated in design. The decision to employ Victor Tsui came at least four years too late in my opinion."

"S1. Where everyone has opinions!"

"You don't agree?"

"Of course I agree. The change between the old cars and Victor's car is staggering. Even the newest fans of this sport can see the impact Victor's design has had."

"You see. Socrates is loyal. The driver he moved on to get you still drives for him."

"Yes, in Series E. It's a good option for him." They'd met a few times at team gatherings, and Lucien Grenville was thriving in Series E where the cars were completely electric and were basically a giant computer sitting on a battery; not too different from an S1 car, honestly. He drove a mechanical engine. Lucien had an electrical one. Lucien had a reputation for being a hothead, but he hadn't seemed to have been in the media much lately.

"Don't worry about Socrates. We know he's already

said he'll make a formal statement in your favour if and when you decide to come out."

"I think I want to do that now."

"You think that is the rumour?"

"I highly doubt it." Ondrej shook his head. "It could be."

"We should get ahead of the rumour and say something first."

"Yeah. Most of all, I am tired of hiding. I'm not worried about what will happen with my seat at Gamble if I do this."

Papa cleared his throat. "Um, there's one problem."

"Hudson?" Ondrej really didn't want to rehash the discussion they'd had last time around Papa's superstitions that Ondrej falling in love would be a fatal distraction. His own superstition around his racing number was the only secret he had from Papa; it wouldn't be fair to tell him that Ondrej believed he had an expiration date.

"Yes. He has no media training and probably has no idea how much the press will hound him if you include him in this announcement."

"Are you saying it's not fair to him? That's a new angle for you."

Papa breathed out heavily. "I'm still worried that falling in love will be a distraction. Your Ma..."

"Papa."

"I'm not saying this to push you two apart. And I'm not saying this to stop you coming out if that's what you want."

"Okay?"

"I just think when you do, it shouldn't include him.

Keep it about yourself, then we can control the narrative. Maybe he can be introduced to the world as your partner at the end of the season, when people are bored with this story. If he's still around then, of course."

"You think he won't be?"

"You said it yourself. It's only sex. You aren't in love with him."

"Sorry, Papa. Is this hard to talk about?"

Papa sighed. "I don't want you to fall in love. You know why, but it's a risk." He shook his head.

"What?"

"It's hard to see my son as an adult sometimes. I know I am your agent and we discuss work all the time, but this is personal. Your mother would've loved... Well, I miss her and I wish she was here to help you navigate this." Did Papa just hint that Ma would've loved Hudson? Or just that she would've supported him in coming out?

"Thanks. I wish I'd known her."

"You are very like her, you know. When our discussions get heated, I feel her presence, as if there is a part of her still with us both."

"Only when we argue?" Ondrej laughed.

"No. You share her sense of humour too. And her driving style. She had an incredible ability to sense risk instinctively, and her reaction times were stunning. She would be so proud of you."

The doorbell rang, saving Ondrej from needing to respond. After Papa got up to answer the door and let in the room service, Ondrej wiped his eyes on the collar of the dressing gown. They ate breakfast quietly, and Ondrej was grateful that Papa didn't talk to him. It wasn't until he'd finished his coffee that he leaned back on the seat.

"What were you thinking around the timing?" Papa asked.

"Of making a formal announcement that I'm gay? Today?" Ondrej wanted to get it done, and there were ten days until he needed to be focused for Imola. Ten days that would become a media circus if he did this.

"Yes. It's good timing as there is time to process all the responses before Imola." Papa understood the schedule too.

"In a just world, it wouldn't matter. No one ever has to announce that they are heterosexual."

Papa reached out and patted him on the shoulder. "I'm sorry that the world is like this."

"It's the same world that pays me to drive very fast in an amazing car, so it's not all bad." Ondrej smiled, even though he didn't much feel like it.

"I have drafted a few different versions of a press release."

"You have?" Even though Papa had told him he was prepared for when Ondrej might be accidentally outed, he wasn't really expecting anything like this.

"I'll bring them up on my laptop and you can select which one feels most comfortable, or if you don't like any of them, we can workshop something else."

Ondrej nodded and focused on breathing slowly as he waited for Papa to grab his laptop and set it up. He tried not to think about how unfair it was that he even needed to do this, but the other side was to hide himself forever, and that option was no longer palatable.

"I've based these on other sports people making similar

announcements. Have a read through and pick one that fits your style."

Ondrej read through the different options slowly. Then read them again. It was all so clinical.

"You hate them all?"

"No. They are fine. Just boring and it grates that I need do this if I want to live openly."

"Most drivers are very private about their families."

"Yes, but they also take their wives to some of the events. I want that one day." He could imagine Hudson in a sharp suit walking into dinner with the royals at Monaco, or the end of season awards night, or standing beside him when next year's car gets unveiled.

"We can write something different if you want."

"Boring is probably best. How about this one?"

Series One has been part of my life for nearly eight years and I am grateful for the opportunities I've had in this sport. Today I proudly announce that I am gay. I'm thankful for the ongoing support of the team at Gamble Racing. I make this announcement knowing my pathway has been made easy by those who've fought for queer rights.

"Yes, that one is my favourite too." Papa nodded. "It's simple and clear and shows you have Socrates' support."

"I like the way it alludes to past gay athletes in S1 too. Socrates might be a major player, but there have been others who've had to hide themselves." Ondrej had flicked through Lucien Grenville's social media and he really didn't bother to hide the photos of himself with semi-naked men on beaches during the various breaks. And there were rumours about Freddy Hiptonstall, one of the press guys who used to be an S1 driver, too.

"Yes, like Mike Butler. He was a good friend of your mother's too."

"He was?"

"Yes. I suppose it was because she was a woman in a man's sport, and he didn't quite fit either."

"Makes sense. Let's do it. Send it out in the world." Ondrej leaned back in his seat and watched Papa send an email to his PA. He called her and gave instructions, and then it was done.

"Do you want me to call Socrates?"

"I'll do it." Ondrej picked up his phone to ring his boss, who answered after a couple of rings. "Good morning, Socrates."

"Ondrej. I hope this is urgent. It's early."

"I just posted a press release."

"You came out?"

"Yes."

"Congratulations. I wish I'd been able to do something like that when I was driving. Instead, it was the worst kept secret on the grid. Everyone knew! The law meant me and a couple of others couldn't really talk about it. You've done a good thing, Ondrej. I'm proud of you."

Ondrej smiled. "Thanks."

"Of course, someone clever is going to add this to the reason you left your last team and make a giant story from it. They will say no comment and then everyone will judge the situation. You'll have to plan to say something."

Ondrej didn't have to think to respond with a convenient lie. "Contracts prevent me from discussing that time in my life."

"Yeah, that's a good one. Stick with that. Their actions tell the story anyway."

"And me turning up here immediately with your support only reinforces it." Ondrej shook his head. This could get ugly fast. "JP supports me too."

"Ten days until Imola. I think that should be plenty of time to let this blow over and then you can focus on a good performance there. Will your cute red head be coming with you?"

Ondrej scratched his head. "My cute red head?" He glanced at Papa who was pointedly staring at his laptop. "His name is Hudson. Yes, like the car, so you should be able to remember that. And no, Papa thinks we should wait a while before going out in public together. Hudson has no media training and Papa worries about my brand."

"He worries too much. You two make a cute couple. The media will love photos of the two of you."

"I'd rather focus on Imola."

"Good. Ignore my teasing. The focus is what I'm paying you for." Socrates boomed out a laugh and Ondrej wondered if Jaxxon was right. Could it be time for a new Team Principal? No. Socrates was a thrill seeker, an occasional alcoholic, and sometimes a little wild, but Gamble was his team. He was the owner, CEO, and Team Principal. It was his money on the line all the time. Socrates was well within his rights to spend his own money on his own team however it pleased him.

"I'd better go then."

"Yes. Go. Get on the simulator and win me a race." Socrates hung up, leaving Ondrej staring at the stream of notifications for missed calls on his phone. One text made him grin.

Alex: Awesome bravery. Makes it easier for the rest of us.

There was one person Ondrej needed to hear from, so he sent him a quick message.

CHAPTER 18

udson groaned as his phone dinged with a new message. Ondrej was in Singapore and probably hadn't checked the time zone back to England. Luckily he was an early riser and while five in the morning was slightly too early, even for him, he didn't mind too much. He put on his glasses and thumbed open his phone to read the message.

Ondrej: I've just sent out a press release.

What was he supposed to do with that text? About what? Hudson's phone rang, so he answered it.

"Ondrej." He hoped nothing was wrong. Ondrej hadn't been injured in yesterday's race, so it couldn't be that.

"Sorry. I realised I couldn't put this in writing."

Didn't a press release do exactly that? There must be something more that couldn't be in the media. Hudson's mouth dried out.

"Sounds serious."

"The press release has just been sent out to media. Papa's PA will put it on my socials in a few minutes."

"About?" Hudson needed confirmation. His heart was a little unsteady when he didn't know what the press release was about.

"I've decided to come out."

All his anxiety fled, replaced with a joy that surrounded Hudson in a blanket of warmth. "Congratulations."

"Yeah."

"What's the matter? You don't sound happy. Did someone force you into this?"

"No. It's my decision."

"Then?"

"It's just that I shouldn't have to, you know. No one announces that they are straight. Did JP put out a formal press release when he first kissed a woman, letting everyone know that he'd figured out his sexuality and it was the default one? No."

"I know. It sucks that the world puts this burden on you."

"Thank you. The other thing is that we aren't going to mention you."

Hudson swayed, glad he was still in bed and not standing, as all the blood in his head drained. "Why?" He wasn't sure he wanted to be mentioned—the S1 press scared him —but to be deliberately excluded hurt too. He'd even been excluded from the whole discussion and decision; Ondrej told him after it was already out there in the world. So much for partnership.

"I wanted to—" Ondrej sighed and Hudson breathed in. It was going to be alright. "Papa felt that it was one thing to make this announcement without complicating things. And to be frank, once he mentioned that you aren't used to being in the spotlight, I agree with him."

"What do you mean?" Hudson's emotions were swirling all over the place. He literally didn't know what to feel, and the unsteady churn in his gut reflected the rushing noise in his ears.

"S1 media is intense at the best of times. This is going to be an utter circus. I have years of practice at this. You don't. I know it's tough because—"

"I want to stand beside you and support you."

"You are. Just not in public yet. Let this settle down first, and we can quietly go out together later."

Hudson swallowed back the frustration at being asked to keep his relationship with Ondrej a secret and tried to focus on the important thing. Ondrej was making a big step.

"You are very brave to do this. S1 hasn't always been good to you on this point..."

"Socrates said the same thing."

"Yes. People will guess at what happened at your former team. Some will side with them. Some with you."

Ondrej growled, the guttural noise echoing in Hudson's ear.

"Think of it this way. This announcement will show you who matters." Hudson tried to not cringe, even though Ondrej couldn't see him. He was always better at giving advice than listening to it.

"It should be live now. I'm glad I don't have social media on my phone."

"Do you want me to look for you?"

"No. It's done. People are going to say what they want." Ondrej scoffed. "My phone is ringing."

"Do you want to get it?"

"No. It can go to voice mail. Not many people know this number, only a few on the team, and Papa, and some friends."

"I wish I could be with you."

Ondrej huffed out a loud breath. "Nah. Singapore is hot and sticky. The opposite of England."

"I'd like to experience that one day."

"Come with me next year."

Hudson wished he could believe Ondrej meant that. Between the nasty comment he'd made months ago back at Socrates' mansion and how he'd stopped Hudson being part of today's announcement, it was hard to trust that Ondrej wanted this thing between them to be long term.

"Okay."

"And Hudson?"

"Yeah?"

"If I don't call for the next few days, it's not you. Once this press release is out, things might get a little busy."

Hudson closed his eyes and swallowed. "I understand."

"Thanks. I miss you." Ondrej hung up before Hudson could say more. He sat down and started to scroll social media.

Formula 1 has been part of my life for nearly eight years and I am grateful for the opportunities I've had in this sport. Today I proudly announce that I am gay. I'm thankful for the ongoing support of the team at Gamble Racing. I make this announcement knowing my pathway has been made easy by those who've fought for queer rights.

The first story had only been online for three minutes and it already had 40,000 likes and over 6,000 comments. Ondrej hadn't been wrong when he said it was going to be a wild ride over the next few days. Hudson probably shouldn't ask this, but he really wanted to be with Ondrej as he navigated the world's response to his statement.

Hudson: Want me to come to you?

Ondrej: Yes. Monaco tomorrow.

Hudson booked a flight online for the next day and began to pack. Ondrej was going to need someone by his side as this story unfolded.

Thankfully, the promised summer storm didn't arrive until after Hudson's plane had landed. He stood on Ondrej's balcony looking out over the bay as the clouds rolled in and dumped an unseasonable amount of rain on the city. He'd managed to walk past the crowded group of media photographers outside the building, unrecognised by them, and he made a mental note to thank Mr D'Grieg for not including him in Ondrej's press release. One of them had asked him about Ondrej, and he'd simply frowned and said, "Who?" which had been enough for them all to ignore him.

"It's impressive, huh." Ondrej leaned against Hudson's shoulder as they stared out at the storm.

"Yes."

"I'm glad you are here."

Hudson wasn't sure how to respond. "Mackenzie wasn't happy about it."

"About?"

"Me coming here. She is concerned that you aren't

being fair to me, requiring us to stay private. But I don't mind." Hudson had argued with her before he'd come. She'd accused Ondrej of keeping Hudson like a pet, only calling him when he needed him and ignoring him the rest of the time. Hudson didn't see it that way. Ondrej had a high-pressure job that involved lots of travel; it wasn't that he used Hudson when it suited him, more than he couldn't be around all the time. Besides, this visit was Hudson's choice.

"It is unfair to you. And me. I want to go out in public with you."

"Why don't we?"

"Says the guys who was stunned by the press hanging out at my front door."

"Yeah, okay. I'm not ready for that." Hudson wondered if he should ask for some media training. "But now that people know, they are going to look for me, or rather, people like me."

"Meaning?"

"Men who visit your apartment block regularly. It's only a matter of time before someone notices that we spend a lot of time together."

"Does that bother you?"

"No. I just think your father is right. I'm under prepared for this. I've been a nobody all my life." And if he was honest, Hudson wasn't sure about their relationship status either. Was he Ondrej's boyfriend? They'd been together for months now on a casual basis. Hudson swallowed down a gasp; they'd never discussed it and he suddenly freaked out that they weren't exclusive. Hudson had been, but Ondrej travelled all the time for work. He must have opportunities. No. He wasn't like that.

"What's the matter?"

"What do you mean?"

"You've just stepped away from me and folded your arms."

Hudson glanced down. "It's nothing. Never mind."

Ondrej gave him such a look that Hudson nearly spilled all his uncertainty on a shaky breath, but he couldn't. Being so insecure would make him look pathetic. The doorbell rang and Ondrej shook his head.

"We will talk about this." He walked back inside, and Hudson forced himself to relax his arms. He turned and followed Ondrej inside the apartment, trying to ignore the way his brain spun with possible ways to explain his concerns, but none of them were any good. All of them made him sound needy or desperate or just pathetic.

"JP is coming up."

"Okay." It would be good to have something else to do, to think about, now that Hudson's anxiety had decided to activate. "Do you want me to go?"

"What? No. Why would you think that?"

"Never mind—" Hudson shouldn't have said anything.

"Hey. Did the press say something?"

"I shouldn't be here."

"Hudson. I want you here."

"But it's just sex." Hudson's lungs hurt as he tried to breathe.

Ondrej rolled his eyes. "S1 is rubbing off on you."

"What?"

"You've taken something I said months ago, combined

it with Papa wanting to protect you from the press, and decided that I don't care about you? Am I right?"

Hudson mumbled. "Something like that."

"I want you here."

"Okay."

Ondrej kissed him hard. "I want you."

Hudson bit his bottom lip, rather than blurt out, 'for now'. A loud knock at the door interrupted and as soon as Ondrej walked to open the door for JP, Hudson let out a huge sigh. Shit. He'd overreacted and still hadn't talked about the issue. Was he Ondrej's boyfriend, or just a temporary fuck-buddy on call whenever Ondrej wanted him? All his life people had abandoned him, so it made sense that Ondrej would do the same as soon as things became difficult.

JP shook his head as he walked inside, spraying water like a drowned puppy. "There is so much press outside your door. I brushed them off as best I could."

"Now everyone know that you are a gay man's friend."

"I am already a gay man's brother, not that it's anyone's business." JP waved his hand dismissively.

"Did you tell the press that?"

"Of course I did. They are making a silly fuss over something that doesn't matter. It doesn't change the way you drive."

Ondrej laughed, and the sound washed over Hudson. "No. I'm paid to drive. Nothing else is relevant."

"True, true, but the world is silly and they care about things that don't matter." JP slapped Ondrej on the back. "Hey, have you got a towel or something?"

"Yeah, in the bathroom. Through that door."

"He's a good friend." Hudson said. "At least the press are getting wet standing in the rain outside your building."

"All to try and get more information about something boring. They should be at home in bed. This rain is perfect sleeping weather."

JP walked back into the lounge, rubbing his hair with a towel. "Who is sleeping with who? Do I want to know what you were talking about when I left the room?"

"What?"

"I overheard you say 'sleeping with her'."

Ondrej laughed. "No. Sleeping weather. This rain is perfect sleeping weather."

"Ah."

"Don't be so dirty, JP."

Hudson felt like an intruder. "Anyone want a drink? Water, tea, beer? Um, soup?"

"Soup would be amazing." JP threw the towel on the couch and plonked down on it. "This rain is something else. Doesn't usually rain at this time of year."

Soup. What the fuck? Why did he say that? Now Hudson needed to figure out how to make soup. He opened the fridge and surreptitiously pulled his phone out of his back pocket to look up a recipe that might work with what he found in the fridge.

"There are some tins in the pantry."

Hudson jumped as Ondrej placed his hand on his back. "Thanks."

"I thought you knew when you mentioned soup as an option. I didn't expect to see you in the fridge. Are you looking up recipes on your phone?"

"I was nervous." Hudson swallowed. He felt like a

naughty toddler who'd been caught drawing pictures on the wall, just like Henry had last week.

"Because of JP."

"Because he thinks I'm your boyfriend."

"You are."

Hudson spun around so fast he nearly knocked himself out on the fridge door. "I am?"

"Of course. What do you think we've been doing for the last few months? It's been six months since we met, and you've basically lived here with me between races since before the mid-season break."

"But you said…"

"I said a lot of silly things while I was working this out. Hudson, make the soup. I'll chat to JP, and later we can sort this out."

Hudson nodded awkwardly. Ondrej reached up and held both of Hudson's cheeks and gently kissed him. It was more than Hudson deserved, but he really wanted to lean into it and believe what Ondrej was telling him.

"Let me make soup. Don't let JP get cold." Hudson had to do something before he ran away in a panic, and that wasn't going to help anyone. People left him. He was loyal, and he'd continue to be loyal by making soup, or whatever. Twenty minutes later, he served up the soup on the small dining table along with a loaf of fresh bread that Ondrej had had delivered in this morning's groceries, and some cheese because it looked pretty.

"How domestic, Hudson."

"I live with my sister and her family, and we all share the cooking duties."

"Right, I remember that you said you were a foster kid. You must be self-sufficient," JP said.

"I guess so."

"JP. Leave him alone." Ondrej rested his hand on Hudson's thigh under the table, a comforting connection.

"It's fine. I have a little cabin in their back yard, so I'm not in their business all the time. Mackenzie and Brian have twins, so their life is a bit hectic at times. I like helping them out because they've made the family that Mackenzie and I never had."

"And you get to be the awesome fun uncle!" JP laughed. "My brother and his husband are thinking of adopting, so I want to be the fun uncle too."

"You don't want kids?" Ondrej asked, and Hudson cringed. It was such a fraught question.

"No. Sofia and I both travel so much for work. If we had kids, they'd end up being brought up by nannies, which isn't fair on anyone. Maybe once we both retire, but then we'll be old, so I don't think it's the life for us."

"Fair enough. I'm in awe of Mackenzie and how well she's adjusted to being a mum, after everything she went through herself. Her kids are so lucky, and funny too."

"Yes. They are very cute," Ondrej said, and Hudson remembered that he'd met them already.

"The other day, Henry drew on the wall. Mackenzie was so mad. She growled at him and pointed at the painting and said, 'what do you think this is?' and Henry just looked at her."

"Was he scared?"

"What? No, of course not. He said, 'dog'."

JP bellowed with laughter. "He'd drawn a dog? So literal."

"So cheeky. He knew he wasn't allowed to draw there. Mackenzie took it all in her stride. She said, 'next time, draw the dog on paper. Let's clean this one off the wall'. She handed him a cleaning rag and they cleaned it up together. I mean, Mackenzie would've done most of the cleaning, because three-year-olds are hopeless at that type of thing, but Henry tried and that's what mattered."

"She sounds like she's a great mum."

"She's a great person." Hudson would need to ring her back later and apologise for being upset with her; once he'd clarified things with Ondrej and he could give her some certainty. She was worried about him. Ondrej squeezed his thigh and changed the subject to some car related thing and him and JP got into a heated debate about a technical rule that Hudson had no clue about. He didn't mind. It was nice to sit here and eat soup on a warm rainy day with the doors open to the balcony and listen to people being passionate about their job.

CHAPTER 19

JAPAN

Ondrej sat alone in another hotel room. He'd let the team down today. Days like this were the hardest to take because it was completely his fault. The only good part was that he'd kept the car out of the wall when he'd spun off at Spoon Curve and had been able to re-join the race. His phone rang. Socrates. He was tempted to ignore it.

"Hello."

"Come to dinner with me."

It was the last thing Ondrej wanted to do, but when the team owner summoned, he was obliged to attend. "Okay. Where?"

"Meet me in the hotel lobby and we can go from there."

"I'll be down in a bit." Ondrej would rather wallow, but he recognised that it wasn't healthy. Instead he changed out of the casual sweatpants he'd thrown on after his shower and put on jeans and a nice shirt.

"Ondrej. Over here." Socrates had commandeered a table in the corner of the hotel bar. Jaxxon, Paulo, Victor, and Paulo's race engineer Monica all sat with him. Ondrej slid onto a chair and barely had time to put his phone on the table when a waiter asked him for what he wanted. He ordered an orange juice, noting that Socrates ordered himself another wine.

"This fucking car is so inconsistent," Socrates said. "Slow in Singapore, then a solid result at Imola, and now this crap."

Ondrej had finished fifth at Imola, and Paulo had driven well to come from P11 in quali to finish in seventh.

"This crap ... You mean this race which was my fault, not the car's fault." Ondrej had qualified in second; his first time on the front row for Gamble. But he'd pushed too hard and lost the back end at Spoon on the third lap, spinning out of the race. By the time he had the car facing the right way again, the whole field had passed him, and he'd had to fight his way back from last to twelfth.

"You pushed a little hard going into Spoon. It's an easy mistake to make here." Jaxxon's soothing answer didn't help much.

"Are you fighting with that man of yours?" Socrates asked.

"What? This has nothing to do with that. Can you keep out of my private business?" Ondrej frowned.

"Ah come on. One gay to another. We can tease each other."

"It's not teasing if it only goes one way." Ondrej wasn't going to look at the others around the table to see how they responded.

"If that's how this works, do I get to tease Ondrej too?" Jaxxon asked.

"What?" Ondrej blurted, only realising a split second later that Socrates spoke at the same time as him too. Ondrej twisted towards his race engineer.

"I'm bi. If only queer people get to tease you, by order of the boss, then that includes me too." Jaxxon's grin was huge and Ondrej slapped him on the shoulder.

"Damn. Anyone else have something to admit?" Ondrej laughed, fully expecting Victor, Monica, and Paulo to say nothing.

"I think we must be the queerest team on the grid." Victor spread his hands wide and grinned. "I am also gay."

"You've never mentioned that." Socrates sounded affronted, which made Ondrej laugh.

"No. S1 isn't exactly the environment to talk about it. I assumed you'd knew, given that you gave the job of Chief Engineer to me. I'm only thirty-one; all my peers are in their late forties and early fifties."

"I needed someone young and fresh to take over from Reginald, so it was obvious to him that I wasn't replacing him with someone like him. We've been tight friends for a long time."

"No one is questioning your loyalty, Socrates. But perhaps your gaydar is off if you didn't pick Victor," Jaxxon teased.

"Ha. I suspected about you though. Bisexual, huh?"

Ondrej leaned back in his chair and contemplated this collection of people. He'd always been comfortable around them and maybe this was a key reason why. "Hudson knew."

"About?" Socrates asked.

"Jaxxon. They had a good chat about Hudson's business after Monza. At first he was worried your questions meant you knew about us—"

"Mate, you brought your boyfriend to a team dinner and had a flimsy excuse about him doing research for your family. We all knew." Jaxxon laughed.

"I didn't." Paulo spoke for the first time tonight. "I took it as face value. Why wouldn't I?" He was so young and naïve that the comment didn't surprise Ondrej at all. Monica glanced sideways at her driver but didn't say anything. She wasn't much of a talker; brief and precise in her work, but Ondrej really wanted to know what she thought about Paulo's comment.

"See. Anyway, Jaxxon, stop changing the subject. Hudson noticed that you were very pleased when he mentioned his business is queer friendly, and he wondered."

"It's not a crime to be bisexual."

"Not anymore." Socrates' comment sobered Ondrej. "You boys have it much easier now." Silence descended on the table, and everyone stared into their drinks.

"It was very brave to come out, Ondrej," Paulo said. Ondrej turned to the twenty-one-year-old rookie and nodded.

"Sometimes necessity leads to bravery."

"I could never. My parents would..." Paulo trailed off; his eyes wide open. "They wouldn't approve of me having dinner with all of you. Only Socrates' because he's the team owner."

"I don't understand. They are one of our biggest sponsors. Surely they know Socrates is gay."

"They bought my seat. No one else wanted someone whose best result was fourth on the S2 table, and they knew

Socrates needed the money. There were at least three drivers faster and better than me who deserved a seat before me." Paulo paused for breath, as Monica squinted at her driver. "Without their money, I'm just another wanna-be driver who isn't quite good enough for S1. When we talk, they remind me of my obligations as a good Catholic, and to make sure I'm not being corrupted by Socrates. I'm supposed to be showing you how to be a real man."

"What a lot of bullshit toxic masculinity. You are a damned good driver." Monica glared at everyone as if expecting them to disagree with her. No one would dare, and it was on the tip of Ondej's tongue to say that her experience as a race engineer was one of the major reasons Paulo had adjusted so quickly to S1 this season.

"Hell. I'm sorry." Ondrej focused on the important message for Paulo. Papa had never put a lot of pressure on him to succeed, always understanding that Ondrej needed to love what he did to be great at it.

"That sucks, man," Jaxxon said.

"I am aware of their beliefs. Running a racing team is expensive and sometimes ethics need to be blurred to gain the finances necessary," Socrates said.

"Don't sacrifice too much."

"I'm not so easily intimidated. Getting rid of Reginald was part of the sponsorship deal, and it pleases me a great deal to learn that his replacement is gay. Paulo's father selected Victor; he was very insistent that Victor was the engineer who could build a car to make his son a champion."

Paulo coughed. "I know. That's why I assumed Victor was straight."

"Are you uncomfortable sitting here with four queer men?" Jaxxon asked.

Monica coughed. "Hey."

"And a straight woman."

"Just because I'm divorced doesn't make me straight."

Socrates slapped his forehead. "You too?"

Monica smirked. "Well, I did have an affair with your niece Xenia before I was married…" She trailed off as Socrates' eyes widened and his jaw dropped.

Victor raised his eyebrows. "Shut it, you two. Jaxxon, you should know better than to ask Paulo such a question. The poor kid is already under enough pressure with his family financing the whole team."

"Did you know they'd hand-picked you?" Jaxxon asked Victor.

"No. I was surprised to get Socrates' job offer, but this makes some sense. In my previous role, I worked with Paulo's S3 team before Paulo moved into S2."

"Father's greatest skill is to find talent. You should be flattered," Paulo said. Ondrej leaned back, listening carefully to the discussion. He hadn't realised that Paulo's family had such a big influence on the team; surely Socrates had taken a huge financial risky by opening having a gay driver on the team when the major sponsors were Catholic bigots.

"Should we? How would your father react if he knew he was sponsoring a bunch of queers?" Jaxxon asked.

"He ignores facts that he doesn't like."

Jaxxon's eyebrows rose so high he looked comical.

"I only want to race, and their money has given me the chance. Senior likes having his name associated with a big brand like S1 and being able to show off his famous son. If I have to be a certain way to keep them pleased, then it's a small sacrifice to be here." Paulo's face was a little flushed. "I could never be brave like Ondrej. There is too much at stake."

"You are gay too?" Jaxxon smirked. "Oh, that would be too deliciously ironic."

Paulo shook his head slightly and his nostrils flared. "Please don't ask me that in public where anyone might overhear." He beckoned Monica closer and whispered something in her ear. She whispered back and Paulo nodded grimly.

"I can't. Don't even mention we had this conversation. Please. I just need to drive. I can't risk him taking away the funds."

"I'm your race engineer, Paulo. It's my job to do whatever it takes to make you as fast and focused as possible. All race engineers know too much about their drivers. And your situation is what someone might call being caught between a rock and a hard place." Monica had a determined expression that Ondrej had learned meant she was going to do everything she could to protect her rookie driver. Ondrej didn't need to know what Paulo had said. He could guess. The rookie was queer in some way and couldn't be because his rich religious parents would likely remove all their money, and Paulo was scared he wouldn't have a seat without their money. S1 was brutal that way. Not many drivers made it to the top without financial backing. Papa had a trust fund thanks to his grandfather investing in Norway's oil industry, and Ondrej had a racing pedigree to boot. He'd made it into S1 on his own ability, although the money had made the pathway up through the junior ranks a lot easier and his mother's name had opened doors when he'd needed them opened.

"Don't stress, Paulo." Socrates shrugged as if Paulo hadn't admitted something to Monica that he was too scared to say out loud. "You got a podium in your rookie season. Less than ten drivers in history have done that. And I've just signed you for the next two seasons. Your seat is safe."

"You'd risk my parent's sponsorship money?" Paulo asked, and when Socrates didn't answer, he shrugged. "I thought as much. It's better if I focus on racing."

"You are young. There is plenty of time to work out who you are later." Socrates said. "And more importantly, how to navigate through a world that isn't always welcoming."

The whole conversation made Ondrej grateful for Papa's support. He couldn't imagine the pressure of trying to live up to impossible family expectations without that support. Papa had always pushed him to honour Ma's legacy, and there'd been a few years as a young teenager when he wasn't sure if he loved racing or if he was doing it for Papa's dreams or Ma's memory, but he'd resolved that question after a break away from racing. He missed it, missed the thrill and the risk, and the feel of a car at speed. He'd missed being really fucking good at something, and as soon as he'd stepped back into a car, he'd known this was his life. Papa was clever, really, allowing him the break when he was a teen, because he'd come back hungrier afterwards. If he'd pushed too hard, Ondrej would probably have given up.

Hudson couldn't focus on work. He'd woken up early to watch the race in Japan on telly with Brian, who was surprisingly invested in all the S1 team politics for someone who worked in environmental management. The time zones meant the race was in the afternoon in Japan, which was very early in the morning in England. When Ondrej had spun out at that long corner, Hudson had held his breath, but the car didn't hit the wall, and Ondrej casually spun the car back around and re-joined the race. Perhaps Hudson wasn't cut out for caring for someone who risked their life in their work because the what if scenarios grew heavier and heavier as he sat at his desk, staring out the window at the overcast sky.

They hadn't really seen each other since that rainy day in Monaco after the race in Singapore when Ondrej had sent out his press release. After JP had left, Ondrej had been open about wanting to be Hudson's boyfriend and make their relationship formally recognised, if only between the two of them. He'd talked about how he wanted to protect him from the wildness of the media and promised to set up a dinner with Sofia sometime soon so Hudson would have someone to talk to who understood what it was like to be a driver's partner. It hadn't happened yet, because of the S1 schedule. Ondrej had rushed off to Italy, and then gone directly from there to Japan. Hudson tried not to let negative thoughts sink in over the past few weeks. He spoke to Ondrej on the phone regularly. And he focused on his own work. The Bugatti mystery was looking like it wasn't going anywhere. He'd found several people who might have old letters sent by Mr D'Grieg's grandfather about the car, but so far, none of the connections he'd made had come up with anything. He was running out of options.

After the race, he'd eaten breakfast with Bruce, then come back to his cabin to work. His phone rang. Ondrej. The bitterness that had been growing on his tongue disappeared.

"Hey. Are you okay?"

"Physically, yes. It was just a silly spin."

"And emotionally?"

"I fucked up."

"Oh?" Hudson's already anxious thoughts spun like Ondrej's car. Out of control. What was Ondrej about to confess? Obviously that Hudson wasn't worthy of him. Now he was an openly gay S1 driver, he must have many people better than Hudson to pick from.

"I came into Spoon too hard, hit the curb inside the apex, and spun. It was my fault."

A racing mistake, nothing else. "I saw. I'm glad you were okay."

"Lots of runoff area there." Ondrej sighed, heavily through the phone.

"What's the matter?"

"Seriously." Ondrej sighed again. "I forget you know nothing about my job. I completely fucked up. I was in P2, going well, and I pushed too hard into Spoon. It was unnecessary."

"You are angry at yourself?"

"Yes. Very. I threw away a podium."

Hudson had no response to that. If he shared his own

anxious nonsense about Ondrej moving on from him, well, it really wouldn't help.

"Are you there?"

"Yes. I just didn't know what to say. I'm sorry." His inadequate response only made his own feelings worse. Ondrej should probably find himself a proper boyfriend. One who understood his job and could help him when something like this happened.

"You don't need to be sorry for my fuck up. I missed the apex."

"This is about the spin?"

"Yes. What part of I threw away a podium with my own mistake don't you understand?"

"I understand. Look, I often blame myself too hard. And I know that it's annoying as hell to have someone give advice when that happens."

"What advice could you give anyway?"

"If you were listening, I said I wouldn't give you advice."

"Good. I don't want it."

Hudson wished they weren't in different countries. "I'd rather—" Not fight.

"What? Sink to your knees and suck my cock. I'd rather that too."

Hudson gasped. "That beats any of my suggestions."

"Put your camera on and show me." Ondrej's command blended with the mess in Hudson's head. He quickly realised that Ondrej didn't want him to show him his tongue licking the screen in lieu of licking Ondrej's cock. Come on, brain. Ondrej probably wanted to see Hudson's body?

"Okay." Hudson moved from his desk to the couch, then switched his phone from audio only to video.

"You look delightfully rumpled." Ondrej's smile filled the screen. "And no glasses. Cute."

"Um?"

"And all flustered. Did I do that?"

"It's my natural state."

"Oh, feisty. I miss you." Ondrej's simple acknowledgement sent a delicious flush over Hudson's skin. He'd spent the morning stressing that Ondrej would discard him for someone better, and to hear that soothed away all his silly worries.

"I—" Hudson almost offered to travel with Ondrej for the rest of the season. He'd just get in the way of Ondrej's job and given how passionately upset with his driving he was right now, it was the last thing Ondrej would want. Some guy hanging around, offering nothing but this.

"You, what?"

"I've never done this before."

"Phone sex? Neither." Ondrej sounded so confident though, as if it didn't matter that this was new to him. Hopefully his ego would carry them both through and it wouldn't be as awkward as Hudson was worried about.

"So, what now?"

"Obviously you get naked and show me."

"Show you the process or after?"

Ondrej sighed. "Put the phone somewhere, aim the camera at yourself, and get undressed. I want to see you getting yourself ready for me. You gave me a show once before…"

"But I could see you then. I could tell that you wanted me."

"I want you. I want to see you stroke yourself until I say stop."

Hudson's cock sprang to life. "Yes." His nerves fled at Ondrej's command, wanting to take himself to the edge as many times as Ondrej told him to. He put the phone on a cushion, pointing towards the wall, and clambered off the couch to strip off his shirt.

"You were in bed when I called?" Ondrej asked.

"No, we watched the race early, and now I'm working."

"This will be the perfect way to get you away from that computer for a while." His confidence wrapped around Hudson like a hug, and he pulled his shirt off over his head. "No pants?"

"I have shorts on." Summer was fading but this little cabin was warm enough that he didn't need to wear pants just yet.

"I know." Ondrej growled a little. "Hold yourself. Tight around the base."

Hudson obeyed with a shiver. "What about you?"

"I will watch only. It's my punishment for driving badly today."

Hudson frowned. "Is that what you want?"

"It's what I deserve."

Hudson leaned closer to his phone screen to try and figure out Ondrej's expression.

"Give me a show, Hudson. Touch your lips, like I would kiss them."

Hudson obeyed. It felt so awkward and weird with only Ondrej's voice to guide him.

"Yes, like that. Focus on the touch. Wet your finger."

Hudson sucked his fingers into his mouth, then ran them along his bottom lip. Ondrej's gasp was exactly what he needed to stop the flow of negativity in his head. He leaned in closer to the screen to give Ondrej a close-up view and did it again. This time he obeyed Ondrej's voice, giving in to the sensation as he pretended it was Ondrej's rough fingers sliding over his bottom lip.

"Now lower but take your time. You can't touch that lovely cock of yours until I say."

Hudson groaned. "Why do I obey you?" He trailed his fingers down his throat and spread his hands over his chest.

"You like it. Grab that nipple. Torture it." Ondrej's nostrils flared and Hudson wanted to close his eyes to absorb the sensation as he twisted both his nipples. "Harder."

Hudson twisted them again, harder this time, and he nearly fell over as pleasure shot through his body. He sat on the couch, and his phone toppled over. "Shit. Sorry." He grabbed the phone and propped it up again, making sure it was secure. Then he sat with his legs crossed, facing the phone.

"Focus on me, Hudson. I want to see your mouth when you stroke yourself."

Hudson wrapped his fingers around his cock.

"Greedy. Now let go. Place your hands on your knees."

Hudson growled as Ondrej's gaze drilled into him. He stroked himself once, because he couldn't help it, and Ondrej's eyes narrowed.

"I saw that. No cheating. Move your hands now."

Hudson swallowed but did as he was told. "Done." His voice was rough.

"You beautiful man. Now touch yourself everywhere except your cock. Show me everything."

Hudson moved his hands slowly up his thighs as he contemplated Ondrej's command. Did he mean to give Hudson the option of cupping his balls, or fingering himself? What would Ondrej do if Hudson disobeyed him? Better yet, he'd give Ondrej his favourite things. He reached up with one hand and pushed his fingers through his hair. The shallow breath from Ondrej was everything Hudson wanted. So he did it again, slower this time, letting his hair flop over his hand, then as Ondrej opened his mouth, Hudson grabbed his own hair and pulled. Ondrej's gasp filled the air.

"Yes. Do that again."

Hudson was happy to oblige, especially when Ondrej's intense gaze glazed over. He bit his bottom lip to stop himself smiling at Ondrej's response, and that only increased the hazy look on Ondrej's face. Oh. He should try that in person sometime.

"Put your other hand on your cock. Stroke it lightly."

Hudson obeyed, leaning back a little, so Ondrej had the full view on his screen. He wished he had abs because when Ondrej did this, his stomach rippled. Hudson's just looked flat with no definition. Merely thinking about seeing Ondrej's fit body pushed him right to the edge and he closed his eyes.

"Look at me."

Of course he obeyed, and the way Ondrej stared back at him through the screen had him gasping for breath.

"You are close?"

"Yes. Please. Let me."

"Hudson." The soft tone cut into Hudson's desire. He didn't want to disappoint Ondrej, so he stopped moving his hand and tried to think of anything else. It was impossible with Ondrej's intense dark blue eyes focused on him. "Hudson."

"Yes?"

"You can come now."

Relief rushed through his veins and he stroked himself hard, twice, before he came in long strands over his belly and chest. His head fell backwards and he breathed hard.

"My Hudson. All painted for me." Ondrej's voice rasped and Hudson lifted his head to look at him. Ondrej's face was flushed, and his mouth hung open. As Hudson stared, Ondrej breathed in deep, his chest rising.

"Well, good night." Ondrej's voice changed from desperate and breathy into an uncaring casualness that sent prickles all over Hudson's skin.

"Wait."

"For?"

"What about you?"

"I'm fine. Like I said, I fucked up today and this is my punishment." Ondrej's eyes narrowed.

"I don't understand."

"I'm not going to come until I can touch you."

"Seriously?"

"Yes. It will teach me control." Ondrej's frown was the only indicator that he didn't want to do this, quite frankly, batshit idea. Hudson swallowed. How was he supposed to react to this? His whole body was sated and he wanted to snooze for a while, but this conversation had taken a very confusing turn.

"Um, if you think that's best?"

"I do. Good night. Hudson. Thank you." The phone disconnected and Hudson sat there alone on his couch, rather awkward for the middle of the day, covered in his own come. He closed his eyes, unable to calculate when they'd see each other again. He probably should clean himself up and try to get some work done.

CHAPTER 20

Ondrej had been back in Monaco for a couple of days, and he itched to call Hudson. He hadn't been wrong when he'd told Hudson he wanted to withhold from release until he saw Hudson again. He needed to practice control; it would benefit his racing. He used to do it during the season when he drove for his old team. Hudson was so giving, so keen to obey him, and it was a precious gift to watch him follow Ondrej's instructions. He'd been so uncomfortable at first with his pale skin flushed pink and blotchy. And then he'd warmed up to the task and obeyed so beautifully. On the other hand, Ondrej had to be in the States in less than ten days; hardly enough time to invite Hudson here. They'd end up with only a few days together. Fuck it. He booked Hudson a flight and then sent him a text.

Ondrej: Check your emails. For ten long minutes, Ondrej paced the room waiting for a reply. If only he had social media to pass the time, but from the summary he'd had from Papa on his latest announcement, social media was the last place he wanted to spend any time. Some of the drivers managed their own accounts and loved it, always posting photos of themselves in cool places, or whatever. He only knew because they showed him sometimes, but he didn't want to spend the time dedicated to dealing with all the comments from fans. It probably made him a bit of a dick. Papa employed someone to run his social media, and that in itself was weird, because fans literally thought that his personality matched whatever brand his social media manager created for him.

Hudson: You have to stop buying me things.

Ondrej: I want you here.

Hudson: Fine. See you tomorrow.

Ondrej: You could try to sound excited.

Hudson: Ha. I want to see you. I don't want to feel like I owe you.

Ondrej: Having you here will make me happy. I'd buy you a horse if you let me.

Hudson: Don't. Please.

Ondrej: I'm kidding. Fuck.

Hudson: See you tomorrow.

Ondrej would rather call because the clipped use of words in text messages always made him wonder if someone was annoyed with him. But then Hudson sent him a couple of smiley faces and a gif of him spinning off at Spoon a few days ago. The gif made him smile and he scoffed out loud. A few months ago, something like this would've pissed him off. What had Hudson done to him that he could find his own mistakes funny? Hudson had infiltrated his life and made everything better. The dogged loneliness from last season had gone, replaced by a warm happiness. It wasn't just because he was getting results at work. He belonged with Hudson.

Ondrej: I can't believe someone made that.

Hudson: Yeah, what a world we live in.

The problem with seeing himself in a gif was that he could see exactly where he'd fucked up going into the corner. On repeat. He put his phone down, screen side down, so he didn't see that anymore. Just knowing that Hudson would be here tomorrow filled his chest with warmth. The apartment was empty without him, somehow suffocating him, so he grabbed his keys and put on his shoes. A long walk might help ease this frustration inside him.

By the time he'd headed down in the elevator and opened the front door to the building his head already felt clearer.

"Ondrej D'Grieg." A lone reporter stood on the front steps. All the others had given up long ago. The person had bright purple hair.

"Yeah?"

"Sam Clippington from the online magazine Queernesszine. Can we talk?"

"I've said everything I want to say."

"We'd really love to run an in-depth interview with you. We have a lot of young readers who'd love to know they aren't alone in pursuing sports while queer."

The idea appealed to Ondrej. He would've loved to have read something like that when he first started out, and he knew that Paulo needed to hear it too. "Let me call someone first. Do you have a card?"

"Yes." They pulled out a card out of their shirt pocket.

Sam Clippington

Queernesszine

European Correspondent

they/them

"They/them pronouns?"

"Yes. I hope that's okay."

"Of course. I might be a sports person, but I'm not totally ignorant." Ondrej noticed the card has a USA address. "They sent you here from the States? Why not wait until the race next weekend?"

"Does this mean you'll talk to me?"

Ondrej held up one finger and pulled his phone out of his pocket. There was one person he needed to call before he agreed to this.

"Papa."

"Ondrej. How are you holding up?"

"Well enough. Trying to focus on the next race now." The mistake at Suzuka had been made. There was no point dwelling on it and letting it affect his next race.

"Good."

"I've been approached by a queer publication who want to do an in-depth interview with me." Even through the phone, Ondrej could feel Papa switch from father-mode to agent-mode. He grinned. The journalist's shoulders straightened, and their eyes sharpened hopefully.

"It might be a good opportunity. I know you don't want to dwell on this, but it might be a way to build new fans for S1," Papa said.

"I'm not going to do this to sell more hats."

Sam chuckled and looked away.

"What would it entail?"

"Hold on." Ondrej pulled the phone away from his ear. "What would the interview include, and can I edit it before it goes out in the world?"

"It'll be a profile of your career and some questions about why you decided to come out now, and what challenges you've had."

Ondrej repeated that to Papa who said what Ondrej was thinking. "Don't talk about your old team. Never burn a bridge in S1; this world is too small. If they sack the boss, they might want you back and they have the best car on the grid." Did Papa know something he didn't about JP's boss? He shouldn't let S1 rumours distract him.

"I know. JP is on track for his third championship, and they've already wrapped up the constructor's title again. Does this mean I should do the interview?"

"If they agreed to edit approval."

"Okay. Thanks." Ondrej hung up. He had plenty of media training, he could manage an interview like this, and it would give him something to do this evening. Better than pace around Monaco waiting for Hudson to arrive. Before he'd met Hudson, he'd gone months without sex, and now the next twelve hours of self-imposed control were going to feel longer than any chaste period in his past.

"Yes. I'll do it on a few conditions."

"Anything."

"Be careful when you say that."

Sam blushed and nodded. "An interview like this will make my career. I'll agree to most reasonable things to get it."

"How long have you been waiting outside my door?"

"When I saw your announcement online, my boss put me on a plane and told me to wait until I had an interview."

Ondrej had made his announcement ten days before Imola, and it'd been a two week break to the race at Suzuka. "You've been here for three weeks. Waiting?"

"Yes."

"Your dedication is admirable. Come to dinner with me and we will talk." Ondrej named a place and a time. "I will walk now."

"I can walk with you."

Ondrej shrugged. If the journalist thought they could match his pace, well good luck to them. "If you want."

———

Hudson had caught the early flight and arrived at Ondrej's building just before lunch. He'd picked up some of Monaco's famous socca on the way, as a treat. With no press outside the building, he used the code to let himself in, and took the elevator up to Ondrej's floor. They'd found a rhythm in the past few months with Hudson living here between races, almost like they'd fallen into a relationship. Having Ondrej confirm that he wanted this to be more than casual helped Hudson remove the doubt seeded by Mackenzie that he was Ondrej's convenient pet. He tapped in the code and pushed open the door. As expected the apartment was empty. This time of day, Ondrej would be doing his stamina exercise with his trainer Amy.

Hudson put the food on the kitchen bench and proceeded to put his suitcase away. The easy domesticity of this life as Hudson pottered about was lovely. He could see himself moving here permanently; flying back to England for business meetings with Mackenzie—and to see her and her family—regularly. If he truly wanted this, he'd have to earn it. He needed to find the Bugatti, to prove his worth to Mr D'Grieg; and he'd need to discuss money with Ondrej. The disparity between their income needed to be dealt with up front. The front door opened.

"Good run?" Hudson asked. The way Ondrej's face lit up at Hudson's voice was the perfect welcome.

"Yes. Come here." Ondrej's shirt was slick with sweat, clinging to his lean body, and Hudson wanted to lick him clean. He moved quickly. Not as fast as Ondrej who wrapped his arms around Hudson's waist and pulled him close. Hudson dipped his head for a kiss. This was why he disrupted his own life and schedule for Ondrej. The two of them were meant to be together. The chemistry in every kiss continued to grow into something special. Ondrej gripped Hudson's hips tight, grinding their cocks together.

"Too much fabric."

"And you taste like sweat."

"I thought you liked that."

"I do." Hudson loved everything about Ondrej. He gasped, unable to control it.

"What?" Ondrej frowned.

"It's nothing much."

"Good. Because I haven't come since Suzuka and I need to." Ondrej kissed him hard, walking Hudson backwards until his spine hit the wall. Whenever they kissed like this, Hudson's one inch of height advantage always seemed to be a disadvantage. Ondrej commanded the kiss, stroking his tongue over Hudson's with such virulent ego, as if he had every right to march into Hudson's space and take whatever he wanted. Hudson groaned. He would happily give it all to Ondrej. His knees buckled as Ondrej continued to plunder his mouth. Hudson was barely able to do anything under this sensual onslaught, just resting his hands on Ondrej's forearms.

"I want you to get naked, get in the shower, on your knees and suck me until I come."

"Now?" Of course, now, Hudson. He had no blood left in his brain to be able to come up with any sort of cognitive thought.

"Yes. Now." Ondrej stepped back with a little wave towards the bathroom. Hudson's legs felt like jelly as he followed Ondrej's directions. He pulled his jeans down over his bare feet—Monaco was a lot hotter than England at this time of year and he'd taken his socks off with his shoes when he'd arrived—then tossed his jeans aside. Hudson yelped as Ondrej tapped him on his bare ass.

"Hey."

"Hurry up."

"I'm going as fast as possible." Hudson put his glasses on the shelf, then pulled his shirt over his head and stepped into the shower. He knelt on the floor. Only seconds after he sat down, Ondrej turned on the water and Hudson gasped as cold water hit his body. Gooseflesh broke out everywhere on his skin.

"Fuck you."

"It's your fault. You could've waited for the water to heat up." Ondrej casually stripped off his sweaty running clothes. Now the sweat was beginning to dry, the smell changed from salty and delicious to slightly rank. The cold water slowly heated up and the warmth in the water exacerbated the scents in the air. Hudson bowed his head, so the stream of shower water hit the top of his head and poured down the sides of his face. Ondrej's feet appeared in front of Hudson and he lifted his head. Ondrej's body blocked the water, stopping it landing on Hudson's face. Instead it streamed over Ondrej's athletic form. How fucking lucky was Hudson to be the one that Ondrej picked. Would he ever lose this sense of amazement?

"Stay." Ondrej squirted some body wash into his hands and soaped himself all over. The sight of lean muscles under Ondrej's own hands would've guaranteed Hudson's obedience alone. He wanted to stay. Forever.

"I'm not your pet." Hudson gulped, needing to say something to get rid of the ugly voices in his head telling he wasn't enough for Ondrej. He was just the first relationship Ondrej had allowed himself to have; one that didn't compromise his career in S1 and one that he could keep neatly parked out of the way until it suited him.

"No." Ondrej lathered up more soap and covered his cock with it. "No. You are my anchor, my support. You keep my ego in check and my feet firmly on the ground."

Hudson swallowed. He did?

"I don't want your complete obedience, Hudson. I have enough people in my life telling me that I'm awesome and I shouldn't have to get out of anyone's way. You don't treat me like I'm famous, and I appreciate that." Ondrej's hands on his own cock drew all of Hudson's attention. How dare he say such beautiful things while tempting Hudson so thoroughly.

"Um, thanks." Hudson didn't know how to respond to

that. And then Ondrej turned around, so his ass was level with Hudson's head. Ondrej tipped his head back under the water. What a glorious sight. Hudson lifted his hands, needing to touch him, but as soon as he was close, Ondrej spun around again.

"Now suck me."

Hudson fought the urge to fall mouth first onto Ondrej's rigid cock, and instead he bent much lower and kissed Ondrej's ankles. He dragged his mouth and hands all over Ondrej's legs.

"You make me want—" Ondrej didn't finish the sentence. Instead he threaded his fingers into Hudson's hair and pulled. Hudson groaned as his scalp came alive with prickles of sensation. He dug his fingers into Ondrej's thighs for balance, and sucked Ondrej's balls into his mouth. The noise Ondrej made was incredible.

"Fuck."

Hudson licked all the way up Ondrej's glorious cock, tasting the salty pre-come already leaking from the end as he lowered his mouth over Ondrej's length. Yes. He hummed around him and Ondrej jerked his hips. Ondrej's cock hit the roof of Hudson's mouth, slight too hard, but also perfect. Hudson held on tight to Ondrej's legs as he sucked him. He gave Ondrej everything he had, everything he couldn't quite say yet, and when Ondrej cried out that he was coming, Hudson kept going. He flattened his tongue and took Ondrej deeper, tears leaking from the corners of his eyes as he gagged on Ondrej's full length. Hudson was filled with Ondrej's hot cock and it was exactly right. He licked and sucked and let himself be filled over and over, loving the way Ondrej's breath quickened.

"Hudson." Ondrej cried out as he came. Hudson rode it out, then swallowed everything. He felt a little dizzy when Ondrej hauled him to his feet. He rested his head on Ondrej's shoulder, and it only took a few strokes from Ondrej before he came too.

"I'm going to miss you." Ondrej whispered in Hudson's ear.

"Why?"

"I have to be in the states in a few days, then Mexico a week later, then two weeks till Brazil, so I won't see you for a month."

"I could come with you?" Hudson saw the shadow cross Ondrej's face. "Never mind. Forget that I asked."

"It's too much to ask from you. I can't ask you to give your life and follow me around the S1 circuit."

Hudson nodded slowly. "No. I will miss you too."

"Papa was correct, you know."

"About?" Hudson's stomach churned. He knew exactly what Mr D'Grieg thought of their relationship and none of it was good.

"Only announcing one thing at a time. I had dinner last night with a journalist. Sam from Queernesszine, and before we'd even got to dessert, they showed me a social media tagging me in photos with them."

"Oh?"

"Like, people are just making up wild stuff because I had dinner with a non-binary person with purple hair. Papa was correct about keeping you away from all of that."

"Because he doesn't like me?"

"No. I mean, what? He likes you just fine. He's just worried about my safety and my career, and he doesn't want you involved in all this media attention when you have no training."

"So he doesn't trust me?"

"What do you mean?"

"If he trusted me, he'd trust me to only say positive things to the media." Hudson didn't say what sat on the tip of his tongue—that if he spoke to the media it would be immediately obvious that Hudson cared deeply for Ondrej.

"It's not about trust. The press is slippery. They'll get you to say things that you don't mean to say."

"I'm really not that interesting. There's nothing for me to say." Hudson didn't know what else to say.

Ondrej laughed and pulled him closer for a kiss. Eventually he lifted his head, allowing Hudson's head to stop swimming.

"You are fascinating. The press are desperate to know who is special enough for me to decide to come out now."

"I don't understand."

"The most common question I've been asked since I wrote that question has been; why now? With the implication that there must be someone special in my life to want to bring all this attention on me."

"Oh." Hudson couldn't breathe as he realised what that meant. "Did you come out because of me?"

"Obviously. Yes." Ondrej kissed him again. "Before I met you, I was content to hide during the season, and in the off-season, to simply pretend that I knew I looked quite a lot like that S1 driver. *Ha ha, you aren't the first person to say I look like Ondrej D'Grieg. I'm virtually his gay twin.* And so on. I was so good at pretending to be some random guy who happened to look a lot like me."

"But?" Hudson wasn't sure what he wanted to ask. He certainly didn't think he was worth all that fuss.

"But nothing. You are worth this."

Hudson's instinct was to argue and say that he really, really, wasn't worth much, but he managed to hold his tongue.

"I'm not sure where this relationship might be going —" Ondrej's admission was a breath of relief because it reminded Hudson that, yeah, he wasn't worth all this trouble. "—but I want to try and make it work. I know my work schedule is pretty difficult."

"We don't need to decide now. Let's just eat the lunch I bought and hang out together for a while." Hudson wasn't worth forever—people didn't stick around for him—but he could enjoy right now before Ondrej figured that out.

CHAPTER 21
MEXICO

It wasn't often that Ondrej got to sit on the front row —only his second time this season—and unlike Japan, he wasn't going to fuck this chance up. He'd started the race in fourth, and had made his way up to second, when JP's team-mate spun out in the light rain. Now Ondrej sat on the front row, awaiting the official restart. The rain had finally gone away, and he'd done a steady formation lap to prepare for this grid restart. He went through a breathing exercise to focus every fibre in his body on the task ahead as he waited for the lights. One, Two, Three, Four, Five. Lights out. The car flew, responding to his commands into a perfect start and he tore away from the field, leaving the lead driver, Etrulius, in his rear-view mirrors as they raced down the long straight at Mexico. His car quickened like he wanted, nice and fast. Fuck. Etrulius was keeping pace well enough that the first corner would be crucial. His tyres had maintained their temperature after the formation lap so he had lots of grip on the drying surface. Slicks was a gamble but so far, it'd paid off as he led

Etriulius into turn one. He hit the brakes as late as possible. The back end shifted slightly, and he adjusted. There was a loud bang—right rear tyre—and the next millisecond he was airborne with zero control. Shit. The car landed with a thump on the front end and slammed into the tyre barrier. There was another loud crunch and a shunt from behind. The engine whined. Whenever he crashed, it felt like time slowed down, even more than when he was racing.

"Are you okay, Ondrej?" Jaxxon's voice was calm on the radio.

"I'm okay." He answered automatically without really knowing the truth. He reminded himself to breathe. Adrenalin soared in his veins. His heart rate would be off the measurement charts. He went through the post-crash process. A quick check for smoke. A few deep breaths to smell the air. Nothing. No smoke. No fuel leaks. No brake fluid. Good. Next step. He checked his body, wiggling his toes in his racing boots, then all the way up, checking each muscle. Yes, everything was still attached, and everything hurt. Time to get out of the cockpit.

"It was my racing line." He knew that much. Etrulius must've turned into his racing line.

"We know. Turn off the engine."

Ondrej followed Jaxxon's instructions, glad for his sensible voice. As he used his arms to pull himself up via the halo, he was able to look around. JP's car was stuck into the back end of his car—that'd explain the extra shunt after the initial crash—and two other cars were scattered across the track. Pieces of carbon fibre were everywhere. His right rear tyre was completely shredded.

"You okay, JP?"

"Yeah. Fucking Etrulius cut you off, and I had no space either." JP must be okay as he was spitting mad. "I'll see you later."

Ondrej started to nod, but his head felt weird so he kept it still. He checked over the car. The front end was fucked and he'd likely need all new suspension and a gear box. Fuck. He'd get grid penalties for the next race now. One of the medics touched him on the shoulder and he let himself be led to their car. He collapsed into the back seat to find JP already seated there.

"I suppose we'll be off to the hospital now?"

"Yeah, gotta get checked out. You'd better send Hudson a text too, once you get back to pits. Let him know you're okay."

"And Sofia."

"She's in the pits today. Besides she's done this often enough." JP breathed out. "Fuck. I needed today's points."

———

It was nearly midnight in England as Hudson watched the replays over and over, hating the way they showed it in slow motion as Ondrej's rear tyre exploded. He clipped wheels with the car beside him, launching Ondrej's car into the air. Ondrej landed heavily before slamming into the tyre wall. If that wasn't enough, JP's car hit the back of him hard. It was Hudson's worst nightmare on repeat. It didn't matter how often the television replayed the radio with Ondrej saying 'I'm okay', Hudson needed to hear from him in person. How did anyone think this was okay?

Ondrej: I'm fine. Lots of protocol to do now. I'll call later

Hudson stared at his phone. Protocol? What did that entail. Should he call? Surely Ondrej would call if he was allowed. A few weeks ago, Ondrej had mentioned that Hudson should chat to Sofia about being a driver's partner, and he wished he'd made the time to do. He really could do with someone who could tell him what was happening.

Hudson: Thank fuck. So good to hear from you.

There were so many other things he could've said, but he wasn't sure how to say them. Instead, he watched as the race resumed. It was surreal watching cars continue to drive while Ondrej was doing 'protocol'; whatever that was. Hopefully it meant he was being looked at by a doctor, although he'd said he was fine. Several laps went by and he heard nothing. The commentators were still analysing the crash and were now blaming Ondrej's tyre for having a suspected puncture. It made sense. On the slow footage, the tyre burst pushing Ondrej's car sideways into the other car and the angle had launched Ondrej's car into the air. JP had clipped the other car too and slammed into the back of Ondrej's car. What a mess. Hudson sucked in a breath as his phone dinged. He needed news from Ondrej.

Unknown: Sofia here. They are being taken to hospital for a check over. You okay?

He probably wasn't but he didn't have words for how he felt.

Hudson: Thanks for checking in.

Sofia: I'm heading to the hospital with them.

Hudson: Okay.

Sofia: Can I call?

Hudson sent her a thumbs up emoji and his phone rang

immediately with a video call and Sofia's face filled his screen.

"JP got your number from Ondrej and said I should text you. I hope that's alright."

"He sent me a text to say he was okay, but protocol meant he couldn't call. What does that mean?"

Sofia cleared her throat and a frown flitted over her brow. "He has a minor concussion. It should be nothing, but the medics took his phone away until they could check him over. It's protocol because they don't want any extra stress on him."

"I don't understand."

"It's standard procedure with potential concussions. The theory is that the light on the screen makes it worse."

"Sounds like rubbish."

"Probably, but the medics have a lot of experience dealing with high-speed crashes, so if they say it's an issue, then it is."

Hudson's chest hurt. "He's not okay?"

"He'll be fine. He's a bit wobbly but that's normal for a crash like that."

"How can you say that?" Didn't being fine mean that he wasn't okay right at this second? How long until Ondrej was fine?

"Hey Hudson." Sofia's voice was gentle and comforting. "It's going to be fine. I've done this a few times now."

"How?" Hudson was barely holding himself together after seeing Ondrej's car fly through the air. Theoretically, he'd known this might happen. Hell, he'd spent the whole race at Monza reading about dead racing car drivers. But seeing it—seeing Ondrej—made it real. His skin was clammy and cold. He was going to puke. The only thing keeping him from completely dissolving was hearing Ondrej's voice on the radio. He'd sounded so clinical, saying he was fine, and then complaining about the other driver. Jaxxon's response had been so calm too, as if a high-speed crash and a chance of death was just another Sunday.

Sofia shrugged. "This part of being in love with a driver sucks. And it's extra difficult when you aren't there because the information is always so slow. There are long periods where you know nothing."

"Yes. It's hard." Hudson just wanted to hear Ondrej's voice. Personally, not on television. One measly text wasn't enough.

"But you want to know how I can deal with this?"

"Yes." Hudson didn't even know what questions he wanted to ask Sofia.

"The first time JP crashed heavily, I was a mess."

Hudson sucked in a breath. "Yes, I'm a mess."

"I almost asked JP to give it up because I couldn't cope with the idea that he might die. Drivers still die doing this, even with all the safety protocols." Sofia closed her eyes for a moment and Hudson waited. His hands were all clammy as he held the phone and stared at her. "Do you know why I didn't ask JP to stop?"

Hudson knew the answer even if he didn't want it to be true. For the first time since Ondrej's crash, Hudson had a clear thought. The answer was simple.

"It would destroy him." Hudson couldn't ask Ondrej to give up the one thing that made him, well, him. Ondrej wasn't reckless when he drove. He was precise and amazing and a life without this would be very difficult for him to adjust to. He deserved to have someone in his life who supported him.

"Yes. For these drivers, racing means more than just the quest for a championship. If it was only that, JP would've retired after his first one. There is something innate in his personality that means he needs this. He needs to push himself and his car to the absolute limits and understanding that meant I had to learn to live with the risks too. If I asked him to stop because I couldn't deal with the chance that he might die, I would be asking him to be someone else."

"And you don't want someone else. You want JP."

"Just as you want Ondrej." Sofia knew. "We have a unique burden, holding someone in our heart who risks their life every time they go to work. Days like this are a reminder of how hard that can be, but I wouldn't change JP for anything."

"Yes." Hudson let out the air in his lungs and it scalded him. "You'll call again if you get an update?"

"Absolutely. When you guys are ready, you should meet some of the other driver's wives and girlfriends." Sofia grinned.

Hudson tried not to cringe. "Does that make me an honorary wife? Weird."

"Husband then. Whatever. Not many people under-stand the challenges in being in love with a race car driver. It's a unique thing to support a driver, and it's hard to do alone."

"Thanks." Hudson must have said that on repeat now, but what else was he going to say? The television commen-tators were still analysing the crash, even as the race kept going, flicking between live shots and then back to the image of JP getting out of his car and walking over to talk to Ondrej. Ondrej climbed out of his car and stood beside JP and the other driver, swaying a little. He moved gingerly as if his whole body hurt. Hudson wished he'd gone with him. Now he was stuck here, far away from Mexico, in England with no news and only Sofia's goodwill—friendship—to let him know anything.

"I'll call you back when I know something. It'll probably be a while. Hospitals always take ages with this sort of thing."

"Okay. I really appreciate the call."

"And turn off the television. Trust me, you don't want to watch the crash on repeat. Stay away from the news and social media. Everyone will have an opinion on whose fault it was and none of them will care about Ondrej as a person. To them, he's a brand name. It's not healthy for you to listen to people talk about him in detached terms."

"That's good advice." Hudson wasn't sure if he would take it, because at least when he watched the crash, he could see Ondrej pull himself out of the car and stand up without assistance. Seeing him get out of the car was reassuring. "Thanks for calling. I hope JP is okay too."

"He's fine. I'll call you back soon." Sofia hung up and Hudson went back to staring at the television. Fine. Everyone was fine. A tiny four-letter word was doing so much work. What did it really mean? How fine was fine? It was getting close to midnight here, but there was no chance he was going to bed. Not while he waited for news on Ondrej.

———

The first thing Ondrej did when the medics finally gave him back his phone was book a flight to England. They'd kept him in the hospital overnight, waking him up every hour because his MRI showed the tiniest concussion. Finally, he was discharged, and he could head to the airport. Jaxxon had gone well above his job description to pack up Ondrej's hotel room and had delivered his suitcase here, so he could change into a fresh set of clothes. His racing suit had gone back to the pits with Jaxxon where it would be packed by the logistics team to travel to Brazil. The hospital discharged all the drivers together and organised taxis for them in a quiet back alley to avoid the press. Being famous had its perks; something Hudson would have found amusing. Ondrej had been waiting for hours to make this call, not wanting to do it in the hospital where every nurse and doctor wanted to inspect him, prod him, or just get his signature. Now he was alone in the back of a taxi, he dialled Hudson's number.

"Hello?" Hudson's voice was all rough with sleep. He always looked so wonderful when he woke up, all rumpled without his glasses. Fuck, Ondrej wished he was with him. He wanted someone to hug him and be with him and care for him at the hospital. They'd put him and JP in the same room and seeing Sofia fuss over JP caused his stomach to yearn for the same.

"Hey. I'm okay."

"Ondrej. Oh my god. I'm so glad to hear from you. Sofia told me hours ago that you'd been discharged. Are you alright?"

"I'm—" Ondrej almost said fine automatically, but he

didn't want to lie to Hudson. "I'm pretty bruised and I have a nasty headache."

"Oh no."

"The doctors did all the concussion tests and sent me for an MRI scan. It's nothing major, just the result of going from one twenty to zero in less than a second."

"One twenty?"

"Kilometres per hour. I guess it depends where you measure it from, since the straight is very long, and I hit three sixty-two before the braking zone."

Hudson laughed softly and Ondrej's skin warmed all over at the unexpected noise. He'd been so worried that Hudson was worried about him, and Hudson's gentle laugh meant more to Ondrej than Hudson would ever know. He didn't want Hudson to worry about him. Crashes were part of the job. If Hudson wanted to be with him, he'd need to learn to shake them off, just as he did. To hear Hudson's laugh gave Ondrej hope that this might work; not just in the good times like the mid-season break, but also in the hardest times. He'd made the correct decision to book a flight and head directly to Hudson today.

"I love it when you talk technical about your job." Hudson was a little breathless. Was he turned on? Ondrej's brain must've been shaken in the crash because Hudson wasn't making any sense.

"You do? I thought you had no interest in S1?"

"I didn't say I had any interest in S1. Just that I love it when you talk passionately about it. I don't understand the technical stuff, but I don't need to get it to appreciate your joy." Hudson paused. "Sofia asked me something yesterday... She wanted to know if I'd ask you to stop racing."

"And?" It was Ondrej's worst nightmare. He held his breath. If Hudson asked that, then Ondrej would be driving for the rest of the season with a broken heart. He couldn't stop.

"I said I couldn't ask you to do that."

Thank fuck. "What?" Ondrej's heart wasn't going to cope with the stop-start way it raced now, as if he was driving with one cylinder misfiring.

"I should start at the beginning. She rang from the hospital to let me know that you were okay and being checked over."

Ondrej breathed out slowly; JP and Sofia were true friends and he'd almost let them disappear out of his life. He had them now, just as he had Hudson. Life was a lot less lonely than it had been this time a year ago. "Yeah?"

"I asked her how she coped with it."

"With?"

"Seeing JP crash, and she admitted that it was hard, but it would be harder to ask JP to stop because he needed to be a driver. He needed this life. And that's when I understood something very important."

"What's that?" Ondrej had a sinking feeling. Here it comes. Hudson was going to dump him. He braced himself for it and his ears filled with a roaring sound.

"Asking you to stop because I was scared about what might happen to you would be a mistake. Asking you to stop driving would change you. I don't want you to change. I love you, Ondrej, and if loving you means that sometimes I'll be scared, that's okay."

Ondrej tried to talk but only a croaking sound came out.

"I love you, Ondrej."

"I'm coming to England." Ondrej could sleep on the plane. He needed to be with Hudson now.

"Now?"

"Yes. I've already booked a ticket."

"No. Don't be absurd. You've just had a massive crash. You need to look after yourself."

"It's too late. I'm in a cab on the way to the airport." Ondrej waited but the silence stretched. Finally, as the seconds dragged out, Hudson scoffed.

"Fine. As if you ever do what I tell you."

Ondrej grinned, glad no one could see him except the taxi driver who was sneaking glances in the rear-view mirror. "No. Why would I when you are so good at doing what I ask?"

Hudson's sudden puff of breath was loud in Ondrej's ear. The perfect sound.

"Are you blushing?" Ondrej closed his eyes to imagine the flush of pink across Hudson's cheeks, making his freckles stand out. A year ago, Ondrej would've scoffed if someone had told him he'd have a thing for red-hair and freckles. Only one red head mattered to him.

"Yes." Hudson swallowed. "You know I am. You caused it."

"I'll be there in twelve hours."

"Please rest on the plane."

Ondrej chuckled. "Of course I will. I have plans for when I see you." The best thing about his fitness regime was that it was designed to help him recover quickly after a crash. His hours on the simulator and his neck strengthening exercises were all done so he could crash in Q1 and get back in the car twenty minutes later for Q2. Training prepared his body to cope with huge G-forces.

"Aren't you sore?"

"Nothing a good soak in a hot bath can't fix." Ondrej grinned. The taxi pulled up at the airport. "Hold on. I'll call you back." He paid the driver, signed an autograph, then went into the airport with his bag. It took him nearly an hour to get through all the ticketing and customs and with every minute, the anticipation in his gut grew hotter as he imagined Hudson pacing with frustration. Ondrej found a quiet spot in the lounge where no one would bother him and called Hudson back.

"What took so long?"

"Airport stuff."

"Okay, you could've warned me."

"Where would be the fun in that?"

"Fun!" Hudson spluttered in Ondrej's ear, and he grinned.

"I want to you do something for me."

"Okay." The switch in Hudson's voice—from irritated to eager—was everything Ondrej hoped for. He spread his legs as his cock hardened.

"Find a hotel room with a massive bath. Book it for three nights. Send me a text with the details and I'll meet you there. My flight arrives at..." Ondrej flicked open his emails to double check. "—just before midnight." Fuck, that timing sucked.

"Okay?"

"I will sleep, then in the morning, you will run me a hot bath with magnesium salts and you will attend to my bruises."

Hudson gasped. "Like actual bruises, or is that a euphemism?"

"Both. Make it good, Hudson."

"I can do that."

"Perfect." Ondrej hung up before he said something sappy. He was exhausted and just wanted to get on the plane and sleep for the next twelve hours. His whole body hurt. As much as he teased Hudson, he really did need to soak in a recovery bath. He'd missed his post-race ice bath because of the crash and his five point harness had left ugly red bruises over his shoulders and thighs. They called his name for the flight and he went through the routine, glad that they boarded the first class passengers before everyone else. For a long flight like this, he just wanted to be left alone, and paying for first class guaranteed that. This was one of those times when his pay cheque gave him more benefits than being famous took away. His body hurt too much, and the only person he could manage to be civil with was Hudson.

CHAPTER 22

Hudson stood on the balcony of the penthouse and stared out over the city. This hotel was one of many created inside the old mill buildings that had built the back of Manchester. The renovation had retained many of the cool old features with exposed red brick walls and vaulted ceilings. Hudson had splashed out with the two bedroom penthouse, not for the extra bed, but for the huge double width spa bath. Satisfaction at finding a hotel room with a bathtub big enough for the two of them blended with the nerve-tingling anticipation of seeing Ondrej again. Hudson had spent an obscene amount of money—for him—on this room, and he wasn't going to let Ondrej pay him back. Ondrej already bought all his flights back and forth to Monaco and all around the place for most of this year. Hudson could do this. It was well after midnight, nearly a whole day since Ondrej's crash. Having something to do—find this hotel room—had helped but now he was here and Ondrej wasn't. The November air was cold; winter was definitely close, and he hugged himself tight. His breath left tendrils of fog as he breathed out unsteadily, pushing away the nasty catastrophising thoughts about Ondrej never turning up. Fucking brain.

The door opened. Hudson spun around at the noise, rushing inside and across the room, because there he was. Ondrej. In one piece. Right here. He opened his mouth to tell Ondrej how good it was to see him and found himself being kissed instead. Hudson wrapped his arms around Ondrej, holding him tight, and slowly with every stroke of Ondrej's tongue against his own, the relief turned into desire. He needed Ondrej inside him, as close as possible. He needed this. Hudson touched Ondrej everywhere, reassuring himself that he was all here, all fine, as promised.

"You look tired." Hudson stepped back for a moment, resting his hands on Ondrej's cheeks.

"I am."

"Come to bed."

"I thought you'd never ask."

"Let me close the door to the balcony first." He didn't want Ondrej to get cold. Hudson reluctantly pulled himself away from Ondrej and closed the sliding glass door to their private balcony. He rushed back towards Ondrej and reached out to hold his hands. Hudson walked to the bedroom in the suite, tugging slightly on Ondrej's hand to guide him towards the bed. Ondrej must be tired because he followed without his usual bossiness, and then he just sat on the end of the bed. Hudson kissed him on the forehead.

"It's great to see you." He gently ran his hands down Ondrej's torso, down his legs, and knelt as he took of Ondrej's shoes and socks. Ondrej half-stood and pulled off his jeans, then sat again, so Hudson could tug them down Ondrej's legs and cast them aside. He stood up again and lifted Ondrej's shirt over his head.

"Oh." Two long ugly bruises started at Ondrej's shoulders, and went down his chest, and out across his waist. "What happened?"

"It's from the harness. Looks worse than it is."

"I hope so because it looks very painful. I'm so sorry." Hudson had clung to Ondrej when he'd walked into the hotel room, pressing himself hard against those mean looking marks on his skin.

"Don't stress about it." Ondrej half shrugged, then shifted quickly under the covers. He nestled in against the pillows while Hudson was still standing there, holding Ondrej's shirt and trying to catch up.

"Good choice. This bed is great." Ondrej's voice was a little husky and it centred Hudson.

"You should sleep."

"So should you. Come here." Ondrej patted the other pillow and the cheeky grin on his face made everything feel alright again. Hudson stripped quickly and dove into bed beside Ondrej. He hesitated, not wanting to hurt Ondrej's bruises, but Ondrej pulled him closer, spooning around him. With Ondrej's hard chest pressed against his spine, Hudson wanted to close his eyes and just breathe in the familiarity of Ondrej's masculine scent.

"You should've been with me." Ondrej's whisper was hot on the back of Hudson's neck and he shivered.

"It was okay. Sofia kept me up to date."

"It wasn't okay. Everyone else had someone beside their bed, except me. I want you with me." Ondrej stroked one hand lazily over Hudson's side, slowly across his waist, and down towards his cock.

"You did?" Hudson desperately wanted to hear this, but the doubt at Ondrej not calling took over.

"I did." Ondrej nuzzled the back of his neck, and then he wrapped his hand around Hudson's cock. "You don't want this?"

Hudson wasn't hard. How could he be when he was so worried about Ondrej?

"I'm here now." Ondrej stroked him gently and every tug was perfection. Hudson grew hard quickly. If Ondrej needed him, that was enough for him to get out of his head and focus on the rough texture of Ondrej's hand on his cock.

"I do want this. I want you."

"You said that you love me."

"I do." Hudson's hips bucked as Ondrej gripped him tight. "I do love you. I was so scared."

"Don't be scared. I'm safe now."

"Okay?"

"And you are safe too. In my arms." How did Ondrej know exactly the right thing to say?

"I am." Hudson wriggled his ass, pressing it harder against Ondrej, and the hard length of Ondrej's cock slotted perfectly between his cheeks. Heat, glorious sexual heat, surrounded him.

"You want this?"

"Please." Hudson couldn't wait another second. He'd been so worried and now all his fears were gone. Replaced with a pure desire. He loved this man who risked his life for speed. He loved him with everything. He rolled over and kissed Ondrej with all the pent-up energy of the last day or so. He threaded his hands through Ondrej's hair, holding him close, and kissed him until he couldn't breathe anymore. With every stroke of his tongue, Ondrej matched it with the same rhythm using his hands on both their cocks. Hudson shifted his mouth and dragged in a deep breath. "I'm going to come."

"Good. Kiss me like that again, and we can come together."

"How do you sound so calm?" Hudson panted out each word, overwrought by the sensations in his body and the emotions since the crash.

"Calm? No. I am controlled, although you are pushing that control." Ondrej's tone lowered, his voice ragged and rough, and it was enough to send Hudson over the edge.

"I love you. I'm sorry." He came quickly, coating Ondrej's hand, and he kissed him because the relief was epic. Ondrej was here with him, and he was ... fine. Ondrej grunted and came too, then collapsed onto his back.

"Don't be sorry. We both needed that."

Hudson breathed out, emptying his lungs completely. "We did." He kissed Ondrej on the cheek. "I love you."

The only answer was a gentle snore. Hudson waited for the spike of anxiety, because Ondrej hadn't said the same thing to him, but it didn't happen. Just as he would never want Ondrej to change by asking him to stop driving, he also didn't need Ondrej to love him back. Simply loving him was enough. He slid out of the bed as quietly and gently as he could to grab a cloth and clean them both up. As he washed Ondrej, his stomach muscles twitched but he didn't wake up. The poor man must be exhausted. Once they were both clean, Hudson got back into bed, making sure he didn't disturb Ondrej's sleep, and just lay there beside him, listening to him breathe. The regularity of his breathing helped soothe Hudson until he slowly succumbed to the warmth of the bed and fell asleep too.

Hudson woke early out of habit. The bed was nice and warm, and it was still dark outside. He grabbed his glasses and his phone, then ignored the notifications on his social media apps. Instead, he checked his emails and sent a text to Mackenzie, apologising in advance for missing a meeting they had scheduled for today. His finger hovered over one of the social media apps. It took a decent amount of control to stop himself looking, but as Sofia had said, too many fans would be talking about Ondrej's crash without considering that he was a person. A real person covered in nasty bruises, and currently fast asleep in bed beside him. The unnatural glow from Hudson's phone made Ondrej's skin look slightly green—ill—which really didn't help the way Hudson's muscles tensed. It was not much fun to be in love with Ondrej. Not just because Ondrej didn't return the depth of his feelings, but also because Hudson had to learn to willingly allow Ondrej to step into danger every time he slid into his race car. Like he'd said to Sofia, he didn't want Ondrej to be someone else. He adored his arrogant commands and the technical precision and ambition he applied to his job.

"What are you reading?" Ondrej's voice was hoarse and sleep filled.

"Please don't laugh."

"Why would I laugh?"

"I'm reading the unofficial biography of Socrates Drayton."

Ondrej laughed, a low chuckle. "That exists?"

"Yes. It's pretty interesting, actually. The author has painted him as a ladies' man who was always surrounded by women."

"Um, yeah, that's not what Socrates says."

"I guess it would be an effective cover back then?" Hudson knew better than most how far queer people used to go to avoid the awful legal ramifications of loving someone. It'd literally been his thesis topic.

"Or the biographer is a bigot who wants to rewrite history."

Hudson frowned. "It wouldn't be the first time." He went back to the chapter headings page and clicked through to the one on Socrates' retirement from racing. Nothing. He breathed in deeply; time for a search. The great thing about e-books was that they made research so much easier.

"Damn it, you are right."

"About?"

"The author. The only usage of the word gay in the book is to say that there were unsubstantiated rumours that Socrates was gay, but no evidence could be found."

"He's fucking married to Mike."

"Yes. The erasure is blatant."

Ondrej sat up and placed his hand on Hudson's cheek, slowly turning Hudson's face towards his own. "Promise me something."

"Okay?"

"Promise me that you won't let this happen to me."

Hudson blinked as Ondrej's gaze pierced him. "I will try. I mean, it's a lot harder for anyone to try this with you, since you've publicly come out already."

"Socrates is married to his husband and still someone wrote this rubbish."

"Yes." Hudson swallowed as Ondrej's gaze intensified.

"I... Write my story now."

"Me?" Hudson cringed at the squeak in his voice. "I'm a researcher, not a writer."

"I trust you." Ondrej kissed him and if the words hadn't already stolen his breath, the kiss finished the job. Hudson's heart fluttered in his chest. This kiss, and hearing Ondrej say he trusted him, was enough for him. Hudson didn't need to have his love returned; he never expected that of anyone. People didn't stick around for him, and he'd learned that he needed to love people anyway. One day Ondrej would realise that he could have anyone and Hudson would be cast aside, like he always was, and Hudson would have to be okay with that. Just like he'd survived every other time someone did this to him. Being with Ondrej was temporary—relationships were always temporary—but he would enjoy every second while it lasted. He would collect memories every day and they would keep him warm when this inevitably ended. Until then, he would love Ondrej because a life without love was worse than the heart ache of abandonment.

"Stop thinking."

"What?"

"Hudson. You are thinking too fucking much."

Hudson let out a shaky breath. It was true. "I think it's time for the bath I promised you." He rolled out of bed and rushed into the decadent bathroom. His hands shook slightly as he put the plug in and turned on the taps.

"I'm serious. I want you to write my story."

Hudson's shoulder muscles were so tight, he could barely shake his head. "I'm not a writer."

"Then don't write it. I'll find a writer to do it and you can review it."

"You could review it."

"I already have a job."

So did Hudson, but he didn't want to fight about this. "Ondrej. Not now, okay? How about we get these bruises soaked and healed instead." He tested the water temperature. Good. Nice and steamy. He added the magnesium salts, following the instructions precisely, and used his hand to swirl it around.

"I don't want to be erased like that, Hudson. After all this fuss declaring myself to the world, I want this to matter to gay kids."

Hudson's heart couldn't take much more of this. "I will try my best. Now, will you please get in and soak?"

Ondrej stepped into the bath and lowered his body gently into the hot water. Every muscle on Ondrej's body was taut, and once again, Hudson was astounded that this gorgeous, incredible man, wanted to have Hudson in his life.

"Get in with me."

"Are you sure? This is supposed to be for your recovery."

"Hudson. Get in the bath. There is plenty of room." Ondrej spread his arms along the edge of the bath, a picture of relaxation. Hudson obeyed, because he'd never be able to resist that tone in Ondrej's voice and slipped into the water.

"Come here." Ondrej spread his legs. "Sit between my legs and lean back against me."

"But your bruises."

"Are nothing."

"They don't look like nothing." Hudson could acknowledge that Ondrej's bruises did look better this morning. Not so red with most of the area turning into a faded purple with green and yellow discolouration along the edges.

"I'm strapped to the car with a seven-point safety harness. It's done up tight enough that I'm not going to move in a crash. Trust me, these bruises would be worst in a normal car crash with a standard seat belt. Now, come."

Hudson shifted so he sat between Ondrej's legs. Ondrej placed his hands on Hudson's hips and pulled him closer, then slid his hands up Hudson's back until they rested on his shoulders. Ondrej's thumbs dug into the tight muscles and suddenly all of Hudson's worries disappeared as Ondrej massaged his shoulders. His head lolled backwards with the combination of Ondrej's touch and the hot water.

"Is that good?"

"So fucking good." Hudson groaned as Ondrej dug his thumbs into the base of his skull.

"You spend too long on a computer. I should get my physio to give you a proper deep tissue massage."

Hudson whimpered. "You can't. You already give me too much." Like now—he was supposed to be helping Ondrej recover from his crash—not being indulged like this.

"Relax. I like to give you things."

Hudson fought the automatic protest that welled up, and instead, swallowed down the roughness in his throat. "Thank you."

Ondrej kissed the back of Hudson's neck and fuck... When Ondrej realised that Hudson wasn't worth this, it was going to take all of Hudson's strength to continue living. Fuck, so dramatic, Hudson. He breathed out. Enjoy one day at a time because he could control that. He forced himself to smile, so Ondrej could hear it in his voice.

"Thank you." He rolled over in the bath, and rested lightly on Ondrej's torso, using the water to keep his weight off the ugly bruises on Ondrej's chest and shoulders. They weren't as red today. Ondrej kissed his forehead and Hudson sighed happily. He closed his eyes and just breathed, letting the soft scent of the bathwater and Ondrej surround him. After a moment, he drew his knees under himself and held Ondrej's hand. He focused all his attention on gently stroking his skin. It wasn't a massage, not like Ondrej's physio would do, more of a demonstration of the way Hudson felt. He slid his hands along Ondrej's arm, over the lean muscles, and down his torso, carefully avoiding his bruises.

"Lower."

"It's too hot in here for sex."

"Yes. You could stand up, hold the wall, and bend over for me."

"I could." Hudson sucked in a deep breath, then ducked his head underwater. He covered Ondrej's cock with his mouth and blew out all the air in his lungs. Bubbles slid over Ondrej's cock but Hudson didn't have enough air to stay and appreciate Ondrej's response. He lifted his face out of the water and hauled in a deep breath of air with a gasp.

"Holy shit. Hudson. That was amazing. Now stand."

Hudson stood up, slightly wobbly, but Ondrej stood with him and helped him balance. He let Ondrej shift his body, until he stood, legs apart with his hands against the tiled wall.

"Stay."

Behind him, Hudson could hear the water splash as Ondrej climbed out of the bath and walked away. He tried to steady his breathing as he waited—presumably for Ondrej to grab a condom and some lube—and focused on the way his body slowly cooled as the hot water dripped off him. His feet were still in the hot water, contrasting to the rest of his body.

"Excellent." There was another splash and then Ondrej's warm hands spread over Hudson's hips. He bent his spine, arching to open himself up, and loved it when Ondrej growled in response. "You are so lovely." Ondrej slid his hands between Hudson's legs and cupped his tight balls. Slowly he toyed with Hudson until he was panting and desperate.

"Please." He wasn't beyond begging at this point. Ondrej gently opened him up.

"Do you want this?"

"Very much." Hudson shivered as Ondrej entered him. He gripped the wall, spreading his fingers wide to hang on to the smooth tiles. Ondrej pounded into him, with one hand splayed on the middle of Hudson's back, and the other wrapped around his waist to grip Hudson's cock.

Every thrust hit Hudson's prostate and his legs trembled as he tried to hold himself in place under the sensual onslaught.

"Come for me now." Ondrej's hoarse whispered command, combined with his hand on Hudson's cock, was all it took, and Hudson came on a shout. He hung his head, unable to keep it up. After shocks of pleasure filled him with every one of Ondrej's thrusts.

"I love you." He whispered it in sated bliss. Ondrej growled loud, then came with his head resting on Hudson's spine. Ondrej pulled out and together they sank back down into the water.

"I'd better clean up."

"I'll do it." Hudson grabbed a cloth, surprised to find his limbs kind of floppy and useless, and twisted around to see that Ondrej had already removed the condom and was cleaning himself.

"I think it's time for breakfast." So much for a slow recovery.

"Not all of us are athletes." Hudson grumbled.

"The water is getting cold. I'm hungry. Come on."

Hudson sighed. "Fine." He let Ondrej pull him to his feet, and managed to get out of the bath first, so he could hand Ondrej a clean towel. The hotel towels were fluffy and soft, and Hudson wanted to wrap himself in one and have a little rest. They got dried and dressed.

"Let's go out for breakfast."

"In public?" Hudson asked.

"Yes."

"But?"

"Are you worried about having your photo taken?"

"No. I'm no one. But aren't you worried?"

Ondrej laughed, a booming laugh. "No. Let them speculate. Fuck, they've spent my whole career writing bullshit articles about me and a bunch of random women. They've already written trash about Sam."

"Sam?"

"A reporter I had dinner with last week in Monaco."

"You mentioned that." Hudson nodded. "If you are cool with it, I'd love to have breakfast with you in public."

"Great. This is your hometown. Where should we go?"

Hudson shook his head. "I don't know. My budget doesn't really stretch to fancy breakfasts. I can look something up on the internet?"

"Yes. Do that."

This part of town had gone through a bit of a renaissance recently with all the old mills being restored and turned into funky hotels and event spaces. "Or we could simply go for a walk until you see something you like? There are plenty of nice places around here."

"Great. Walk with me."

CHAPTER 23

UAE

"Looks like another podium." Mr D'Grieg stood beside Hudson at the back of Ondrej's pit garage in Abu Dhabi, both watching the various television screens all showing different sections of the track. Ondrej was currently in second place, about three seconds behind JP who only needed to finish in the top ten to win his third successive world championship. Gamble's rookie, Paulo, was in fifth.

"Yes." There wasn't much Hudson could add to it. Hudson couldn't see Ondrej beating JP from here, although there was a lot left in this race with forty laps still to go. Ondrej had finished third in a thrilling race in Brazil, and Hudson had watched on television from home. Every day he spent with Ondrej was precious; those few days together in Manchester, and then after Brazil, Hudson had gone to Monaco where they'd had ten days before Ondrej had to be here in Abu Dhabi for the last race of the season. The last thing he'd expected was to be invited here as

Ondrej's guest, not Mr D'Grieg's guest, and to be given his own set of Gamble Racing branded earmuffs.

"How is the search for the Bugatti going?" Mr D'Grieg reminded Hudson that he hadn't put together a report for him in over a month. There wasn't much to say.

"I'm mostly waiting on responses to enquiries I've sent out." None of the relatives of people on his list had replied to him. It nagged at him that he couldn't solve the puzzle. There was one thing he could do though. Let Mr D'Grieg down gently, like he'd promised so many months ago in Bahrain.

"I suppose you think I should let go of this dream."

Hudson tilted his head and considered how to phrase this. "It is looking increasingly unlikely. I'm so sorry that I haven't been able to resolve this for you." He pinched his lips together before he said something needy; something about how his best wasn't good enough.

"I might have my doubts about you and Ondrej and the wisdom of letting Ondrej indulge for so long with one person, but I have no doubts that you are a fine historian. You've approached this task with diligence and have looked at it from several perspectives that are unique."

"Thank you." It was high praise indeed, and Hudson chest swelled. "I do wish I had something more concrete for you."

"As do I, but in life, we don't always get what we want." Was that a warning?

"No. That is certainly true."

"You probably think my superstition is silly, worrying about Ondrej falling in love..."

"Not at all." Hudson tried not to gasp; perhaps Mr

D'Grieg hadn't been talking about getting rid of Hudson. "Belief systems don't have to be logical, and it seems to me that you have a very good reason for thinking the way you do."

"Yes." Mr D'Grieg wiped away a tear. "I miss her the most during Ondrej's races. She would've loved this."

Hudson's own eyes prickled with heat. "I think Ondrej carries her with him."

"Yes." There was a short pause. "Fuck."

Hudson stared at the screen in horror as a Gamble Racing car caught fire. "Is that?"

"Paulo." Mr D'Grieg's voice trembled slightly. "It's Paulo."

"We have a fire. Pull over and turn off the engine, Paulo." Monica's voice crackled over the radio. It was surreal to hear it via the television when Monica sat on the pit wall only a few metres from where he stood with Mr D'Grieg.

"Okay." Paulo stopped the car and jumped out as marshals ran towards the car. Flames shot out of the back of it. One marshal guided Paulo away from track. Others covered the car in fire retardant.

"He looks okay?" Hudson asked.

"Yes. They'll have to red flag the race now. It's good for Ondrej as he won't need to pit for tyres, so he won't lose any places."

Hudson wasn't quite sure what to make of that comment. The pragmatism surely meant that Paulo was fine. He looked fine, as much as Hudson could tell from the television anyway, as he stood beside the track. The fire had stopped, and now the car looked very sad, sitting on the edge of the track covered in white foam. Around him, the pit crew leaped off their chairs and rushed into the pit lane. Ondrej's car drove in and was immediately surrounded by mechanics. A strong hand landed on Hudson's shoulder.

"You'll have to stay here. It'll be a short red flag, so he won't get out of the car—"

"And I shouldn't distract him." Hudson hadn't even realised he'd started to walk towards Ondrej.

"Yes. You'll get used to this."

Hudson spun around to stare at Mr D'Grieg. "You think I'll be here often enough to get used to it?"

"Of course. I know my son, Hudson, and he cares a lot for you. I know I said that love would distract him from racing, that I was worried that he wouldn't be safe if he fell in love, but I was wrong. He's happier than I've seen him in a long time and that's valuable to me."

"Oh." Hudson knew it on some level, but it'd been more than a fortnight since Hudson had told Ondrej he loved him, only to get nothing back. "Thank you."

"He hasn't told you, has he?"

Hudson wasn't going to cry or anything. He just wished that his pale skin didn't tell the whole world what he was feeling, because from the way his cheeks burned, he knew Mr D'Grieg could see his blush.

"My son is a complex man. I've seen him grow up with the burden of living up to his mother's dreams for him without having her to guide him. He carries a lot of his grief deep inside."

"I know. I don't need him to tell me anything. I'm content to wait."

Mr D'Grieg smiled softly. "I had my doubts for a long

time. I don't have them anymore. Welcome to the D'Grieg family, Hudson."

Hudson pressed the heels of his hands against his eyes. He held his breath until this need to bawl left. Eventually, he was steady enough to drop his hands. He breathed deliberately, a few long slow breaths to help control his pulse. "Thank you."

"I'd like to meet your family sometime, after the season is done."

"There is only my sister and me."

"Oh?"

Hudson appreciated that Ondrej hadn't shared his story with Mr D'Grieg. "I'm a foster kid. My parents were not as good at parenting as you are with Ondrej. My sister is a few years older, and she adopted me when she was old enough to be my guardian."

"She sounds incredible."

It was the easiest thing in the world to smile. "She is."

"I would be honoured to meet her." In the background, Ondrej's car engine roared and his tyres squealed. "Red flag must be ending soon. It's time to get racing." Mr D'Grieg turned back to the television. Two laps after the re-start, a thin plume of smoke was visible from the back of Ondrej's car.

"Are you seeing that?" Hudson gripped Mr D'Grieg's bicep then immediately let go because it was super weird to be clinging on to his ... soon to be father-in-law?

"Yes." In the few seconds since the first pillar of smoke was seen, Ondrej pulled the car over and the television broadcast Jaxxon asking Ondrej to pull over and turn off the engine.

"How can this happen to both cars?"

Ondrej pulled himself out of the car, both hands on the halo. Hudson held his breath. Once again, the marshals ran over and covered the car in fire retardant. A few licks of flame were still visible out of the back of the car, but they were quickly put out by the marshals. Ondrej paced around the car. The focus and intensity in the way he moved was enough for Hudson to breathe again. Ondrej was fine. Angry. But fine. Hudson preferred this to the sinking feeling when Ondrej had crashed, then he immediately shook his head to get rid of that insidious thought. Yes, Ondrej wasn't hurt this time, but he could've been. Now he was getting onto the back of a motorbike with a marshal, who would drive him back to the pits. If Hudson was going to be in a proper relationship with Ondrej, he needed to learn how to deal with all the emotions caused by any racing incident. If this was going to be his life now, he couldn't make this about himself and his reactions. He had to learn to support Ondrej. Mr D'Grieg believed in him. Hudson could learn to believe in himself too.

———

Ondrej late braked into the hairpin, lining his car up to overtake JP for the lead. This was his moment. A win was within his reach. He stepped on the accelerator, and the car lagged for a split second; just enough for JP to pull away again.

"Fuck."

"Fire." Jaxxon's voice was clear in his ear. "Pull over and turn off the engine."

"What the fuck, man?" His engine started to lose power and his dash lit up with warning lights. He growled as he went through the motions of doing as Jaxxon said. As soon as the car came to a stop, he unclipped his safety belt, and pulled himself out of the car. Flames licked the back end of the car, coming out of the exhaust. A marshal pushed him aside and blasted the car with fire retardant. Another marshal moved him away from the car off the track. Ondrej wanted to punch something. He should be winning this race. Not standing here helplessly watching his car go up in flames. First Paulo's car, and now his. Victor was going to hear about this. His fucking tinkering with the setup all season had gone too far. Two DNFs in his last four races wasn't good enough. Fuck. He could hardly blame Victor for a busted tyre.

He swung onto the back of a motorbike behind the marshal for the ride back to the pits. Cameras followed him, so he kept his helmet on. It provided a good barrier so the press couldn't see his scowl. The long walk down pit lane was useful, as his frustration dissipated with each step, until he was able to walk into the garage without wanting to shake Victor.

"You okay?" Jaxxon jumped off the pit wall and walked the last few steps beside him.

"Yeah. Fuck."

"Yeah. It's a shit show. Both cars."

"What the fuck happened?"

"We don't know. There was nothing on the metrics and then suddenly a hot spot in the exhaust pipe, smoke, and fire."

Ondrej stopped, mid stride. "That makes no sense."

"No. Victor has insisted that no one touch the cars until he's examined them."

"What?"

"I don't know. Perhaps... Not here." Jaxxon waved his fingers at the press who stood at the edge of the Gamble Racing garages. Ondrej followed him inside, past the mechanics who all looked stunned, past Victor who was whispering frantically to Socrates. He ripped off his helmet and fire protection, then stepped into the media-free zone out the back of the garage.

"I'm so glad you are okay." Hudson grabbed his hands.

"I'm fine." Ondrej ripped his hands away. "The car is fucked though."

"You'll still finish sixth on the table." Papa's contribution didn't help. The midfield was quite tight this year, since JP and Etrulius had won most of the races between them, putting them far above everyone else in the championship race.

"I could've won today." It stung to be so close to victory, able to taste it, have it stripped away by a technical fault. Sweat ran down his temples, stinging as it touched the corners of his eyes. Fuck. He grabbed a towel and wiped his face.

"I'm sorry." Hudson said.

"Don't be. You didn't build a shitty fucking engine that caught fire." Ondrej forced himself to stand still. The temptation to have a crack at Victor was something a hot-headed young driver would do. He'd been in the game for eight years; he should have more control over his emotions than this.

"Is there anything I can do?" Hudson asked.

"About?"

Hudson shrugged. "I don't know. You look upset. I want to—" He cleared his throat. "—care for you."

Ondrej glared. "I don't need care. I need a fucking winning car." He needed to get rid of this energy somehow. All this tension and aggression inside needed an outlet.

"Excuse me, Mr D'Grieg. Can you please leave us alone for a while and make sure no one comes in? Thank you."

To Ondrej's surprise, Papa did as Hudson asked, leaving the room in record speed.

"Ondrej." Hudson spoke softly, the opposite of what Ondrej needed.

"What?"

"I would like you to angry fuck me. Please."

Ondrej's heart accelerated, if that was fucking possible. "Yes." It was the perfect way to get rid of all this frustration. His cock went from resting to rock hard instantly.

"Fuck me hard. You know you need it."

Ondrej grabbed Hudson by the arm. "Over here." He pulled Hudson towards a table and shoved him over it.

Hudson gasped. "Harder. Please." His voice was all breathy. Fucking perfect. Ondrej unzipped his racing suit, then dragged his hand through Hudson's hair. He tugged a little; not too hard, but enough for Hudson to moan and spread his legs wider.

"Patience. Let's get you naked first."

"Okay."

"No. You do it." Ondrej had a few condoms in his locker, so he left Hudson to sort out his own clothing and turned to grab one and roll it on. When he turned back, Hudson had pulled his jeans and undies down to his ankles, effectively tying his ankles together. He still wore his shirt. Only his naked ass and legs were bare for Ondrej. Fuck, no lube. This fucking day. He brushed his hands through his hair.

"Wait there." There had to be a solution. He had lube in his hotel room. Fucking lot of use that was. A bottle of aloe vera sat beside the first aid kit. The mechanics often used it for helping heal minor burns. It was slippery, surely it would work. He squirted a bunch on his hand and covered his cock in it. The cool gel added to his desperate need to be inside Hudson.

"Ready?"

"I'm ready for anything you need." Hudson's voice shook a little and Ondrej paused. "Please."

The one word undid Ondrej. Knowing that Hudson wanted this as much as he needed it was fucking perfection. He grabbed Hudson's hips and used one hand to guide himself into Hudson's ass. Perhaps it was a little rude not to prepare him, but he'd asked for this. An angry fuck.

"You want this hard?"

"Give me all your anger. I can take it."

Ondrej cried out as he slammed into Hudson, holding Hudson's hips tight. This was going to be fast and furious. Hudson spread his arms across the table and moaned. A loud moan that rumbled. The sound of absolute pure desire. Hudson was so tight, so impossibly perfect, and Ondrej needed this release more than anything. He threw all his anguish into this, focusing only on the way his cock slid in and out of Hudson's perfect hole. Hudson's ass gripped him tight, centred him. He should be winning a race right now. This was almost as good. Definitely as good.

Hudson lifted his head and Ondrej stroked one hand up his spine until he could thread his fingers through Hudson's flaming red hair. The decadent moan when he tugged on Hudson's hair pushed Ondrej all the way to the edge.

"Fuck." He came on a yell, collapsing forward onto Hudson. "I fucking love you. That was everything I needed."

The noise Hudson made—a happy moan—warmed Ondrej all the way through. He kissed the back of Hudson's neck, and slowly eased his way out. Hudson stood up slowly.

"Um, is there a towel? I've made a bit of a mess." Hudson's face was bright pink. Ondrej grinned and threw him the towel he'd used earlier to wipe his sweaty brow. Hudson knelt down and used the towel to clean up his come off the floor. Well, that answered that question then. Hudson obviously enjoyed himself too.

"You are coming to all my races now."

"I am?"

"Yes." Ondrej had already said too much. Blurting that he loved Hudson right after angry fucking him over a table in the room behind the pit garage was a lot to process. Now it was done, Ondrej could think properly. Hudson hadn't just offered him refuge for his frustration, he'd cleansed out the negativity too. Hudson pulled up his jeans, then walked over to Ondrej, removed the condom and used the towel to clean up Ondrej too. It was a lot. Getting that gentle care right after Hudson had offered the one thing Ondrej didn't know he'd really needed. Phew. He collapsed on one of the chairs.

"Shall I unlock the doors?"

"Give me a moment." Ondrej wasn't quite ready to have Papa walk back into the room when it was rather obvious that Hudson had thrown everyone out so Ondrej could fuck him. What a gift Hudson was. "Hudson, come here."

Hudson placed the dirty towel on the table, then walked over and stood awkwardly beside him.

"I love you." He didn't need to complicate it. He stood up and wrapped his arms around Hudson, pulling him closer for a kiss. Ondrej poured the truth into this kiss, using all his skill to show Hudson that he meant it.

CHAPTER 24

Hudson sat on the couch in Monaco, cuddled under a blanket as he chatted to Mackenzie on the phone. Ondrej was massaging Hudson's feet, although his version of it was to taunt Hudson by stroking his hands up Hudson's thighs and almost touching his cock whenever he spoke to his sister.

"Are you coming home for Christmas?" Mackenzie asked.

"Yes. Would it be okay if we invited Ondrej's Papa as well?"

"Absolutely. Ondrej is family now. His family is our family." Just like Hudson, Mackenzie liked to collect people into her family.

"Great. I'll ask him."

"Awesome. Hold on..." Mackenzie mumbled something, presumably to Brian or one of the twins. "Brian has just reminded me. There is a parcel here for you."

"Open it." Hudson didn't care if Mackenzie saw whatever someone had sent him.

"Okay." There was a rustle of paper and then Mackenzie gasped. "It's from the great-niece of Robert Benoist. There's a key."

"Read it out." Hudson had given up on ever solving the Bugatti mystery.

Mr Lockley,

Thank you for your kind letter regarding my uncle's correspondence. I'm sorry that it took me some time to respond, as his letter collection is rather extensive and it took me a while to find the relevant one. I've enclosed a photo of the letter, and the key that was in the envelope. As you can see, the letter from your client's great-grandfather, there is no mention of what the key opens, although it does say that it is the key to keeping the car safe from bombs.

I do wish you all the very best with your puzzle and I hope you figure out what this key opens.

Yours,

Nancy Benoist

"Holy shit, Hudson. Does this key open a garage or something?"

Tingles broke out all over Hudson's body. If he could find the garage, he might find the car.

"Yes. Keep it safe. We will come and collect it."

"What?"

"Ondrej and I will fly from Monaco to England tomorrow and collect the key." His heart raced and his body was flush with the thrill of maybe, maybe, having solved this mystery.

"Why rush? Maybe work out what it opens first."

Hudson sighed. "So bloody logical, Mackenzie."

Her giggle was everything. "You two love birds work

out what you want to do and let me know. The key and the photo of the letter is safe here, so take your time."

"Okay." Hudson hung up.

"You found the Bugatti?" Ondrej's eyes were wide.

"No."

"Fuck. I almost got excited there."

Hudson grinned. "All this fuss over a rusty old car."

"Tell me what she told you."

"Okay. I wrote to a bunch of people who might have kept letters from your great-grandfather, and one of them just replied. She also sent a key that opens a place that will keep the car safe from bombs, whatever that means."

"Like a bomb shelter."

Holy shit. That was it. Hudson gasped. "Hold on a second." Ernie Trew had a photo hanging on the wall in his stable office, a print of a famous photo of the stallion Nearco walking out of his WWII bomb shelter. Hudson threw off the blanket and jumped to his feet to grab his phone from where it had been charging. He did a quick internet search. Yes, that was it.

"Look at this."

"It's a horse?"

"Not just any horse. Nearco."

"So?"

"The farm built him his own bomb shelter in WWII. Look at it." Hudson vibrated as he waited impatiently for Ondrej to see it too. Ondrej peered over his shoulder.

"I don't get it."

"It's the same shaped hill as the one behind William Grover-Williams' house in France. The house—"

"—where my great-grandfather was supposed to collect the car."

"Yes. What if the key opens the door to the bomb shelter under that hill?"

"Hudson. You are a fucking genius." Ondrej wrapped his arms around Hudson's waist as Hudson blew out an unsteady breath.

"Assuming the hill is a bomb shelter."

"You think it is."

"Yes. When I first went there, the hill bugged me for some reason. It was so out of context with the surrounding land, but I couldn't make it make sense. This photo of Nearco holds the key."

"The horse?"

"Yes. The hill is the same shape as Nearco's bunker."

"Get in the car."

"Now?"

"Yes."

Hudson paced around the room. "Are you suggesting we drive to this house and just start digging? Shouldn't we go to England and get the key first? If I'm right, you are going to want the key."

"Why doesn't your sister meet us there?" Ondrej's suggestion made a lot of sense.

"Hold up a minute. The car, if it is there, has been there for seventy years. An extra day or two isn't going to help. This isn't a movie where we are racing against the clock to beat someone else to the car."

Ondrej burst into laughter, the sound ricocheting around his apartment. "True. And it's nearly dinner time."

"Yes, you promised me pizza and a movie."

"And sex."

Hudson grinned. "Obviously."

Ondrej picked him up and spun him around. "My clever fucking historian. I can't believe you've found the car. I love you."

"Might have found the car." Hudson couldn't protest any further, as Ondrej kissed him.

———

"Are we ready?" Ondrej unloaded the small excavator from the hire truck and drove it into the backyard of Grover-Williams' house. Mackenzie and Brian stood to the side, holding the twin's hands who were both super excited to see the excavator. Mr D'Grieg had bought the house last week, as soon as Hudson had told him his idea, and although it wouldn't technically be his until the paperwork was settled, he'd paid the current owners an exorbitant rental fee to ensure he got access to the property immediately. Hudson had been in contact with several local historians but there wasn't really a process around this type of discovery. If he'd been wanting to develop the area, then the government would order surveys to determine if there was anything historical in the area that they cared about. People stumbled across old war relics all the time and unless they had some significance to the war narrative, then no one really cared, especially if it was just in someone's backyard. There were so many WWII bunkers around France that people even converted some of them into boutique hotels.

"You just want to drive machinery."

"Of course." Ondrej was at home behind the wheel of

anything mechanical. This excavator was small enough that it hardly warranted the name, it was more of a tiny digger.

"Shall we dig?" Papa asked. Mr D'Grieg had invited Hudson to call him by his first name, but since he shared it with Ondrej, it'd been a bit weird the first few times he'd called him Ondrej Senior. Papa had laughing said it made him feel old to have the senior tag, and Hudson struggled with having two Ondrej's in his life, so the solution had been for Hudson to call him Papa. Having someone who wanted to be a father figure for him was the greatest gift Ondrej—both of them—could have given him.

"Are you impatient for your Christmas present, Papa?" Ondrej teased. It was still three weeks until Christmas, but the weather had already become decidedly wintery.

"Yes. I have been looking for this car for decades, and to think it could have been right here all along..."

"Where do we start?" Ondrej asked. Hudson paced around the edge of the little hill. Over the past week, he'd learned everything there was to know about the construction of WWII bomb shelters.

"The dirt covering it is probably thinner at the top, so we should start there, except I don't think we should drive up the hill."

"You want me to hand dig first?"

"Yes. If we find concrete, then we know we're on the right track and we can use the excavator to try and find the door."

Ondrej jumped off the excavator, grabbed a shovel, and marched up the little hill. He started to dig. Having a boyfriend who was an athlete had many benefits but being able to dig quickly hadn't been high on Hudson's list of boyfriend requirements until right now. It only took a few shovel loads before Ondrej created a decent sized hole.

"The dirt is fucking hard."

"It is the beginning of winter. It's probably frozen."

"I keep thinking, yes this is it, I've hit concrete, but it's just more solid dirt." Ondrej tipped out another shovelful of dirt, then dug in again. It was astounding to watch him dig so rapidly and chat about it without him breathing heavily at all. You'd think he was going for a casual walk in the park.

"Oh shit. I think this is it." He scooped out more dirt and sure enough, there was concrete. Ondrej tapped it with his shovel a few times.

"That's definitely concrete."

"Holy shit. You did it." Ondrej kissed him on the mouth, once, then dug a bit more to widen the hole. The others ran up the small hill to join them and they all stared at the concrete.

"Knowing my luck, the bunker will be empty."

Mackenzie shoved him. "Stop talking like that."

Ondrej leaned on his shovel and laughed. "Yeah, Hudson, listen to your sister. Twelve other historians tried to find the fourth Bugatti Atlantis—La Voiture Noire— and failed. None of them noticed the fucking bunker in the backyard of Grover-Williams old house."

"Okay." Hudson paced around the edge of the oddly square shaped hill amazed that he hadn't made the connection to a bunker earlier. He pulled out his phone and stared at the image of Nearco walking out of his bunker. For the last week, he'd told himself that the odds of two self-built bunkers having a similar design were very low. Now that he stood on the top of this one, he realised the similarities. This one was angled differently to the house, as if it was designed with the door facing the house and built around the car.

"I think the door will be here."

Ondrej jogged down the hill, with the shovel over his shoulder. Soon enough the excavator roared to life, and Ondrej was making short work of digging out the area that hopefully was the entrance to the bunker. Dirt piled up to the side. After about half an hour, the excavator bucket made a nasty scraping sound.

"I think that's concrete." Hudson grabbed a shovel and stood awkwardly to the side so he could clear away some of the surrounding dirt.

"Get out of the way." Ondrej called out. "Fuck, are you trying to get injured?"

"I'm trying to help."

"Then stand back, damn it."

Mackenzie grabbed his arm and pulled. "You two have the cutest love language."

"Shoosh." He let himself be walked back to the top of the bunker and Ondrej carried on with his digging. By the time Ondrej had enough dirt cleared for them to see the concrete structure of the opening, the fog had cleared, and Brian had gone to the shops to grab everyone some lunch. Two long angled walls lead up to the top of the bunker, and old metal doors hung precariously from rusty hinges. Between Hudson helping to clear the smaller sections with the shovel and Ondrej removing most of the dirt with his digger, they could now stand on a concrete ramp and stare at the doors.

"Mackenzie. The key?"

Mackenzie pulled it out of her pocket and walked up to the doors. "The keyhole is filled with dirt."

"Hang on." Hudson poked at it with a screwdriver until most of the dirt was loose. "Can you pass me some water?"

Mackenzie handed him a bottle of water and he poured it on the keyhole then used the screwdriver to finish cleaning it out.

"Hopefully it's not rusted shut."

"Let's try it." Mackenzie put the key into the lock and turned. "It works." She twisted it more. "Damn it, not quite."

"There's some lubricant here in the excavator." Ondrej handed the spray can to Hudson who squirted it into the lock, and Mackenzie tried the key again. The lock opened reluctantly.

"I think Papa should do the honours." Hudson stepped aside, so Papa could open the door. He closed his eyes, not wanting to know if the car was there or not, but quickly decided that was silly and opened them again. The door made a grinding sound as Papa and Ondrej pushed it open.

"It's bloody heavy."

"I think it's dragging against the concrete."

"No shit. But I can't lift it, so this will have to do." Ondrej gave it one last shove and everyone crowded around to peer into the dark. Hudson grabbed his phone from his back pocket. The torch function would be really handy right now, so he turned it on and lifted it up over Ondrej's head. Inside the bunker was a car shaped object covered in dark canvas tarpaulin.

"Is that?" Ondrej and Papa marched inside and pulled the tarpaulin. It came free in a cloud of dust. Hudson sneezed. When he opened his eyes again, there it was. An ancient car in pristine condition.

"You did it."

"You fucking did it. Oh my God."

Hudson couldn't believe it. He just stared at the car without moving as everyone around him screamed with joy. Papa ran his hands reverently over the bonnet of the car. He'd found the car. He'd solved an impossible puzzle. Hudson let out a deep satisfying breath from the very bottom of his lungs. His whole body floated, light as air, as contentment and something like gratification spread through his limbs. He'd done it. No one believed the Bugatti known as La Voiture Noire existed, let alone could be found, and he'd found it, only metres from where it'd last been seen in 1939. This was the absolute pinnacle of his career.

"Well, brother, you are never allowed to doubt yourself ever again." Mackenzie patted him on the shoulder.

"Yeah." He pulled her close for a hug. "We found it."

"You found it. You did this."

"Fuck yeah." Ondrej hugged them both. "Hudson is the greatest."

"Settle down."

"We will not. Have you seen what you just found?" Ondrej waved his arms at the car, then turned back to Hudson and kissed his cheek. "Do you think Papa will let me drive it?"

"I think you'll have to fight him for the honour."

Papa had already opened the car with the spare key from his precious letter and was sitting in the driver's seat.

"The battery will be dead anyway. We'll have to get it on a truck and taken to a workshop first."

Hudson swallowed. "There is so much to organise now. Insurance. Ownership papers. Registration. Getting it out of here and taken somewhere."

"Slow down. It's been here for more than seventy years, a few more days isn't going to matter," Mackenzie said.

"I guess so."

"Technically…" Ondrej drew out the word.

"What?"

"Well, it's incredibly dry in here which will have kept the car in optimal condition, but now that we've opened up the doors, we are letting in moisture which will start to have an impact on the car. We should move it quickly to a specialist restorer, and we'll need to wrap it in the cloth again for the journey."

"How will we do that?"

Ondrej laughed. "I might know someone."

"You do?"

"Hudson, Gamble Racing has an entire logistics team who move two S1 cars and their pit garages all over the world. I'll give Helen, she's the logistics manager, a call. She'll know exactly what to do."

Hudson followed Ondrej as he walked out of the bunker and leaned against the excavator. He only half-listened to the phone call. The thrill of actually finding the car when everyone believed it was impossible was still sinking in. He'd done it. Holy mother of goodness.

"Helen has it under control. She's going to fly here

today." Ondrej picked up Hudson and he squeaked with surprise. His butt hit the tracks on the excavator and he sat there with Ondrej standing between his legs. "I'm so fucking proud of you, Hudson."

"Thanks."

"Having you in my life this year has been amazing. I love you."

"I love you too, Ondrej." Hudson almost didn't get to finish his sentence before Ondrej kissed him. He'd never get bored with Ondrej's kisses. For some reason, Ondrej—one of the best drivers in the world—wanted to have Hudson as his lover. It was such a thrill, and after today's discovery, Hudson could believe that he was worth it.

"Do you think Papa would leave us alone with the car so we can christen it?"

"You want to do what with the car?"

Ondrej leaned in close and gently bit Hudson's earlobe. "I want to fuck you on the bonnet of the car."

Hudson shivered. "Please."

———

If you enjoyed this book, and you want to know why the Gamble Racing cars caught fire in the last race of the season, the next book in the series is DRIVEN BY PASSION, featuring Victor Tsui and Lucien Grenville.

Engine fires, sabotage, and two friends falling in love....

Engineer Victor Tsui needs to figure out why his race cars keep failing. Being Gamble Racing's Chief Engineer is his dream job and he's built a fast car. But there is something wrong with his design and he needs to understand how to fix it before next season.

Hot headed driver Lucien Grenville has nowhere to go over the winter break, so when his friend Victor expresses frustration at the recent run of engine failures, he decides to hang out and offer support.

Things get awkward when Lucien gets an intense urge to kiss Victor, and they need to decide if this is going to remain a friendship, or become something more.

Want a bit more romance? Would you love to know how Socrates met his husband? Their story is available as an exclusive bonus when you sign up for my newsletter at reneedahlia.com.

ACKNOWLEDGMENTS

I pay my respects to the Wangal people of the Eora Nation, who are the traditional owners of the land on which this book was written.

To my children, who are huge F1 fans, for their constant help with all the F1 details. Most especially, thank you to kid3 who discovered the mystery of the missing Bugatti and wanted me to make up a fictional version where a character found the $100million car. Unfortunately, the real one is still missing.

As usual, thanks to my readers and my writing friends who have helped me believe in my writing. Thank you to Lina, Rachel and the rest of the Carina writers group, D and Kris and the rest of the Wordmakers, MV Ellis, and Ebony Oaten.

AUTHOR NOTES

This book is based on the missing Fourth Bugatti aka: La Voiture Noire.

"Bugatti gave the car to racing driver Robert Benoist as a prize after winning the 1937 24 Hours of Le Mans. After a while, he gave the car to his close friend and race teammate, William Grover-Williams. Despite Chassis #57453 being regularly used, it never had a registered owner. In 1937, Williams and his wife fled to England after World War 2 had broke out. The car was last seen after being returned to the Bugatti factory in Molsheim, France. The last mention about Chassis #57453 was on a list of cars sent to Bordeaux, France during the French Exodus in 1941." www.drivetribe.com

Socrates' mansion is loosely based on the Goodwood Estate in West Sussex owned by the Duke of Richmond and Gordon. The property houses a car racing track and a horse racing track, so it's the perfect inspiration for Socrates and his horse loving niece Xenia, but perhaps on a smaller scale than Goodwood itself!

ALL BOOKS BY RENÉE DAHLIA

Thanks for reading DRIVEN TO DISTRACTION. I hope you enjoyed it. Reviews can help readers find books, and I am grateful for all honest reviews. Thank you for taking the time to let others know what you've read, and what you thought. If you write a review for DRIVEN TO DISTRACTION and email me with the link, I will send you a free copy of any book from my backlist.

If you'd like to know more about me, my books, or to connect with me online, you can visit my webpage www.reneedahlia.com and if you sign up to my newsletter, you can grab a free book.

Twitter:
https://twitter.com/dekabat
Facebook:
https://www.facebook.com/reneedahliawriter/
Instagram:
https://www.instagram.com/reneedahlia_author/

You've just read a book in my Gamble Racing Series.
Contemporary Series: Gamble Racing

1. Driven to Distraction (mm)
2. Driven by Passion (mm)
3. Driven by Ambition (mm)
4. Driven to Protect (mm)

Contemporary Series: Seraph's Burlesque Club

1. Show Up (ff with bisexual heroine)
2. Show Off (ff with bisexual heroines)
3. Show Queen (ff)
4. Show Time (mm)
5. Show Dance (mm)

Contemporary Series: Kapow!

1. Out of Her League (fm with bisexual characters)
2. His Buxom Beauty (fm)
3. Craving His Spotlight (mm)
4. Her Pregnant Rival (ff)

Contemporary Series: Farrellton Foster Family

1. Betrayed (fm)
2. Forbidden (fm with bisexual characters)
3. Liability (ff)

———

Contemporary Series: Margaret River TV: Boxed Set

- Homage (fm with bisexual heroine)
- Uplift (ff with bisexual heroines)

Contemporary Series: Merindah Park

1. Merindah Park (fm)
2. Making Her Mark (fm with bisexual heroine)
3. Two Hearts Healing (fm)
4. Racetrack Royalty (fm)

Contemporary Series: Rainbow Cove

1. His Christmas Pearl (fm)
2. His Christmas Pride (mm)

Historical Series: Great War

1. Her Lady's Melody (ff)
2. Her Lady's Fortune (ff)
3. Her Lady's Honor (ff)
4. His Lord's Soldier (mm)

Historical Series: Bluestockings

Prequel: The Shipwrecked Earl's Bride (fm with bisexual hero)

To Charm a Bluestocking (fm with bisexual hero)

In Pursuit of a Bluestocking (fm)

The Heart of a Bluestocking (fm)